THE
RED VIRGIN

A novel inspired by the life of Simone Weil

CLARK McCANN

Author's note: *The Red Virgin* reimagines the life of the French philosopher Simone Weil (1909-43) through the character of Sabine Arnaud. The novel does not presume to be an accurate portrait of Weil, or any member of her family. In cases where I quote from Weil's published work, or paraphrase her ideas, my sources are referenced in the appendix.

ISBN: 978-0-578-52261-6

This book is a work of fiction. Names, characters, places and incidents either are the product of the author's imagination or, if real, used fictionally.

Cover illustration and book design by Tim Kimble Design

Printed and bound in the United States of America

Published by Solesmes Press
P.O. Box 1601
Issaquah, WA, USA 98027-9998

Visit: https://www.simoneweilnovel.com

*This book is for my grandsons
Ryan, Weston and William,
with gratitude for the joy you have given me.*

May you all be lifelong readers, free thinkers and free spirits.

THE
RED VIRGIN

PRELUDE

Near Lasta, Ethiopia

It was not true that they worshipped her. They regarded her with the respect given a tribal elder, though she was not one of them—and a woman. No one knew where she came from, or why she chose to live high on the plateau, so far from the village, in a mud hut she had built with her own hands. She tended goats, planted beans and maize on a terraced field. Her harvest was small, but she shared what little she had with those in the village who had less. No one ever saw her eat. But she was strong for an old woman, which stirred gossip that she was not human and practiced witchcraft.

Her skin was burned brown like theirs, but her lion's mane of hair was as white as an egret. When she spoke their language, she pronounced each word carefully, but sometimes mistook one word for another, which made people laugh. Then she would smile too, the lines in her face cracking like furrows in the parched earth. They called her "grandmother" in Amharic, which seemed to please her.

Women brought their sick children to her; men came with wounds from battle. Inside a rusted metal box she kept bandages and medicine. She was not a doctor, but she was educated and knew how to treat fevers, sew torn flesh, and splint bones. Those she could not cure, she comforted by her touch. With the dying she was patient and suffered with them until the end. No one ever saw her weep. She said that all her tears had been shed long ago.

Though she covered her head like a good Muslim, she often prayed in the stone grotto that had once been an ancient church. When asked about her God, she always replied: "When you find God, tell me where He is, and I will follow you to Him. Until then, I am content to wait."

All this was long ago, before the rains stopped, and the famine came, and the war drove people toward the cities, where there might be food—and peace.

It was then that other men, her own people, came looking for her. But they found only what she had left behind: a Greek Bible with the Old Testament torn out. Inside the Bible was a folded sheet of paper, written in her own hand, which ended with the words:

> *I am the honored one and the scorned one,*
> *I am the whore and the holy one.*
> *I am the wife and the virgin....*
> *I am the barren one,*
> *And many are my sons...*
> *I am the silence that is incomprehensible...*
> *I am the utterance of my name.*

CHAPTER ONE

Nothing can have as its destination anything other than its origin.

North Hollywood, California. November 1976

She was an odd choice for an obsession, the bone-thin woman with the beak nose, wire glasses, and unruly hair. In Craig's favorite photo, she stands on a street corner in Marseille in 1942, just before she sailed for New York, sporting a black beret and wearing a cape that falls to her ankles and dirty feet in sandals. In the background a trolley, pedestrians in drab clothes, a boarded-up *boulangerie*. It is Vichy France, in the dark days of the Nazi occupation. She squints at the camera, her smile thin, bemused. Sabine Arnaud is thirty-three and will be dead in sixteen months from tuberculosis and self-starvation.

Craig Martin closed the dog-eared biography of Arnaud, with its precious photos, and tossed the book in his suitcase. Then he ran his finger over the postcard that his mother had received from Arnaud, just days before Arnaud's death in an English sanitarium. Seeing his name penned in Arnaud's firm hand helped quiet the voice that told him he was about to make the biggest mistake of his life.

Craig returned the card to the briefcase that contained his research, photographs, and correspondence with Sophie Daudin, an Arnaud scholar at the Sorbonne who was writing the definitive biography of the great philosopher. When he met with Daudin, he would advance his theory about Arnaud's mysterious sojourn to New York in 1942—a theory that, if he could prove it, would rewrite the narrative of her extraordinary life and change the course of his own.

He checked his watch for the third time in ten minutes. He'd told Rita that his Air France flight left an hour earlier than it did, expecting her to be late to take him to the airport, which she was. He parted the drapes to scan the traffic flowing under his window, hoping to spot her smoke-belching Comet sweeping down the hill past Universal Studios. If she wasn't there in five minutes, he'd call a cab.

Craig's friends thought he was crazy to quit his job as a staff writer for *The Tonight Show* to take an extended vacation in France. After years of bouncing from one cancelled sitcom to the next, he had steady work as a comedy writer. His agent, Saul, was furious. You didn't quit Johnny Carson—writers killed for those jobs. It could ruin his career. Craig didn't disagree. He'd told Saul he was burnt-out (true) and needed a break. If he disclosed the real reason, Saul would think him a lunatic.

A horn beeped twice and Craig bolted down the stairs. Rita was double-parked, traffic snarled behind her, angry horns blaring. He tossed his bag on the back seat and she swung out into traffic, accelerated, then pulled a U-turn, triggering more outrage.

"You're late," Craig said.

"Not so, Marty. You lied about the flight time."

Rita was always one step ahead of him. It was one of the things he loved and hated about her. And she never called him Craig. He was "Marty," or a playfully pejorative nickname that struck her fancy.

Rita was decked out in a white blouse, black pants, high heels—not her usual jeans and sandals. She had put on belly fat, and her pants, shiny with wear, bulged around her abdomen. Dear old Rita, sometime lover, longtime friend—ace deli clerk at Vons.

"What's with the fancy outfit?" Craig asked.

She shrugged and lit a cigarette.

"You said you quit."

"I did. I'm celebrating."

"Celebrating what?"

"Maybe I'll tell you." And she didn't.

Rita was pushing forty, with a Mayan face, an outlaw smile, and a short fuse. She didn't suffer fools, and had less patience for the pedantic wise. Craig thought she was smartest person he knew, despite her ninth-grade education and checkered past, which included prison for transporting drugs.

When she pulled to the curb at LAX, Craig kissed her, grabbed his bag, and rushed for the terminal. He was in line at the Air France counter when he saw her strolling toward him, dragging an enormous suitcase.

"What the hell are you doing?"

"What does it look like? I'm going to Paris."

"No, you're not."

"I got my ticket—one-way." She waved it under his chin. "You can fly me home. That's fair. Besides, you *owe* me, big time."

"You *can't* go. This is *serious* for me."

"I can help."

"Your goddamn car will get towed!" Craig shouted, for want of a stronger argument.

"Like my photo?" She flashed her passport.

"What about your job?" he tried, lamely.

"I make sandwiches. I'm going."

Rita stepped in front of him, hefted her suitcase onto the scale, and proudly handed her ticket to the smiling attendant.

Six hours later it was night and they were somewhere over the Arctic, swigging champagne and eating *coq au vin* from plastic trays. Craig was buzzed and half-glad Rita was there. She would make the trip more fun, if also more trying. But they would inevitably share a bed, which made him happy, thinking of it. He touched her hand.

"What about your car?"

"It's in Donny's name. Let him pay the impound fee, the prick." Donny was her live-in for the last year, the produce manager at Vons, eight years her junior.

"I thought you liked him."

"It was time. I didn't like the way he was starting to look at me, like he could do better."

"Smart man."

"Fuck off." She was angry.

"It was a joke."

"No it wasn't."

"I'm *sorry*."

"Ohhh, you're *sorry*. What's that supposed to mean? You're a sorry, selfish fuck?"

Craig said nothing. He could feel her eyes on him. Maybe it would pass; maybe it wouldn't. You could never tell with Rita. But she was right when she said he owed her.

Two months before, after Craig's mother, Alice, died of breast cancer, Rita had helped him clean out her apartment. He'd often described Alice as a celebrity mom who had never been a celebrity. She was vain, theatrical, seductive, cold, narcissistic, and often cruel. In some ways, Alice was another casualty of the war. The Sunday Japan bombed Pearl Harbor, Alice was performing in a Broadway musical, her first juicy role, with the promise of more to come. She was single, talented, and gorgeous—with a real shot at stardom. Four months later, after marrying a dashing naval officer, she found herself alone and pregnant in New York, with a husband in the South Pacific.

In the summer of 1942, she was befriended by a new neighbor, a refugee from occupied France: Sabine Arnaud. When Craig was growing up, Alice seldom spoke of Arnaud, except in the context of famous people she claimed to have known. She said she'd gotten drunk once with Scott Fitzgerald, dated Tommy Dorsey, and was pursued by Frank Sinatra. Arnaud was just the "oddball Jew philosopher down the hall" who refused to wear makeup, smoked like a chimney, and sometimes helped with baby Craig, "who wailed incessantly."

Craig had first read Arnaud when he was twelve, during the misery of adolescence. Bullied at school, ignored at home, and tormented by sexual urges he thought demonic, he thought seriously of suicide. In this state, the solipsism of puberty, he stumbled on Arnaud's *Gravity and Grace* in his mother's bookcase. He would never forget the first words he read when the book fell open in his hands. *To wish that the world did not exist is to wish that I, just as I am, may be everything.* She had put a name to his agony.

Much of the book was beyond him, but there were lines that rang true, like the pure melody of a song that touched your heart. *Those who are unhappy have no need for anything in this world but people capable of giving them their attention.* And the fact that she, the famous philosopher, had held him in her arms when he was an infant made the words that more poignant, as if she were whispering comfort into his ear. By the time he reached college, Craig had read every word Arnaud had written, and much of what had been written about her.

It was sad going through his mother's things. And more so his father's, who'd died ten years earlier, crashing his car drunk into a telephone pole, perhaps on purpose. There were ancient copies of *Variety*, playbills, and boxes of letters, most from his father during the war and some from his father's missionary brother in Africa. Craig saved the family photo albums, wartime letters, and his father's Navy Cross, which he'd won for rescuing sailors from a sinking ship—suffering burns that disfigured his face. Rita took the gold jewelry, fox fur, and antique silver. The furniture and clothes went to charity.

As they were cleaning up, Rita spotted a yellow envelope in a box of tax records Craig had marked for trash. Inside were two Kodak transparencies of Sabine Arnaud and his mother, along with a postcard from England, dated August 9, 1943.

Dearest Alice:

  I am not supposed to write (doctor's orders!), but wanted to let you know I am getting stronger by the day and hope to take part in the war effort soon. Please kiss little Craig for me. There is nothing to forgive. I know he will be safe. The world is a dangerous place, but also beautiful. Yours, Sabine

When Craig read it, his heart jumped as he beheld his name drawn in Arnaud's hand. She had thought of *him*, even close to death. It gave his life a sudden new dimension—like the fleeting glimpse of an unknown god. He'd read enough about Arnaud to know that she often lied in letters to friends about the actual state of her health, and the postcard was no exception. *I am getting stronger by the day*. Arnaud had sent the card two weeks before she died, and so it was historically important—perhaps the last words she'd written.

The color slides held more proof that Arnaud and his mother had been good friends. In one shot they walked arm-in-arm in Times Square, his mother in a flowery sundress and Arnaud in her gray cape and beret. They looked happy, like two girls out on the town. The photo must have been taken a month or so after he was born, because his mother looked postpartum plump. In the second photo, they were pushing a baby carriage, his mother beaming at the camera. Sabine was looking down into the black carriage. She was looking at *him*.

Craig had prints made from the transparencies. There were no known color images of Arnaud, and he wanted to share them with the world—or at least that small part of the world that cared about her life and work. He resolved to contact the best-known Arnaud scholars about the photographs, the postcard, and the friendship between his mother and Arnaud. The matter might have ended there, if not for Rita.

When he showed her the color prints, she was smoking a hash pipe at his kitchen table. Rita glanced at the photo of his mother and Arnaud in Times Square, and said: "She looks pregnant."

"My mother was still carrying some weight."

"No, Sabine."

"Oh, the cape. She always dressed like that, in a tent. To hide her shape, her sex. I'll show you." He opened a biography of Arnaud, which included a dozen black-and-white photos of the philosopher taken in Paris and Marseille. In every shot she wore a long cape and beret—virtually the same outfit as the photos taken with his mother in New York. Unimpressed, Rita took another hit, squinted close to the book photos, and compared them to the color image.

"I think she's pregnant. She's fatter in New York. Besides, she's got that glow, that smile women get when they're pregnant."

"You're crazy. She was a virgin. In France, they called her the Red Virgin—because of her politics and asexual nature."

Rita shrugged, closed her eyes, and exhaled a satisfying hit.

"Just because you think a lot, Marty, it don't mean you're smart."

After Rita left, Craig examined the Times Square photo with a magnifying glass. Arnaud did look healthier than she had in Marseille. As for the "glow," the shot was in color, so her face had flesh tones, not grainy shades of white. And the smile? She'd escaped the Nazis and was standing on the most dazzling street corner in New York. The Red Virgin pregnant? Rita had smoked too much hash.

Craig noted a theater marquee that touted the premier of a movie he'd never heard of, *Footlight Serenade*, starring Betty Grable and Victor Mature. Perhaps Alice and Arnaud had gone to see it. Curious, he looked it up in his *Encyclopedia of American Film*. What he read set his heart pounding. The film had premiered in Hollywood and New York on August 1, 1942, six weeks before his birth. Alice didn't look eight months pregnant, but Arnaud, under the cape, could have been. *Just because you think a lot, Marty, it don't mean you're smart.*

Craig rushed to the closet and dug out his birth certificate. It looked official, issued by the State of New York and signed by one Julius Epstein MD, indicating that Craig Louis Martin was born to Mrs. Alice Jane Martin, at 9:30 a.m. on September 17, at her residence; his father listed as Earl Robert Martin. Alice always said she'd chosen his middle name, Louis, for no particular reason, but it was a French name. The home birth was one of Alice's favorite, self-dramatizing stories. When she went into labor, she claimed, she called an ambulance, but emergency services were delayed because of a big fire in Harlem. So Alice soldiered on bravely, despite ungodly pain, bearing her ungrateful son with the help of a midwife in the building, who eventually summoned a neighborhood doctor. When mother and child finally reached the hospital, the staff all marveled at Alice's courage in giving birth without an anesthetic.

The next morning, Craig was at the library when the doors opened. Microfilm records of the *New York Times* made no mention of a fire on the day he was born. Alice had lied about that. What else had she lied about? He hired a private investigator to dig deeper. Three weeks and five thousand dollars later, he got the report. Alice had not been admitted to any New York hospital on the day of his birth, or the day after. But she had been in July, the treatment records lost. Was her baby stillborn? There had been a Dr. Julius Epstein, with his practice several blocks from Alice's building. He was seventy-eight at the time of Craig's birth.

So Craig shaped a possible narrative: Dr. Epstein arrives at the apartment of a woman who has just given birth. Mother and child are healthy, but the mother—a woman with black hair and stubborn as a mule—refuses to go to the hospital. There is another woman present in this manger, the "midwife" who delivered the baby. She helps the doddering physician complete the paperwork he will file with the State of New York. The mother is listed as Alice Jane Martin, but in fact is Sabine Arnaud—who has bestowed upon Alice the gift of her child.

When he told Rita his theory, she remained skeptical. "If Arnaud had a kid, maybe she gave it to somebody else. Alice had her own baby—*you*."

At a loss to find more clues in the US, Craig looked to France.

It would all depend on his meeting with Sophie Daudin. He'd sent her copies of the photos and postcard, but had yet to advance the case that Arnaud was his birth mother. That could only be done face- to-face. If he could enlist Daudin as an ally, he might uncover a new trail of evidence that would prove what he already believed in his heart was true.

Craig awoke from unsound sleep, startled by sun and bustle in the cabin. Rita was alert, smiling—last night's snit forgotten—digging into an omelet and stealing glances out the window at green fields shadowed by cloud. It was her first glimpse of the Europe she had only read about. She was excited, happy. Craig yawned and rubbed his eyes.

"Get with it, Marty. We're almost there."

"I'm starving."

"I've decided—I want to make love in Paris."

"Who with?"

"You're first in line."

He kissed her on the cheek. "Then I better get some food in me—before I eat."

Craig hailed the stewardess, impeccably dressed in a gray tailored suit with red and blue accents. She sniffed with Gallic condescension at the American in jeans, and delivered his foil-wrapped meal with a smirk. *Welcome to France.*

Rita studied him as he buttered his stale croissant.

"You ever look in the mirror?"

"Why?"

"You'd know you're not Jewish. You're a cute WASP."

"My hair's darker than my parents'."

"What, brown? Hers was black, like a crow."

"Well, the father …"

"Was an albino, a Nazi blond beast?" Rita laughed with her mouth wide, exposing a wad of yellow omelet. Craig looked away, feeling suddenly foolish, knowing she was the voice of reason. He'd examined his face many times, looking for a resemblance to Arnaud and found none—except perhaps for his sad brown eyes.

"You don't know and I don't know," he said. "That's why I'm here."

Rita studied him, sensing his mood, and took his arm.

"You're right, baby. You could be a Jew. You got the nose for it. And you're cheap."

CHAPTER TWO

He stood in the cold drizzle and looked up at her birthplace. The Beaux-Arts building at 19 boulevard de Strasbourg, with its slate roof and stone facade, had probably changed little since February 3, 1909, when Sabine Arnaud took her first breath. On the top floor, where the Arnauds had rented a flat, there was a window open, shutters wide to the weather. With no way of knowing, Craig imagined this was the room in which she was born. It seemed fitting—the open window, curtains billowing inward on the wet breeze—for a woman who would choose suffering over comfort her whole life.

Craig turned up the collar of his coat against the cold and headed south toward the Seine. He walked briskly among the Parisians, woolen scarves wrapped around their necks, faces white, cheeks pink in the cold. Pound's famous lines about the metro came to mind; *The apparition of these faces in the crowd:/ Petals on a wet, black bough*. There was a bounce to his step. He was one of them, by *blood*; he belonged to this greatest of all cities.

Craig had been in Paris once before, in summer, and toured the Louvre, strolled the Luxembourg Gardens. But he loved the city even more in winter, now that he was in search of his past. The gray skies and diffuse light seemed to erase color and time, as if he were a part of a black-and-white photograph of Sabine Arnaud.

His next stop was 37 boulevard Saint-Michel, on the Left Bank, where Sabine had grown up in the shadow of the Sorbonne. After reading two biographies of Arnaud, Craig knew the family history well. Sabine's father, Bernard, was a kindly doctor; Selma, the driven Jewish mother, showered Sabine and her brother, André, with love and worry, pushed them to excel in school, and was certain they were destined to achieve great things.

As a child, Sabine was never selfish—just perversely unselfish. When her uncle brought Sabine a beautiful ring for her seventh birthday, she refused to accept it. "I don't like luxury," she said sternly, to her mother's embarrassment. On another occasion, as the family lugged suitcases from the train station in winter, Sabine sat down in the snow and refused to budge—until she was given a bag to carry that was as heavy as her brother's. Selma exhorted Sabine, who was always sickly, to eat and rest, but the child seemed oblivious to the needs of her own body.

Sabine's brother, André, her senior by three years, would rush home from school to share all the wonders of math and science he learned so easily. He taught his sister to read the newspaper when she was five. A year later, Sabine could recite long passages by heart from Racine, standing on a chair as though it were a stage, to the delight of her parents. The two gifted children were inseparable. They laughed, fought, competed for bragging rights in memorizing poetry, and debated philosophy. André was even tempered, eager to please. Sabine was willful, maddeningly stubborn on matters of principle, and her mother's favorite. When Selma learned of Sabine's death in 1943, she spiraled into inconsolable despair and took her own life.

Craig moved on to inspect the schools Sabine attended—the Lycées Fenelon, Victor-Duruy, and Henri-IV—and, finally, the exclusive *École Normale Supérieure*, where she achieved the highest qualifying score for entry, besting Simone de Beauvoir. The two met only once. Simone was intrigued by Sabine's mannish clothes, radical politics, and rumored genius. Simone introduced herself, and a philosophical discussion ensued. Sabine argued that what mattered most was a revolution that would feed the world's starving masses. Simone countered that what mattered more was to find a reason for man's existence. Sabine ended the conversation, snapping: "It's easy to see that you've never gone hungry." Simone felt she had been dismissed as a high-minded *petite bourgeoisie* and never spoke to Sabine again.

By all accounts, Sabine had infuriated all those who might claim her for their own. She was a Christian who refused baptism, a Jew who denied her own heritage, a Marxist who denounced communism, and a towering intellect who condemned the intelligentsia for their social privilege and moral cowardice. Perhaps most telling, she was a prophet of love who shrank from the touch of man or woman.

Craig checked his watch and headed for Saint-Germain-des-Prés to meet Rita at *Les Deux Magots*, which she'd read about in *A Moveable Feast*. Unlike most women, she liked Hemingway, because, as she concluded, "he cuts to the chase and don't write to hear himself think. Of course he's a prick and hates women—but so what? He's a man."

Rita was late as usual. No doubt still shopping for a winter coat, with his money. She was shocked by how cold and dark it was in Paris in late November. "City of Unholy Night," she called it. The weather had put her in such a foul mood that she'd refused his touch after their first day of sightseeing. Craig didn't much care.

For the first time in years he felt excited by the *possibility* of life, by what he might become, though he could not put a name to it.

With time to kill, he headed south to Daudin's address on the Rue de Sèvres. In her last letter, she'd agreed to meet at her apartment on November 23—tomorrow. Since arriving in Paris, he'd called her repeatedly to confirm the appointment, but nobody picked up. He was getting worried.

Daudin's building was bland, institutional, the street door locked. He found her name on the list of tenants and hit the call button. The intercom erupted at once, as though he were expected—a male voice talking rapidly in French. Craig didn't understand a word, but the door buzzed open and he stepped inside. Her apartment was on the second floor. When he topped the stairs, there was a priest standing in the doorway at the end of the hall.

"Qui etes-vous?" the priest asked.

"I don't speak French. My name is Craig Martin, from Los Angeles. I'm here to see Dr. Daudin. She knows who I am."

The priest went back inside and a stern woman with glasses and gray hair replaced him in the doorway.

"Professor Daudin?" Craig ventured.

"You don't know?"

"Know what?"

"My sister is dead. What do you want?"

Craig told her of his correspondence with Daudin and their appointment. He wanted to ask how she died, but thought better of it.

"Yes, yes, the *book*," she said bittterly. "It was all she cared about. It killed her, the pressure... pressure..." Her voice trailed off. "I am sorry you came all this way, for nothing." She stepped back into the apartment and shut the door.

"Get over it, Marty. Let's fly to Rome, or Greece, where it's warm. If you want to believe Sabine was your mother, believe it. You was never going to find out for sure. This was always a wild-goose chase—I knew that. You didn't. It's over."

They sat in wicker chairs in the crowded *Deaux Magots*, their table scarcely big enough for two cups of espresso. The heat was turned up and the windows fogged.

"Think of it this way," Rita said, "you're the son of a *bitch*, as you call your mother, or the son of your saintly Sabine. Either way you're sad-eyed Craig sitting at a café in Paris with coffee spilled on your shirt. I've seen Paris. Let's go to Rome. "

Craig checked his shirt, noted the stain, and shook his head. "You still think I'm rich, don't you? Fly you anywhere, wine and dine you?"

"You are rich."

"My net worth is about ten grand."

"Your Porsche's worth more than that."

"It's not a *liquid* asset."

"You're rich."

"I'll buy your ticket home. You can stay on in Paris with me, if you like. But I'm not leaving until I get what I came for. I want the names of every living soul who knew Arnaud and where to find them. And if it takes every last cent I've got, *and* my fucking Porsche, so be it."

Rita said nothing. But Craig thought he detected something in her shrewd eyes that looked like respect, if not admiration.

The receptionist at Gallimard said it was out of the question. Craig had asked to see the legendary Jacques Rédon, the editor in chief of the most respected publishing house in Europe, where Daudin had a contract. He directed his California looks and boyish charm at the attractive receptionist, hinting at secrets only he knew about Sabine Arnaud that Rédon would be eager to learn. But she wouldn't budge. She told him to write a letter requesting an appointment. He insisted she announce his presence and purpose to Rédon's secretary. She picked up the phone, punched in a number, rattled off something in French, smiled, and replaced the receiver, immensely pleased with herself. "Monsieur Rédon is not available. I must ask you to leave."

"I'm an optimist. I'll wait." Craig took a seat and settled in for the afternoon. Life was simple when you couldn't take "no" for an answer. He closed his eyes, concentrating on the calming mantra he used to meditate.

Ten minutes later his reverie was interrupted by a security guard who escorted him out of the building. Craig found a *brasserie* across the street and took a table by the window with a view of the entrance to Gallimard. He'd seen Rédon on TV, interviewed by Dick Cavett. With his large head, wire glasses, and mane of white hair, Rédon was the quintessential French intellectual, railing against the evils of America's cultural imperialism. It was four o'clock. He would wait and corner Rédon when he left the office. Craig settled in and ordered coffee, then soup, and finally a bottle of wine to hold the table.

It was six thirty when he saw Rédon's white head bobbing among the crowd leaving the building. He was tall, in a black raincoat, and walking fast, talking and gesturing to another man, who had trouble keeping up. Craig rushed out, darting through traffic to keep Rédon in sight.

After three blocks, the two men pushed through the doors of the Hotel d'Angleterre and headed for the bar, where they were greeted by a starched waiter who escorted them to a choice table near the fireplace. Craig found a seat at the bar and studied Rédon. Though he said nothing, the force of his personality seemed to dominate the room. Rédon sipped his drink from a frosted martini glass, composed but not bored, while his companion talked.

Craig slid the photo of Arnaud and his mother in Times Square out of its folio, crossed the room to the table, and stood over Rédon. As the leonine head swiveled to glare at the intruder, Craig placed the photo in front of him. Rédon snatched it up angrily and was about to speak when the image registered. He glanced at Craig and returned his attention to the photo, his eyes moving searchingly behind wire glasses. When he was satisfied, he motioned for Craig to sit. Five minutes later, Rédon's friend had gone and they were deep in conversation.

"Sophie called me the night she died," Rédon said. He spoke perfect English, but with a strong accent, perhaps to show he was deigning to speak an inferior tongue "She didn't sound upset, just tired. She told me to publish the book as it stood. She was done. Not another word. A few hours later, she took an overdose of sleeping pills, but didn't leave a note. Perhaps she felt, with the book finished—her life's work, really—she had nothing to live for."

Craig told Rédon about Alice's friendship with Arnaud, but held off on advancing his theory that Arnaud was his birth mother.

"Sophie never told me about you. She was secretive about her work—obsessed, I should say. The manuscript has been complete for almost a year, but she would not let go of it."

"The Times Square photo would make a great cover, don't you think? Just crop out my mother and it's the best photo ever taken of Arnaud—and in color."

Rédon's mood turned suspicious. "We already have an image for the cover, which is quite powerful. I imagine, being an American, you want compensation for the right to print your picture?"

"Not a sou. But something."

"And what might that be?"

"Something that could make Daudin's book a global best-seller."

Craig related the clues that led him to suspect that Arnaud was his birth mother, and asked for access to Daudin's manuscript, research, interviews, and living sources as a condition for publishing the photograph. Rédon was incredulous. He shook his big head in a resounding NO, and slammed his fist on the table.

"My God, that's delusional! Arnaud an unwed mother—your mother? Absurd. You seem like a sensible sort, but really… I have no time for this." Rédon motioned for the check. "And out of the question, what you want. I don't need you—or your snapshot."

Craig surprised himself by placing his hand gently over Rédon's. "You need to listen to me, Monsieur Rédon—for two more minutes. I've come a long way. And I can help you sell books." Rédon was startled by Craig's touch, but then relaxed—a little.

"You're right," Craig said. "The idea is crazy. The Red Virgin the mother of an American? But it's not absurd—because it's *possible,* given the evidence. I'll sign a nondisclosure agreement before you give me access to the manuscript and research. I won't write about Arnaud, or upstage Daudin.

"I can help you sell books. Your author, no disrespect, is dead. She can't do media interviews, lectures, or book tours. So, you print my photograph, explain where it came from in the introduction to the book. An American, a TV writer for God's sake, with a crazy theory about Arnaud being pregnant when she came to New York, shows up at your door. You say my pregnancy theory is surely false, but the photograph is *real,* and beautiful, and you thank me for my contribution to Daudin's monumental biography of Arnaud. You debunk my theory, but *mention* it. The media will run with it, believe me. Distance yourself from me, but if the media wants an interview—I'll do it. In France, or in the States, at my expense. You said an English translation was in the works. I can promote the hell out of your book by stirring up interest in Arnaud on both sides of the Atlantic—and it won't cost you a franc. That's the worst-case scenario—you sell more books. Best-case scenario, I turn up credible evidence *before* you publish that Arnaud *was* pregnant when she came to New York, and you put *that* in the book—the Red Virgin and her American love child—and you've got a best-seller. Either way you win big with me on your team, Jacques. May I call you Jacques?"

Craig was out of breath, perspiring; he'd slipped into Hollywood pitch mode. He wiped his face and considered Rédon, who drummed his fingers thoughtfully on the table.

"I'm sorry," Rédon said, finally. "I can't dignify your motherhood theory by mentioning it in my introduction to a serious work of scholarship. I'd look the fool. So keep your picture."

Rédon stood and started for the door. Craig caught up and blocked his path.

"Counter offer, Jacques. You publish my photo, no conditions. And I pay you, for your trouble, five hundred dollars for the name and address of every person alive who knew Arnaud during the last two years of her life. The living sources that Daudin interviewed."

Rédon considered the offer with furrowed brow.

"Five hundred for all the names, or each?"

"Each—if the list is short, as I suspect it is."

"In cash, off the record, just between you and me?"

The next morning, after a brief meeting with Rédon, in which Craig parted with fifteen hundred dollars (wishing it was more), he was introduced to Daudin's research assistant, Claire Brion—pale, thin, with moist palms—who would supply the names. She suggested they go to a café to talk.

In the elevator, he stole glances at her long face and knots of stringy blond hair. She carried a valise, but no purse.

Craig followed her into a Tabac, empty except for an old man smoking at the bar. She took a table in the rear and removed a sheaf of papers from her valise. "Jacques will allow you to read the manuscript, English translation in progress, if you sign this." He scanned the nondisclosure agreement and signed it.

"How much do you know, about me?" Craig asked

"I was Sophie's assistant for five years—and her friend for eight. Jacques told me why you want the research. I share his view that your pregnancy theory is nonsense. That said, I *am* very interested in the material you sent to Sophie. In fact, you are the reason she went to London—the week before she died."

"I don't understand."

"Did you show Jacques the postcard?"

"No, just the photograph."

"Good. I'm the only one who knows."

"Knows what?"

"Please, may I see the originals?"

Craig removed the photographs and postcard from his portfolio. She ignored the photos and examined the card with a magnifying glass.

"It is as Sophie thought," she said. "She could not be sure from the copy. Did you examine the postmark?"

"The note was dated August 9."

"Not August. Arnaud wrote eight—nine—forty-three, which

you assumed was August 9. In France, we write the day first, then the month—which caught our attention."

"So, she reversed it. She was sick. She didn't write the card after she was dead. What's your point?"

"The postmark, very faint, with the numbers in conventional order, confirms it was mailed on September 8. It is easy to miss. Here, look." She pushed the card toward him and held the glass over it. "And the postmark is from Guildford, fifty kilometers from the sanitarium in Ashford where she died. Odd, don't you think?"

"Maybe she gave the card to someone to mail—and they forgot. Then mailed it later."

"Perhaps. But Sophie tracked down a new source—after your letter. That's why she went to London. Mavis Osborn—an aid at the sanitarium in 1943. No one knew she existed. The other principals from that time—Sabine's doctor, the medical examiner who signed her death certificate—are long dead. Sophie called me after the interview, very excited. She said she had it all on tape. She gave no details—just that Osborn told her Sabine was making progress in early August, eating more, gaining weight. And then she was taken away—for tests somewhere. Osborn got word she was dead about a week later, from an infection. Sophie was going to interview the philosopher Denis Colson again, at Cambridge."

"He was Arnaud's closest British friend, was he not?"

"Yes. He arranged her transfer from Middlesex Hospital in London to Grosvenor Sanitorium in Ashford—because she wanted to be in the country. Sophie interviewed him at length two years ago, but now questioned his story. She wanted to dig deeper. I never heard from her again."

"Rédon said Sophie called him the night she died."

"But she didn't call me—which wasn't like her."

"Well, she was depressed… suicidal."

"After I heard what happened, her sister let me search the apartment. There was no tape recorder, no record of her interviews in England. That's when I began to feel something was… not right."

"Meaning?"

"The bottle of sleeping pills found by her bed was from a pharmacy in London, prescribed by a doctor there. When Sophie telephoned me from London, she made no mention of needing to see a doctor. And she shared everything with me."

"We all have secrets."

"Not Sophie…not from me." She choked up, then gathered herself. "Sophie's sister is a doctor. She demanded a copy of the actual autopsy report."

"And?"

"The report stated she died of an overdose of barbituates. But there was something else. In the routine description of the body, the coroner wrote that the area around the pubis had been recently shaved, with superficial cuts and abrasions."

"She shaved her…that area?"

"Sophie was not vain. She rarely used makeup and did not shave her legs. And certainly not there."

"You're sure?'

"Yes, certain," Claire said curtly.

"Well, there's some explanation."

"Obviously. In any case, this is for you." She stood and handed him the manuscript. "This is the English translation, in progress. Also, contact information for the three people left alive who knew Arnaud during the time period you requested. I found a phone number for Mavis Osborn in Sophie's desk. I tried the number, but it had been disconnected. I included her address. She lives in Swindon—west of London. Colson's phone and address in Cambridge are here as well. The third name you will know, Father Cartan, who wrote of his friendship with Sabine. He's quite feeble now, and lives in Trieste. He remained in Paris during the occupation, and had virtually no contact with Sabine after she left for Marseille. So I suggest you see Osborn and Colson first—to complete the interviews that Sophie thought most vital to her book."

"I'll record my interviews. You'll know everything I find out," Craig said. "You can finish the book the way Professor Daudin would have wanted."

"One more thing," Claire said. "And this keeps me awake nights. The last thing Sophie said to me—when she called from London—was 'maybe Agnes was right.' Agnes Baseden was—"

"The Arnauds' housekeeper," Craig said. "She lived in their Paris flat during the occupation."

"Correct. Sophie interviewed her eight years ago, when she was ninety-two, senile—incoherent. She claimed that Sabine knocked on her door in 1944, after the liberation of Paris. Agnes said she told her, and I quote, 'You may not come in because you are dead.' Naturally, Sophie discounted the story as the ramblings of a demented old woman."

Claire extended her moist hand and managed a smile. "Thank you for your interest in Sabine Arnaud. She was not your mother, but she was an inspired philosopher and a great soul."

CHAPTER THREE

The North Atlantic. December 1942

The Atlantic crossing on a Swedish freighter took two weeks. The handful of passengers—terrified of U-boats—kept mostly to their cabins, but Sabine paced the decks on clear nights, when the threat of attack was high. She was not without fear, but the fear was bracing, like the icy air. It eased the guilt she'd felt in the safety of New York. At last, she was in danger, in reach of the same Nazi war machine that oppressed her countrymen.

She scanned the dark ocean and imagined the enemy beneath it. The stars took her breath away. At the bow, cold hands on the iron railing, she watched the hissing apron of surf spread away from the ship and die into foam on the black waves. Each rolling surge of the ship took her closer to war-torn Europe, where her destiny lay.

When the ship docked in Liverpool, Sabine was bussed to a ref-ugee center on the outskirts of London, known as the "Patriotic

School," fenced by razor wire and guarded by soldiers. There, confined to barracks, she was fingerprinted, photographed, and interrogated by military intelligence about her political loyalties. The vetting process—to ensure she was not a German or Russian spy—took more than two weeks.

Sabine used the time to work on her proposal to form a corps of front-line nurses that she hoped to present to General de Gaulle. She also wrote a letter to her parents in Montreal, apologizing for her cruel silence in New York.

> *Please forgive me for not writing more. I was consumed by the tedious appeals and permissions required to secure a visa to England in time of war. Now that I am in London, I know that you will worry even more about my safety. But here I must be. The suffering of my brothers in France obsesses me, to the point of annihilating my faculties. It is only by securing for myself a large share of danger and hardship in the fight against Hitler that I can find peace. I do not expect you to approve, or to fully understand. Just know that if I had several lives, I would devote one of them to you.*

When released from the Patriotic School, Sabine moved into the flat of Denis Colson, whom she'd met in Paris when he was a philosophy student at the Sorbonne. Now he was attached to the foreign office, rejected for military service because of a bad heart. Colson offered her the one bedroom in his small flat, but Sabine—ever the ascetic—insisted on sleeping on the floor in the pantry.

Sabine turned to her old friend from the *École Normale Supérieure*, Maurice Schumann, who was de Gaulle's spokesman in London, broadcasting inspirational messages on the BBC to Nazi-occupied Europe. They met in a pub near the Savoy and Maurice reviewed her proposal for a corps of front-line nurses. The document, written in her clear and precise hand, ran to more than thirty pages. Sabine sat patiently as he read, observing the other patrons.

She was struck by how reserved and polite the British were, not shouting at each other as people seemed to do in France.

Maurice took off his glasses and wiped his eyes. He seemed deeply moved by what he had read. "So very beautiful, *mon cher*, and of course brilliantly argued. I shall get it typed and give it to de Gaulle. He may think you quite mad, or he may love it. I can not predict his moods in these dark days. But read it he shall."

Two weeks later, Sabine was summoned to Free French headquarters at 4 Carlton Gardens, near St. James's Park. The building was nondescript, but surrounded by elegant mansions that bordered the park.

De Gaulle's adjutant warned Sabine that the general had allotted only ten minutes for the interview. She should not sit unless invited to. The adjutant opened a heavy door and Sabine entered a high-ceilinged room with a chandelier, fireplace, and four armchairs in front of an enormous desk. The general glanced up at the intruder and went back to the papers he was signing. On the wall behind his desk was a large map of the world and a larger map of France. Pale winter light, streaked with dust, flooded through the floor-to-ceiling windows that faced the green expanse of St. James's Park.

After a long minute, pen scratching on paper, de Gaulle stood, as if coming to attention, and smoothed the wrinkles on his immaculate uniform. He came around the desk, towering over Sabine, bowed slightly, and took her hand in his enormous paw. "Welcome to Free France," he said gravely, and patted the leather chair where he wished her to sit. His long face reminded Sabine of a medieval knight, chivalrous and somber. De Gaulle returned to his desk and studied Sabine, his palms together. "Maurice tells me that you are the most intelligent woman he has ever known."

"In my experience, General, the exalted praise of my intelligence is usually intended to evade the question of whether what I say is actually true. Have you read my proposal?"

"Only the first page—enough to be mystified. You want to put nurses on the front line. But we have soldier medics who serve in battle. Surely you see how impractical—"

"A woman's life should not be valued more than a man's. To be sure, these women volunteers would have to be exceptionally brave, treating the wounded in the midst of battle, and inspiring the troops with their willingness to die to save lives. Just as the fanatical SS are prepared to die in the service of brutality and murder, we would embody a higher moral calling for self-sacrifice—one that would illustrate with supreme clarity the two roads between which humanity is forced to choose. This corps of heroic women would also capture the imagination and boost the morale of the general public—far more than any slogan."

De Gaulle seemed at a loss for words. "Go on," he said.

"Certainly there are risks in such a plan. The women's courage might fail under fire. And their presence among soldiers at the front might have undesirable moral effects."

De Gaulle laughed. "*Might,* my dear? You know very little about soldiers deprived of the company of women."

"These volunteers would, of course, be selected for their high moral character, as well as courage. I do not believe our soldiers would show disrespect to a woman who was brave under fire. And when the front line was quiet, the women could be sent to the rear."

"I take it you are volunteering to serve in this corps of front-line nurses."

"I am, sir."

"But you are an academic, not a nurse."

"I completed a Red Cross course in first aid in New York. An elementary knowledge of nursing will suffice, because nothing can be done in battle except dressings, tourniquets, and perhaps injections. I know there are risks, but the plan could be launched on a small scale, as an experiment, with as few as ten volunteers—"

"Enough," De Gaulle broke in and stood up, extending his hand across the desk. The interview was over. "Your proposal is well-intentioned, but absurd."

"Sir, if you took the time to read it, I think all of your objections would be satisfactorily addressed. The risks are slight, but the potential great. Why not try—"

"Time I do not have—for this kind of high-minded folly. But you are a patriot and have crossed the Atlantic to serve. And serve you shall. You have my word."

Sabine was put to work in the administrative arm of de Gaulle's fiefdom, drafting papers on the political and social ideals that should govern post-war France. Though bitterly disappointed, she threw herself into the job, working long hours at her cramped desk in the basement of Free French headquarters. Sabine wrote in long hand, each letter perfectly formed—each thought indelibly expressed. She seldom revised, filling notebook after notebook with thoughts on the human condition.

> *There is a reality outside the world, that is to say, outside space and time, outside man's mental universe, outside any sphere whatsoever that is accessible to human faculties. Corresponding to this reality, at the center of the human heart, is the longing for an absolute good, a longing which is always there and is never appeased by any object in this world.*

Sabine had a persistent cough now, an ugly hacking cough that she attributed to smoking. *I must quit*, she thought, *or I will not be of use*. But she had tried and failed many times. It was her one vice. She could do without food or warmth or sleep, but not her cigarettes—which seemed to drive the engine of her mind. Often, just before sleep, an idea might seize her, and she would chisel bone to bear the flesh of another essay. *Risk is an essential need of the soul. The absence of risk produces a type of boredom which paralyzes in a different way from fear, but almost as much.* Then she would smoke one last cigarette and look out the window at the stars glittering over blacked-out London.

Frustrated by her desk job, Sabine begged Colson to use his influence to help her return to France to aid the Resistance. He promised to do what he could, but only if she took better care of herself and ate the nourishing meals he wanted to cook for her. She rejected the bribe: "I will not eat the food of the English without taking part in the war effort."

Against his better judgment, Colson recommended Sabine to Carlton Hays, who was attached to the Special Operations Executive (SOE), a secret organization that recruited refugees from Nazi-occupied Europe as spies. Colson thought she would be rejected, but he had to try. Sabine was the only woman he had ever loved—though the love was that of a man for an older, wiser, braver sister whose approval he craved. Some weeks later, Sabine received a buff-colored envelope from the Ministry of Pensions. Inside was a letter from the War Office, Room 55, embossed with a gold seal, inviting her to attend a meeting the following Tuesday in the Sanctuary Building in Westminster. It was signed C. Hays.

Colson explained that the interview with his friend, Charlie Hays, would evaluate her suitability to serve in the First Aid Nursing Yeomanry, an all-volunteer women's organization that supported the war effort. He could not tell her that the FANYs, as they were called, also provided cover for SOE women recruits. "Look your best," he advised her. "Wash your clothes. And eat something for God's sake. You look like a scarecrow."

On the appointed day, Sabine rose early and spent time in front of the mirror, scrubbing her face and brushing her intractable hair, which flared from her skull like crow's wings. She did not own makeup, so she pinched her cheeks hard to give them color—but the color drained quickly away. She remained a ghost, stranded between life and death.

The pants and blouse she'd washed the night before were still damp, but she put them on anyway—the fabric cold and clammy on her skin. She threw on her wool cape, stained but dry, and walked nine blocks in the rain to the brick office block on Great Smith Street. By the time she entered the Sanctuary Building, she was drenched and shivering.

In the cavernous entry hall, a rat-faced man in a black suit sat at a desk reading the *Daily Telegraph*. Sabine composed herself, willing her teeth to stop chattering so she could speak. The man looked up at the cadaver in front of him, smelling of wet wool, and lifted an eyebrow. When she showed him her letter, the eyebrow descended.

Without a word he stood and led her up a marble staircase, then down a carpeted corridor, where he opened an unmarked door, gestured for Sabine to enter, and closed the door behind her.

The room was small, with bare floors and a single desk. Behind the desk was a man in a tweed jacket, scraping the bowl of his pipe with a penknife. To his left, a matronly woman in uniform sat against the wall with a notebook on her lap.

Sabine shivered under the cape, waiting for the man to speak. He did not. Nor did he look at her. His attention was focused on filling his pipe with tobacco from a leather pouch.

"Mr. Hays?"

"Sit down." He waved at the chair in front of his desk, his eyes fixed on the match flame dipping into the bowl of tobacco as he sucked at the stem. When the pipe was uniformly lit, glowing red, he exhaled a pungent white cloud and shifted his gaze to Sabine Arnaud. He was struck immediately by her Semitic features.

Carlton Hays was twenty-six, but projected the authority of a man twice his age. His dark complexion reflected his Welsh heritage. Raised in poverty, he'd won a scholarship to Cambridge, and worked hard ever since to adopt the speech and manners of the upper class, which he despised.

"Oh dear," he said. "You're all wet. Did you not escape France with an umbrella?" Hays chuckled at his own joke and glanced at the woman against the wall, who smiled appreciatively. "I speak passable French," he continued, "if you would prefer to chat in your native tongue."

"I am in England. I will speak English."

"Commendable. Your friend Colson tells me you want to help us win the war—after you dry off, of course."

"Yes. I want to return to France—to fight with the Resistance."

"In that case, perhaps you shouldn't have fled the country."

"I regret leaving with all my heart."

"But you did. And now you are in Britain, with temporary papers. The lady to my left, Mrs. Avery, is a member of the First Aid Nursing Yeomanry. She represents a group of women volunteers who serve where needed—freeing up our men to fight. Our ladies work in hospitals, as wireless operators, translators, typists, drivers, parachute riggers, and many other jobs. I am here to determine your skills. I'm not in the cloak-and-dagger business—in case you harbor some romantic notion of being parachuted into France as Joan of Arc."

Sabine said nothing. But her bemused smile unsettled Hays.

"I know your age and education—from the papers you filled out at the Patriotic School. I understand you work in de Gaulle's organization now, drafting policy papers, so I assume you can type."

"I can not. I write in longhand."

"Do you have practical skills—other than teaching Plato to schoolgirls?"

"I worked in a Renault factory, as a drill press operator."

"Why, for God's sake?"

"I wanted to know the life of the laboring class."

"How noble. For how long?"

"Two months. I was fired for not being fast enough. It was piecework, with an hourly quota for finished parts. I could not have tried harder. I also worked at a plant that manufactured components for streetcars, for six weeks. The cutting tool I was assigned to broke down repeatedly. The foreman said my poor technique was to blame. He fired me—I thought unjustly."

"A bit clumsy, are we? Do you have manual skills of any kind? Can you drive a car, a lorry? A motorcycle?"

"I could learn. If it was essential to my mission."

"Do you have domestic talents?" Hays asked impatiently. "Baking, sewing, pattern making? Some of our ladies cook for the troops, mend uniforms, tents, that sort of thing."

"I have no such skills. And I will not be content until I secure a job in the war effort that involves both hardship and danger. Surely there cannot be such demand for dangerous jobs that one is not available? I would accept any degree of risk, even certain death if the objective was sufficiently important."

"Indeed."

Hays drew on his pipe, studying this strange creature who seemed without fear and without guile. He noted her nicotine-stained fingers.

"Would you like to smoke?"

"Not now."

"Tell me about the circumstances under which you fled Paris in 1940."

"I left by train with my parents, for Marseille, in June, when it was clear there would be no defense of Paris."

"Did your family fear persecution by the Germans? Are you of Jewish heritage?"

"My parents subscribe to no religion. My grandparents were observant Jews."

"Then I'm afraid Herr Hitler would consider you and your family full-blooded Jews."

"I have never set foot in a synagogue. And I detest the Hebrew bible, with its vengeful God and the idea of a 'Chosen People'—as abhorrent to me as Hitler's 'Master Race.'

"So you consider yourself a Christian convert?"

"I feel—in my soul—that I belong to Christ. But I have not been baptized. I believe God wants me to remain outside the church, on the threshold, not *inside*."

"How jolly for you, knowing what God wants," Hays said. "I'm afraid I've never had a clue what that old gentlemen in the sky wants of me, or of anybody else. Did you leave family behind in France—siblings, a husband, child?"

"No one. My brother went to Switzerland before the war."

"Not even a lover? An attractive woman like you?" Hays asked contemptuously.

Sabine glared back, but said nothing.

"I have one more question. How did you feel about the French collapse, after less than six weeks of fighting the Germans?"

"I believe the armistice was an act of cowardice."

"More than a few Brits agree with you. Including most certainly our dead at Dunkirk. What other grand thoughts did you have when France surrendered?"

Sabine reflected on the question. "As I recall, I remarked that it was a great day for Indochina."

"Indochina?" Hays asked, incredulous. "Oh, of course. The fall of an oppressive, colonial power. You have an extraordinary mind, Miss Arnaud. But I am not at all sure we have a job to match your talents. I will be in touch if we can find one. You may go now."

Hays did not stand to shake hands. When Sabine had gone out and closed the door, he drew on his pipe and blew a perfect smoke ring that drifted toward the ceiling. "Don't bother to open a file on her, Miss Avery. Colson sent us a bloody useless kike."

CHAPTER FOUR

With the wipers of the Mini Morris slapping furiously, they drove in silence through sheets of rain. Craig hunched over the tiny wheel, following the white line through watery glass. The boxy car rattled like a tin can, though the rental agent had sworn it was last year's model. Rita was sullen, holding her belly. He'd pulled over twice for her to throw up on the side of the road. Her black hair was wet and tangled.

"It must have been those eggs," Craig said. Their flight from Paris to Heathrow had landed late and they spent the night in an airport hotel—which included a greasy breakfast.

"I called Donny last night," Rita said. "He wants me back."

"All is forgiven? Running out on him, leaving his car at the airport? I knew you called long distance. The charge was on the bill. It cost more than the room."

Rita shrugged. "We said what had to be said. He told me he can't live without me. Which you don't understand. Because you never loved no one. Have you? Except your dead, sexless Saint Sabine. Poor Marty, dead lover of the dead."

"I'm sorry about last night. I shouldn't have woken you up."

"You said you wanted to make love."

"I thought I did."

"Until I got naked."

"I was lonely. I guess I just wanted to snuggle."

"Snuggle your fag hag, Sabine."

"Knock it off, Rita. You're sexy as hell."

"Stop the car. I got to barf."

He pulled over and she opened the door and leaned out. Craig steadied her as she retched and coughed, cars swooshing past in the rain. He handed her the towel she'd taken from the hotel to wipe her mouth. She was breathless, panting, hair soaked. "Still think I'm sexy?"

"I will when the puke smell dissipates."

"Sorry. I'm a stinky bitch."

They drove for a while in silence. Rita sprayed her hands and face with a nauseatingly sweet cologne.

"I wasn't just lonely last night," Craig said. "I was nervous—about Daudin's death, her shaved pussy, about what the fuck I'm doing here."

"Well, you should be nervous. There's a car tailing us."

"You're crazy."

"Every time you stop, I see the same black car go past."

"Christ, all the cars here are black."

"Not with the same license plate. You've led a sheltered life, Marty. There is *evil* in this world. I know. I can feel it, smell it when it gets close."

Rita crossed her arms, closed her eyes, and leaned her head against the window. She dozed off quickly, her lips parted, snoring her distinctive catlike purr. If she did think they were being followed, which he doubted, she wasn't losing any sleep over it. Still,

Craig found himself checking the rearview mirror.

Forty minutes later he pulled into a gas station in Swindon, bought a map, and found his way to an old part of town near a steel mill. The Osborn address was on a brick row house coated with soot.

When he switched off the engine, Rita stirred. "This is it." Craig said. "You coming?"

"To do what?"

"Knock on the door. What else?"

"It's your show. I'll wait."

Craig nervously gathered up his notepad and tape recorder while Rita looked on, amused. He got out, squared his shoulders, and crossed the street, stepping over black puddles. At the door, he took a deep breath, rehearsing his ingratiating spiel, and knocked. Waited. Knocked again—harder. Waited, then went back to the car.

"No luck," he said in disgust. "Not home."

"She's there. The curtains moved while you was on the porch. Somebody checked you out."

"So I'll knock again."

"Should I help him, God, or not?" Rita lifted her palms toward the heavens. "Oh, what the hell." She drummed her fingers on the dash. "We need a story, a scam. What?" She examined the contents of the glove box, studying the leather folder with a plastic window that held the registration. Then she tore off a page of the rental car contract, folded it, and slid it into the folder. She held it up. "You paid for car insurance on this wreck from Hollister Insurance. There they are in big red type, and your signature."

"So?"

"I'll do the talking." Rita fussed with her hair and put on orange lipstick—which she swore complemented her "caramel" skin.

43

"Follow me and keep your mouth shut."

She led the way with purposeful strides and pounded on the door with explosive force. "Police! Open up! Police!" The door cracked open, chain in place, and a woman's frightened face appeared.

"Mavis Osborn?" Rita sneered with cop-like scorn. "Hollister Insurance, private investigators. Detectives." She flipped open the folder and waved it past the woman's wary eyes. "I'm Mrs. Gaona, Deputy Investigator. This is Chief Investigator, Mr. Craig Martin. We need to ask you a few questions about Professor Sophie Daudin. If you won't cooperate, we'll come back with our friends from Scotland Yard—who won't be so nice. But you're not in trouble, *yet*. Can we come in? A minute of your time?"

The chain came off and they entered a dark room that smelled of fried eggs. Osborn, thin with gray hair, clutched her pink bathrobe tight.

"May I call you Mavis?" Rita asked sweetly.

"My husband is coming soon. He don't like me here alone."

Rita pulled up a chair and leaned in close. "Mavis, dear, we know that Sophie talked to you about two weeks ago—"

"I don't know nothing about why she died."

"Did I say she was dead?"

"I saw it on the news. On the BBC."

"Mavis, dear, Sophie Daudin died of a drug overdose. She had a life insurance policy with our company. Her family claims it was accidental. We think it was suicide. And we don't pay off for suicide. You get the picture? Detective Martin will take your statement—which you must swear is the God's truth. Do you solemnly swear, Mavis? Do you?" Mavis nodded.

Craig winced at Rita's Perry Mason theatrics, but the woman was cowed. He snapped on his tape recorder. "Before I ask you about Professor Daudin's mental state, I want to confirm that you met with her on or about November the tenth. And you discussed your memory of Sabine Arnaud in August 1943."

"I didn't say nothing."

"But you knew Arnaud? You worked at the sanitarium where she died."

"I was just a girl. I cooked, cleaned. She was kind to me, Miss Arnaud. I was nobody. But she was curious about my life. Even gave me advice, she did, about boys. Be a good girl—she said. So I wouldn't, you know, get in trouble."

Craig's heart jumped. He took a deep breath to steady himself. "Did Arnaud say she had a child out of wedlock, or give you reason to believe that she had?"

"Oh, no. Miss Arnaud was very proper. Never talked about a man in her life. She was so sick, hardly ate. I cooked special things for her... pudding, sweet cakes. But she couldn't keep nothing down."

"You told Daudin that Sabine *was* eating, getting stronger in August of 1943. You also said she was taken away somewhere—to another hospital. You were surprised, shocked when you heard she had died."

"That's a lie. I never said such a thing."

"Why should it matter if you did?"

"I told you what I know."

Rita excused herself to go to the bathroom. Craig changed the subject. "Was Professor Daudin depressed when you saw her? Did she seem upset by what you told her?" A car horn beeped three times. Mavis jumped to her feet.

"It's my husband. You must go now. Please." She rushed to the door and opened it. A red Triumph at the curb, a stocky man beaming beside it, shouting for Mavis to come look. Craig stood as Rita came back into the room.

When they got outside, the man came toward them, scowling. Craig gave him a wide berth, but Rita walked by close enough to brush his arm. And then lingered under his withering gaze to inspect the sports car.

"Right off the showroom floor, I bet. What'd it cost you?"

"None of your goddamn business."

Rita slid her finger over the gleaming paint. "Or maybe it was gift? You look like a man with rich friends."

As they roared out of Swindon, patches of blue appeared behind scudding clouds. Craig felt good behind the wheel, in control again, after the tense scene with Mavis. He wished he could have questioned her at length, about what Sabine was like, what they had talked about—no matter how mundane. Still, it was progress to have been in the same room with someone who had actually known Sabine. He would focus on that. The rest of it made him queasy. Mavis and her pink bathrobe. The smell of fried eggs, and *fear*. Hers *and* his own—which he could no longer dismiss with logic. His eyes returned again to the rearview mirror.

Rita punched his arm. "Relax. I was wrong. We didn't have no tail this morning. At least we don't now. But then again"—she grinned—"if they're *really* good, you don't see them. When I got busted in '68, I drove from Nogales to L.A. with forty-three keys of weed. I was paranoid as hell and checked behind me the whole way, took side roads, made U-turns. But I never saw the Feds. And they followed me the whole fucking way. They use three, maybe four cars. Change drivers. Radio ahead. Invisible. They came out of thin air when I parked in my dealers' garage in El Monte. I was just a stupid-ass mule."

"She lied to us."

"Sure."

"The BBC wouldn't run a story about Daudin. She wasn't famous enough. And that Triumph—in this neighborhood?"

"When I went to the can," Rita said, "I checked out her meds. A new prescription for valium, other shit to sleep. Mavis is a mess. But that's not the worst part. You notice how she kept pulling her robe tight? I got a peek at one thigh, high up. The skin was raw, like a burn, or a scrape."

"So maybe she's got a rash."

"And maybe your dick is ten inches long and I never noticed."

"You saying it's like Daudin—"

"I'm saying you're in over your head, Marty."

"You want to go home?"

"No. I want to go to Rome."

"I can't. Not until I see Denis Colson. He was Sabine's closest friend in England. If she shared the secret of having a child with anyone—he'd be the guy. We'll stay in a nice hotel in London— you can see the sights. Then we'll fly to Venice and I'll see the old priest in Trieste. And on to Rome."

They turned off the main highway and drove the back roads to Ashford, to visit Sabine's grave. The clouds had dispersed, the day cold and bright. In Ashford, Craig bought a dozen white roses and got directions to the cemetery from the shop girl, who had never heard of Arnaud and had no idea the town was once home to a sanitarium for tuberculosis patients. They found the graveyard adjacent to a Gothic stone chapel.

"It's creepy here," Rita said, as they walked the rows of weathered headstones invaded by weeds. "You see that movie *The Omen*, where they go to the devil's graveyard that's guarded by wild dogs that rip them apart?" Craig didn't answer. He held the roses against his chest and looked patiently for Arnaud's name. They searched the cemetery twice before they found the flat stone half-hidden under a bordering hedge. The inscription read:

SABINE ARNAUD
3 fevrier 1909
24 aout 1943

"Born February, died August," Craig said. "Not a word about who she was. All of her work was published after the war, from notebooks she left with friends. When she died she was a no-body—just an outcast who died alone."

"Like Jesus," Rita said, without her usual irony.

"Yeah, like Jesus."

"I lied when I said Donny wants me back. He told me to go to hell."

"I kinda guessed."

"Nobody wants me."

"What am I—nobody?"

Craig put his arm around her and kissed her cheek. Then he laid the roses on the moss-covered stone, spreading them like a white fan, or perhaps a veil. *The Red Virgin*. He felt strangely moved. This was as close as he would ever get to the real Sabine Arnaud. He thought about her body, her bones, her frayed burial clothes, whatever was left of her after over thirty years in the ground. Death always had the last word, mocking every sentiment and question with silence.

"I'm cold. I'll wait in the car," Rita said. "Stay as long as you want. You think she's your mom—you should spend time with her."

After she left, Craig knelt on the damp earth and whispered, *Our father, who art in heaven...* It was Arnaud's favorite prayer. He repeated it twice with his eyes closed, then kissed the cold gravestone.

They warmed up in an Ashford pub, downing pints of Guinness and chasers of whisky. Craig was pleasantly buzzed, energized by the emotion he had felt at the grave. He suggested another detour—to Guildford—on the way back to London. "Guildford?" Rita said. "You going to dust the post office for prints?"

"It's research. Besides, it's not far."

Rita smiled, then kissed him on the lips with surprising tenderness. Her kind heart always surfaced when she drank.

Guildford proved to be a lovely town, the post office dating back to Queen Victoria. When Craig showed the postmistress Arnaud's postcard, her grin exposed rows of yellow teeth. "Yes, sir, sent from this very station it was, in 1943. Long before your time. A relative of yours by chance?"

"Yes, my mother." But the words rang false on his lips. He was out the door before she could respond.

Beyond the town, a number of large estates perched on the hills like castles. Not far from the gated entrance to one of these mansions was another inviting pub, the Wanborough Inn.

While Rita flirted with the bartender, Craig drank whisky and reflected on the irony of his quest. If his beloved Sabine *was* his mother, she was a piss-poor one, abandoning him at birth. At least neurotic Alice had *tried* to be a good mom, if ill suited to the task. And she was *there*. Maybe it was just an ego trip, wanting to believe he had the blood of a great philosopher in his veins, because it made him think that he might yet do something more with his life than write jokes for tube boobs.

Feeling he should sober up before getting behind the wheel, Craig browsed the old photos that lined the walls. Gentlemen and fine ladies on horseback. Men with shotguns and dead pheasants.

Croquet matches. In the rear, next to the dartboard, his eyes locked on the caption under a photo of the estate that overlooked the pub.

Wanborough Manor, the ancestral home of Lord Kensington, was used during World War II by the Special Operations Executive, an arm of British Intelligence, to train spies and saboteurs. Most of these brave men and women were sent to Nazi-occupied France to aid the Resistance—and few survived the war. Wanborough Manor is open Tuesday and Thursday, 10 a.m to 2 p.m., from May through September, for house and garden tours.

Craig shouted at Rita to come look. "This must be where Sabine wrote the postcard," he said. "She was in training. But why write to Alice, if she knew she was officially dead?"

"Maybe she didn't know. She was locked up in spy school. And probably not supposed to write to anyone."

They asked the bartender about Wanborough Manor, but he was young, new in town, and clueless about the war. All he wanted to talk about was whether the Beatles would get back together.

When they left the pub it was dark, drizzling. Craig removed a flyer that somebody had stuck on their windshield. Only it wasn't a flyer. It was the crude drawing of a cat hanging from a noose.

"Jesus Christ," Craig said, looking up and down the deserted street.

"You won't see nobody." Rita said. "Real pros—"

Back on the road, they didn't talk much. They'd spend the night in London and plan their next move. It was dark now, moonless, few cars on the road.

Craig kept his eyes on the white line as he took the curves through bordering woods, eager to reach the main highway. He constantly checked the rearview mirror for following cars. Rita didn't seem too freaked out by the dead cat drawing, but he was.

The headlights of a big truck appeared behind them, coming fast. Craig slowed, rolled down the window, and waved the truck to pass. The truck held its ground, and edged closer.

"We got company." Craig said. "A big ass truck."

"Don't crap your pants. Hold your speed."

The truck closed in until it was on their bumper, but made no move to pass.

"Shit...shit," Craig said.

"Don't panic, baby. That's what they want."

He couldn't see a driver in the truck; the cab was too high above the Mini Morris. Whatever kind of truck it was, it had a big wheelbase. Too wide for the narrow tracks they'd been passing, dirt roads that branched off the highway. He saw one coming up on his right.

"Hang on!" Craig floored the tiny engine and put fifty feet between him and the truck's bumper.

"Slow down!" Rita yelled.

Having driven his Porsche in a number of rallies, Craig fancied himself a race driver. He turned the wheel sharply and cut down a narrow path with thick woods on either side. Dust boiled up behind and he felt sure the truck had stayed on the highway.

"I fucking lost them!" Craig screamed in jubilation, but didn't see the sharp curve coming up in the dark woods. The car skidded as he turned and braked, went down an embankment, rolled over, and slammed into a tree.

CHAPTER FIVE

When the train pulled into Victoria Station, they waited for the other passengers to collect their bags and file out. Craig got Rita to her feet, braced by crutches, and guided her down the aisle. Her broken left ankle was casted halfway to the knee, her face a mass of purple bruises. He hailed a porter to help them descend the steps to the station platform. Rita was out of breath from the effort, and the porter offered to fetch a wheelchair. Cold air swept through the cavernous station, which seemed to offer no protection from the elements. By the time the porter returned with the wheelchair, they were both shivering.

Craig had fared better than Rita in the crash. The impact with the tree was on the passenger side, and she wasn't wearing her seat belt. Rita was unconscious, bleeding profusely from a head wound, one leg pinned under twisted metal. Craig managed to stop the bleeding and run to a nearby farmhouse. The police, along with an ambulance, arrived in minutes to extract the now conscious Rita from the car—her first words were directed at Craig: "Nice driving, butthead."

What followed were five nightmarish days in Guildford. Rita had an operation to repair her shattered ankle, and Craig was charged with driving while intoxicated. He pleaded his case before a local magistrate, who waived jail time in exchange for an outrageous fine. Hollister Insurance refused to pay for damages to the car—which was totaled—or for medical costs, citing fine print in the contract that relieved them of responsibility in cases of "criminally negligent driving." So Craig was out more than four thousand dollars, his net worth reduced by nearly half (not counting his non-liquid Porsche). He was starting to feel poor, foolish, and lucky to be alive. The only rational decision was to catch the next plane back to LA.

On the train to London, Rita had been curiously quiet. She didn't complain about her crutches, the pain, or blame him for the crash. Craig had never seen her so taciturn; it unnerved him. He tried to get a laugh with a comic riff on Hemingway, which he thought inspired. Rita had read Papa's *oeuvre* at least twice during her five years in federal prison and could recite famous passages from memory, like a pastor quoted Scripture.

"Get this, Rita, I thought of a great feminist sequel to *Sun*. Jake is hurt in the war, but it's not his dick that gets blown off, it's the tip of his tongue. Brett can't orgasm and runs off with Romero, who fights the bulls truly, and gives great head. At the end of the book, after Romero leaves her, she says, in the taxi, in Madrid: 'Oh, Jake, we could have such a damned good time together.' And you know what he says?"

Rita just looked at him.

Craig tried a lisp: "Izzn id preddy da zink so?"

"You think that's funny?"

They checked into a budget hotel near the station and Craig went out for wine and sandwiches. Rita wasn't interested in food, but drank the wine, and had another bout of nausea. Craig steadied her as she knelt at the toilet and heaved until there was nothing left to expel.

After helping her wash up, Craig joked that maybe she had morning sickness, and wished he hadn't. Rita was hurting and he didn't know what to say. Extending comfort to others had never been his strong suit. *A lack of empathy* was how his last serious girlfriend had put it when she broke off their engagement.

The small room felt cold and damp, even with the radiator hissing. They sat on stiff chairs by the window, coats on, gazing out at the red lights of a Chinese restaurant. The streets were slick, traffic slow, black cars glistening wet.

"What do you know?" Rita said, almost in a whisper. "What do you *think* you know?"

"Somebody wants us dead."

"You're the one who almost killed us—with your Steve McQueen getaway. If they wanted us dead, I think we'd be dead. We're dealing with heavyweights. They want to scare us, scare *you* mainly, because they think you're a wimp writer who'll run home to LA. Me, I don't scare so easy."

Craig was hurt by the "wimp writer" dig, but let it pass. "Suppose Arnaud *was* recruited as a spy. Why fake her death? And the war ended thirty years ago. Who would care now?"

"Big shots with dirty secrets."

"If I had facts, reliable sources, I could go to the media—make the story public. Pressure the government to investigate. Maybe dig up Sabine's grave to see if it's empty. But I got nothing—a postcard. I came here to find out if Sabine was my mother. I thought it would spice up my otherwise boring life. I'm no coward, Rita. But I'm scared, I admit it."

She looked at him coldly. "You may be scared, but I'm pissed.

I've been pushed around all my life by fat cats with money, power. College boys, like you, who want to fuck me, but only marry college girls—*white* college girls—"

"I asked you to marry me."

"That's beside the point. I'm *pissed*. Have you ever been royally pissed, Marty? I don't mean *annoyed*. I mean filled with the righteous wrath of God—to see your enemies burn in hell?"

"Not quite."

"You believe Arnaud was good, don't you? I mean *really* good. Almost like a saint?"

"Well, Camus called her the only great spirit of our time."

"Where you find good, *pure* good, you also find evil. Because the Evil One wants to destroy it."

"Oh, come on. The Evil One—the devil? "

Rita said nothing, just looked out the window. "Open that second bottle of wine, will you? I'll tell you a bedtime story."

Craig refilled their plastic cups, moved his chair close, and put his arm around her. He expected her to pull away, but she didn't.

"I never told you, but I met a true saint in prison, maybe like your Sabine. Rene Long was her name. I loved Rene more than I ever loved anybody. I didn't want to sleep with her, nothing like that. I loved her because she was good, *truly* good, a holy righteous woman. When Rene looked at you her eyes was full of love. But she wasn't weak, she was strong. Rene had done bad things, but she was the saint who brought me to the Lord. And not by preaching at me—I always hated that. I went to Bible study because she went, because the love of God flowed out of her, I swear it did."

"I can't picture you in Bible study. You're too smart."

"That's because you're a snob. I think I could of stayed in prison for life if I saw Rene every day, and prayed with her. It sounds silly—to you, maybe—but for the first time in my life I felt *free*.

That nobody could hurt me, ever. I was safe, *saved*."

"It's not silly if that's what you felt," Craig lied.

"Well, nothing good ever lasts, Marty. You know that. There was this guard that ran Bible study, we called her Dyke Doris. She lusted after Rene, because she was blond and creamy-skinned, beautiful, and innocent somehow, not hard and twisted by hate like the rest of us. Rene didn't go for that lesbian shit, told us it was a sin. But she treated Doris like she treated everybody, with kindness and love."

"What happened—something bad?"

"Good guess, college boy."

Rita said nothing. She sipped her wine and stared at the window beaded with rain.

"So how did it end, with Rene?"

"Oh, you want the touching climax?"

"Yeah. I do."

"Why not—the true and final end of my saintly tale. You'll love the irony. One day we was in the in the showers, and Doris was watching Rene—like she always did. And you could see the evil hunger in that ugly fat face, like her cheeks was filled with green pus. Doris told us all to get dressed and leave, except for Rene. I knew what was going down, so I talked out—and got roughed up by the guards and dragged back to my cell.

"Then Doris had her way with Rene, or tried to. I don't know for sure. But we heard later that Rene was dead. They found her naked, beaten, with her head stuffed in a toilet. You like that? The beautiful saint who drowned in a bowl of turds? We all knew Doris done it, but she blamed it on another con who was doing life for murder. I think the warden believed her, at first. That's when I first felt that holy righteous wrath and knew I would kill that evil bitch if I could, kill her with my bare hands, my teeth, and send her to hell for what she done. I wanted revenge even more than when I was raped."

"You never told me you were raped."

"I had no reason to. And don't ask me for no details, ever. I mentioned it because the rage I felt then was just about me, my own pain and shame. I wanted revenge more with Rene because she was *innocent*, and pure, and didn't deserve to die like that. So I wanted to kill, torture, give Doris what she had coming for the evil thing she done. But I never got the chance, or I'd still be in the can. Because Doris confessed and went to prison. Not mine, of course. I heard later she hung herself in her cell. Like Judas. I never believed in God after that, not the way I did when I loved Rene. Because I never met another Christian who wanted me to believe who wasn't a jerk."

"But you believe in evil?"

"I got a question for you, Marty."

"What?"

"Will you cry when I die?"

"What kind of question is that?"

"A serious question. My mama always told me if just one person cries for you when you die you can go to heaven."

"You know I will. Why ask me now?"

Rita patted her abdomen. "You live in your head, Marty. Can't you see my belly looks like I swallowed a football?"

"I noticed you put on a few pounds."

"It's a tumor. Cancer."

"Are you sure?" Craig took her hand.

"Probable, sayeth my doctor. The X-ray shows a mass. They won't know until they cut me open. And then they'll put me back together and tell me there's nothing they can do. It's ovarian cancer, I know. Same as killed my mama. So I'm not having no surgery. That's why I came with you, to see Paris. I thought it would be fun. Are we having fun yet?"

"I don't know what to say."

"You never do, when it counts."

"Let's go home, Rita. Maybe the tumor's benign. You don't know. But I'll do whatever you want. Do you know what you want?"

"Like a told you, I'm pissed at these big shots who think they can push us around. I've never seen London. Why don't you show a poor, dying woman the fabulous sights? Do the Christian thing, take pity on me."

"Where should we start—the Tower of London? Buckingham Palace?"

"No, just the library. A good one."

Craig stole glances at Rita across the reference table, in the hushed reading room of the London Library. She'd been at it all afternoon, scrolling through old newspapers on microfilm, searching for stories about former SOE agents. These legendary heroes were often feted at public ceremonies, or the subject of inspirational profiles. The goal was to find a surviving agent who might have been in training around the time that Sabine mailed her posthumous postcard from Guildford. With a living witness that Sabine Arnaud was very much alive in September 1943, Craig could pitch the story to the press and rest easy in the media firestorm that would certainly follow.

Glasses perched on her nose, casted leg on a chair, Rita embraced the task with the concentration of a Zen monk. When she paused to make notes, her tongue budded through her lips as she drew the words in her slow, rounded hand. He sometimes forgot

Rita's lack of formal education. She wrote with the heartbreaking care of a schoolgirl taking her first exam.

Maybe I do love her, he thought. She certainly knew him better than any of the women he'd professed to love. And she still liked him well enough to tease him with her playful digs. Perhaps she even needed his company in some nontrivial way. You could never tell with Rita. Maybe she'd seen too much to believe in love. And now she was dying of cancer—or so she thought. Eyes welling with tears, he went back to his own book, the official history of the SOE in France.

It was all there: organization, staffing, training sites, and the names of male and female agents, along with their ultimate fates. Much of the material had been classified until the 1960s. Wanborough Manor was the first stop for SOE recruits, where their fitness for clandestine service was evaluated. Those that measured up went on to other secret sites where they learned spy craft, combat tactics, escape and evasion, the use of small arms, and the art of blowing up railways and bridges with plastic explosives.

Out of seventy-one agents sent to France, only nineteen were known to have survived the war. The rest were arrested by the Gestapo, tortured to extract information, and shot—or sent to concentration camps, where they typically died of starvation or disease. The fate of some was never known, victims of Hitler's policy of Nacht und Nebel (Night and Fog). Those who resisted German occupation would vanish into the "night and fog," their families never knowing if they were alive or dead. These "N + N" prisoners, as the Nazis called them, were taken to secret camps and executed, their deaths unrecorded.

Craig studied the names of women agents, along with their fake identities used in the field. He didn't expect to find Arnaud listed, but he knew Sabine was fond of anagrams. Perhaps she'd invented a false identity by scrambling the letters of her name. He spent an hour looking for matching letters and found none. He wasted two more hours playing with permutations of the names of her father, mother, and brother.

Craig did discover a link between Denis Colson and the deputy director of SOE in 1943, Carlton Hays, who was now a prominent member of parliament. They had both graduated from Cambridge about the same time, and may well have known each other when Sabine was recruited by SOE. Hays had gone to France himself in early 1944, where he was captured, tortured, and escaped from a Nazi prison—killing a sentry, putting on his uniform, and fleeing over the rooftops of Paris. He was one of the most celebrated British heroes of the war.

After a dozen calls, Craig reached Denis Colson in Cambridge. He was curt, then effusively warm when Craig explained who he was.

"So sad about Sophie," Colson said. "A colleague at the Sorbonne called me the day she died. By all means we should meet. And I'd love to see your photographs. I do have a spot of time later this week. Would it trouble you to come my way?"

So Craig was taking the morning train to Cambridge. Rita thought it was a waste of time. "If he knows something, his hands are dirty and he'll tell you nothing. And he'll find out what you know. Use your head, college boy—you want to learn a secret, you ask somebody who don't know they *know* the secret. You dig?"

CHAPTER SIX

Under gray skies, Craig arrived at the Cambridge campus and found his way to the Wren Library of Trinity College. He pulled open the heavy doors and entered the cathedral-like interior, replete with stained-glass windows. He found the bust of Isaac Newton, the appointed meeting place, and paced. A handful of students hunched over their books in the Gothic gloom. He felt he was on holy ground, a sanctuary that evoked a bygone era when God was the foundation of all truth. Hadn't Newton himself written more on the nature of the divine than the mechanics of the universe? He recalled a philosophy teacher who had marveled at this—that one of the great intellects in all of human history was foolish enough to believe in God.

Shortly after noon, a lanky student entered the library and strode toward him, heels clicking on the stone floor. He bowed, shook hands, and apologized for Professor Colson, who was delayed by the oral examination of a doctoral candidate. Lunch was now out of the question. But Craig was invited to join the professor for dinner at his home. Say about seven thirty?

Furious, Craig walked to town and booked a room, knowing he'd miss the last train back to London. He called Rita, who wasn't worried. "I'm better alone. Besides, I got things to do." Before he could ask what, she said, "Don't spill your guts to this dweeb" and hung up.

With time to kill, Craig mapped out his strategy to question Colson. And he called Claire at Gallimard to brief her on his meeting with Mavis, and what he'd learned about the SOE presence in Guildford in 1943. He left out the threatening note left on his windshield and the embarrassing car crash. Claire had news of her own. "I tried to reach Father Cartan in Trieste, to tell him about you and your wish to see him. A nun at the retirement home informed me that Father Cartan has had a massive stroke and is unable to speak. He is not expected to live."

And then there was one, Craig thought. Denis Colson was his last, best hope of solving the mystery of Sabine's death, or of acquiring more evidence that Sabine might have been his birth mother.

Colson's Edwardian home was set back from the road, with a gravel path that led through a rose garden to the front door. Craig was greeted by a beautiful young man in a cashmere sweater who introduced himself as Robert. He ushered Craig into the plush interior, furnished with oriental rugs and antiques. There was a fire roaring and a silver tray with glasses, ice, and a selection of liquor. Robert explained that Professor Colson would be down shortly, and excused himself.

Craig set his folio of photographs on a wing-back chair and poured scotch into cut crystal. He wandered the room, examining the oil portraits of dead royalty and immortal philosophers. He heard Colson before he saw him, "Ah, you're inspecting my mausoleum. Not my taste, I assure you." He was bald, blue-eyed, with an impish grin. Craig liked him at once. "This house is the curse of holding the Knightbridge Chair in Philosophy. Live here or else. But I do enjoy the space—it's a bloody mansion. Please, sit. And tell me about yourself. I'm fascinated."

Craig stuck to his cover story. He was taking a break from TV work to research a projected novel about his mother and Sabine Arnaud. He hoped that some of Arnaud's surviving friends might recall her speaking of his mother and the life they shared in New York. Daudin had promised to help, but her death forced him to carry on as best he could, running down leads supplied by her research assistant, Claire Brion.

"The photographs of Sabine and your mother. May I see them?"

Craig spread them out on the coffee table. Colson was transfixed by the images.

"Extraordinary! Sabine looks happy—and healthy. I never saw her cheeks that rosy—she always looked like a cadaver. And your mother was quite the beauty, wasn't she? I can't recall that Sabine ever mentioned her. She told me precious little about her months in New York, except her struggle to secure a visa to get to London. Sabine and I talked and argued politics, religion, philosophy, the war, but the past, *her* past, was not of interest to her. You'd be surprised by how many Arnaud admirers seek me out. What was she *really* like, and all that rot. People worship her today like a bloody saint. And I tell them what I'll tell you. She was a marvelous intellect, and a dreadful person. Selfish, intent on suffering, morally superior. And a frightful bore to be around for any length of time. She sucked the life out of you and pushed you away when you tried to save her from herself. Today she'd be treated for anorexia—a disease we didn't understand then."

"Did you know Daudin was in London the week before her death?"

"I did not."

"Claire told me. She didn't know why she went—some additional interviews, she guessed. So Daudin didn't call you?"

"Heavens no. We were not close. I thought her devotion to Arnaud bordered on the religious—and told her so. She took offense. That was two years ago. I spent hours with Sophie, answering tedious questions. Biographers are typically bores—without insight or original thought. Did Sabine write to your mother?"

"Just one short letter, after arriving in London."

"Do you have it?"

"I left it with Claire—it was not revealing."

"Really? I've never known Sabine to write a single sentence that was not, as you say, *revealing*. But surely she wrote other letters to your mother, perhaps after she'd become seriously ill."

"Nothing that my mother saved. Not even a postcard."

Colson's face betrayed him. Sophie had told him about Sabine's "posthumous" postcard.

"What a pity."

"You were my last hope, Professor Colson, of learning more about Arnaud and my mother. So, I'll be heading home in a day or two. After showing my lady friend the London sights. This is her first trip to Europe. "

"I'm terribly sorry, Craig. May I call you Craig? Shall we repair to the dining room? Robert has cooked us a lovely dinner."

"Does Robert have a last name?"

"Jeeves?" Colson giggled. "Robert is one of my starving students. I supply room and board in exchange for housekeeping duties. He's quite the gourmet cook."

Robert served plates of underdressed salad and overcooked

salmon, but did not join them at the table. Craig surmised that Robert's talents lay more in the bedroom than the kitchen. After failing to elicit anything of interest about Sabine with polite questions, Craig cut to the chase. "Did Sabine ask for your help in joining the French Resistance? That was her obsession—from what I've read. You must have known people in British intelligence."

"On the contrary, I had no contacts in that arena. I was a paper pusher in the foreign office. And I wouldn't have recommended her if I had. She was totally unsuited for that kind of clandestine work—few were. The woman was half-dead from self-starvation, clumsy beyond belief, blind as a bat without her glasses, and looked like what she was: a Jewish intellectual. If an SS man saw her on the street in Paris, he'd ship her off to Auschwitz without bothering to check her papers. If I sound harsh, or anti-Semitic, so be it, but the war years were desperate times in London. We were fighting for our very lives, bombs falling on us daily, which is something you Americans can never understand."

"Quite true. And whereof one cannot speak, thereof one must remain silent."

"Ah, Wittgenstein—an educated man from Hollywood."

"I majored in philosophy, but quit before getting a degree. I wanted to write a great existential novel, like *Nausea* or *The Stranger*."

"Did we not measure up?" Colson inquired with pleasure.

"I never finished my novel. But the first sentence, I thought, was brilliant: *Everything bored him, himself most of all.* Boredom is an underrated catastrophe, don't you think? It's the Black Death of our affluent age. But maybe only the French can write well about ennui. My attempt was profoundly boring."

Colson laughed. "And now you write for TV—perhaps not so boring."

"I discovered my true gift was in writing for an audience I held in mild contempt. If I cared deeply about what I wrote, I couldn't sell it. But the lower I aimed, the more praise I got. And the more money I made."

"But writing comedy—it can't be easy. I couldn't do it."

"Sure you could. It's simple. You just pretend that what's important isn't, and what isn't, is."

"I don't follow."

"I wrote a sitcom episode about suicide. No laughs there, right? But my bit was about a vain young woman who was driven to thoughts of suicide because she couldn't find the perfect shoes to go with her perfect new handbag. Shoes are of no importance, really. So it's funny. If she thought of killing herself because it suddenly dawned on her that her life as a mindless consumer was utterly without meaning—that would ring true, and reflect what many of us feel, but would not be funny. In fact, that's why people *watch* TV, to keep them from thinking about the emptiness of their existence. Anybody can write comedy, believe me."

"And *you*, young man, have the mind of a philosopher. Perhaps you should have stuck with it. I was a student of Wittgenstein—a tortured genius, repressed homosexual. God, I would have loved to see Sabine and Ludwig argue a point! They might have killed each other. I'm sure you've read about Witt threatening Karl Popper with a hot poker!

"Philosophy is the synopsis of trivialities, said Ludwig, with which I quite agree. But I'm off next week to Stanford to lecture for a quarter, where I can at least explicate the trivial under the California sun. I'm much too old to endure another English winter."

They were interrupted by a phone ringing. Colson ordered Robert to take a message. He came back quickly and whispered in Colson's ear, and Colson excused himself to take the call in the kitchen. Craig heard him say, "Fine, yes, fine... as we discussed, yes, absolutely." When he came back to the table, Colson looked tense.

"Anything wrong?" Craig said

"Just a boorish colleague who wants me to use my influence to get his inane book published."

After a dessert of stale cookies and ice cream, they sat by the fire, sipping a glass of port. Colson checked his watch and smiled. The evening was coming to a close. It was now or never.

"I'm afraid, sir," Craig said. "I've not been entirely honest about why I came to see you."

"And now, I presume, you will be?" Colson grimaced, perhaps thinking he was about to get grilled about Sabine's death. But Craig knew he would get nothing on that subject.

"You were struck by one of my photographs, where Sabine looks happy, rosy-cheeked. I think I know the reason why."

"Indeed."

"You're a philosopher in the British rationalist tradition, so I'll work up to my thesis with some hard facts. When Sabine's parents left Marseille for Montreal in January of 1942, she refused to go with them. Yet a month later, she sailed for New York. Why? If her goal was to secure a visa to London to join the Free French Forces, there would have been less red tape in securing one from a member of the commonwealth. And while she was in New York, she made no attempt to visit them. Her letters to her parents were infrequent, and she never supplied a return address—claiming she moved around a lot. In fact, she lived next door to my mother for the eight months she stayed in New York. Would you agree her behavior was curious, as if she was hiding from her mother and father, whom she clearly adored?"

"Very odd, yes. I remember asking Sabine why she separated from her parents, and never got a satisfactory answer."

"I believe I know the reason."

"What, for God's sake?"

"She was pregnant when she left Marseille—with me."

Colson winced. "You're joking."

"Hear me out, Professor Colson." Craig presented the circum-stantial evidence that supported his claim. When he was done, Colson said nothing, just gazed at the crackling fire, stroking his chin thoughtfully.

"It's absurd, of course, your theory. I can assure you that Sabine never alluded to a man in her life, or the desire for a child. She disliked being touched, as I'm sure you've read. And her greatest fear was of being raped. Though, curiously, she was not a prude, when it came to the sex lives of others, even mine. I'm afraid you've come a long way for nothing, young man. I knew her as well as anyone."

"My theory is not absurd, it's possible, given the facts. Like God is possible, even if there's no absolute proof."

"Yes, it's possible, like God, because you can't prove a negative. I don't wish to encourage your motherhood fantasy, but I did recall something as you were arguing your case. As you probably know, Sabine shared my flat for a time, when she first came to London. As I helped her unpack, I made a silly joke—silly for any number of reasons—that I remember distinctly to this day, perhaps out of embarrassment. I told Sabine that, given the tight quarters of my flat, she should worry about me taking advantage of her, 'compromising her virtue,' as we used to say. Sabine laughed and said: 'It doesn't matter anymore.' I thought it an odd remark, but didn't press her for clarification. Was she telling me she wasn't a virgin? Or telling me that, in a time of war, her virginity was simply of no importance? I guess we shall never have the answer to that question."

CHAPTER SEVEN

Grosvenor Sanitarium, Ashford, England. July 1943

"Milk is for English children," she said, refusing the cup. "You bloody fool!" Colson shouted. "There's a war on, if you haven't heard. Food is *rationed*. Every child in England gets his bloody glass of milk before you do. If you don't eat, you'll die! You *are* dying." In a rage, he seized the cup and held it over the vase of roses beside the bed. "But let's truly waste it, if you like, Sabine. I shall refresh your flowers."

She watched him from the bed with her dark, sunken eyes as he tipped the cup slowly until milk trickled into the water.

"Stop! Please don't. Give it to me."

She took the cup and lifted it with both hands to her lips. After a few sips she put it down, grimacing, and rolled onto her side, holding her stomach.

Colson touched her shoulder. It was all bone. Her body convulsed in spasms, her breath rapid and shallow.

"My dear, my poor, poor dear. I'm sorry I got angry. Will you forgive me? I just can't bear to see you this way. If you would just eat, you'd get strong. You would. Why can't you do what you must? Why *won't* you? It breaks my bloody heart. I swear it does." Colson began to sob and buried his face in his hands.

Sabine touched the top of his head with cold fingers. "I don't want to die, Denis. I try to eat. I do. Mavis poached me an egg this morning, with sherry. It was lovely. I ate some of it, I did. But when I eat the cramps start, and then the headaches. I am an utterly useless woman, you see. I can't even drink my milk, like a baby. Will you do something for me?"

"Anything. Of course."

"Take me outside. I want to feel the sun on my face."

He helped her from the bed into a wheelchair and took her out on the balcony. The day was bright and cool. There was a view across the broad lawn and garden to fields of corn bordered by poplars, with the glimpse of a distant pond that caught the sun. She tilted her head back to the sky and closed her eyes, breathing deeply. Colson tucked the blanket around her. When she opened her eyes, she smiled blissfully.

"Thank you, Denis. Thank you for bringing me here." At his own expense, Colson had arranged for her transfer from Middlesex Hospital in London to the sanitarium, where she now had a private room. In the hospital, she'd complained about the noise, that she could neither rest nor sleep. She also longed to be in the country, with clean air and greenery, and the sound of birds. But the change in scene had made no difference. Her condition had only deteriorated.

"Your doctors say you are not gravely ill," Colson lied. "Only part of one lung is infected. But you *must* fight, Sabine, fight the fever with nourishment. If you eat, you can recover. There's no medical reason why your body should reject food. They think it's all in your mind, that you are determined to starve yourself."

"*Cher ami*, I would do as you ask, stuff myself like a pig, if only to please you. But I am utterly broken, beyond all mending, quite apart from Koch's bacillus. I feel as though I am outside the truth, and no human agency can bring me to it."

"Don't talk rot."

"But I am useless. Don't you see? I came here to fight, to die if need be. And now I can barely stand. It's comical. Not even tragic. I have always had the fear of failing, not in my life, but in my death. And now my worst fear is coming to pass."

Colson paced the balcony. There was always an element of negotiation, of bribery, in persuading Sabine to take care of herself. Without a reason to live, she preferred to die. He must give her hope. One of his Cambridge friends, a brilliant mathematician, was engaged in secret work for military intelligence. When Colson guessed the job was code-breaking, his friend played dumb, but winked. Sabine had the most original intellect he had ever encountered. She might, if healthy, be useful in such work. It was a long shot, but so was her recovery.

Colson debated the ethics of what he was about to do, then went to her. He dropped to one knee and took her hand, like a suitor proposing marriage. "Look at me, Sabine. And listen very carefully to what I have to say." She stiffened at the closeness of him, but looked compassionately at his long face and imploring eyes. "My dear, dear Sabine. You have much to offer England in our fight. But not from a bed, and not from the grave. I *promise* you, I *swear*, I will get you into the war if you regain your health. I will get you a job that's vital to the war effort. But you must *eat*. I don't make idle promises. I know people. Important people."

"Like your friend Hays?" she said dryly.

"More powerful," Colson lied. "Men who can pull strings, who will do what I ask."

Sabine removed her hand from his and looked out over the fields to a line of poplars rippling in the breeze, their leaves fluttering white and green, like schools of fish changing direction. "Aren't they beautiful, Denis? My trees. Don't you see, it is the sun falling from heaven that gives them the power to put down roots? The tree is really rooted in the sky."

Colson laughed in exasperation. "Ah, Sabine, how can I argue with poetry? Your mind is sublime—and mine is a sputtering machine, with one gear, or two, on my best day. But now, I fear, I must take my leave. I've said my piece. And London calls. I shall be in touch."

"I have three more notebooks for you. I write every day now. I must—as long as I am able. I've been working on the problem of evil. The paradox of a loving, all-powerful God who creates a world rampant with chaos, suffering, and evil. I think I have the answer."

"You would be the first."

"*De-creation.*"

"I beg your pardon."

"God didn't *create* the world. He *removed* himself from creation, so that the world could come into being, that we might exist separately from Him. *De-creation.* Don't you see, Denis? That's why we see God as an absence, a void, and long to be reunited with Him. On God's part, creation was not an act of self-expansion, but of restraint and renunciation. He permitted the existence of things distinct from Himself and worth infinitely less. By this creative act, God denied Himself for our sakes in order to give us the possibility of denying ourselves for Him. Thus, the existence of evil here below, far from disproving the reality of God is the very thing that reveals him in His truth."

For the next week, Sabine managed to take tea and toast for breakfast and broth at lunch. Mavis pureed potatoes and carrots for dinner, because it reminded Sabine of what her mother made for her as a child. But after consuming a fraction of the bowl, she would drop the spoon and double over in pain. It was as if food was the poison that kept her spirit imprisoned in the flesh from which she longed to escape.

Sometime after midnight, she woke with a brutal headache. The pain was relentless, merciless, beyond anything she had yet known. And it grew stronger, until it was terrifying, unendurable. She wanted to scream in agony, but could emit only a whimper that seemed to come more from her body than her lungs. She wanted to pray, but words would not take shape in her mind or form on her lips. Her consciousness was obliterated by a pain so demonic that it seemed to consume her entire being, until there was nothing left of her to think or speak or will or hope.

It was then, at that moment of utter devastation, that she felt a loving presence in the room. It was a presence more real, more certain, than a human being. She had always scoffed at the idea of a direct encounter with God, but now she found herself on her knees beside the bed, praying. The pain had not gone, but it was no longer hers alone to bear. As her senses returned, she noticed moonlight streaming through the closed blinds, bathing the room in a milky glow. She felt the presence closer, close enough to touch, or to touch her. But she was afraid to look, afraid of what she might see, or not see. She wanted to keep the feeling safe inside her. So she stared at the blinds more white than white and prayed Our Father over and over in her beloved Greek. She prayed until the pain abated and she was taken by sleep, or dream, or spirit, to another place.

When she woke it was late morning, sun flooding the room with warmth and light. And she was ravenous. For the first time in years she *hungered* for food. She wanted to smell it, taste it, feel it in her mouth as she chewed, feel it slide down her throat and into her hollow, rumbling belly.

She cried out for Mavis, who came running into the room, fearing the worst. Sabine barked her breakfast order to an incredulous Mavis. She wanted tea and toast and jam and an egg—no, two eggs, and bangers, or ham, or any meat. *Please, hurry.* And something to write in *now*. Mavis fetched a notebook and pencils and flew out of the room, tripping over her own feet, laughing with glee as she ran down the corridor toward the kitchen.

Sabine wrote furiously about her experience in the night. She wanted to get it down while it was fresh and real and still lived within her. Was it a dream? If it was, if was like no other dream she had ever experienced. Was it real? If it was, it was a reality not of this world. The pencil scratched, sped over the paper, her normally neat and rounded script a spidery scrawl. When the pencil grew dull, or the lead broke from the force of her hand, she grabbed another.

When Colson got the call that Sabine was eating normally and gaining weight, he couldn't believe it. He'd tried to push her out of his mind in recent weeks, with mixed success, and was determined not to see her again. It was too painful to witness her slow, willful suicide. He caught the next train to Ashford.

When he arrived, Sabine was in the garden, notebook in hand, sitting on a stone bench, no wheelchair in sight. She waved cheerily and stood to greet him. Though she was still painfully thin, the color in her cheeks had returned. Even more remarkable, she was eating an enormous, bright-red apple. Colson embraced her, squeezing her arms, delighting in the soft flesh covering bone.

She tried to explain her experience in the night. "I've not read the mystics, and had never foreseen the possibility of a real contact, person to person, here below, between a human being and a god. All I can say is that in the midst of excruciating pain, I felt this sudden possession of me of by something infinite and wholly other, perhaps Christ. But neither my senses or my imagination had any part. Who can understand such things? I only felt in the midst of my suffering the presence of love, like that which one can read in the smile of a beloved face."

"A smile?"

Sabine bit into the shiny apple, wiping the juice from her lips. She chewed it slowly, with relish, turning her face toward the sun. Colson was dumbfounded. He had never seen her eat anything with genuine pleasure.

"I still write, of course," she said. "But I love to walk. I walk until I tire, and then I sit and write, and then walk some more. I want to read you something. I wrote it yesterday, about apples of all things, which I've come to love more than any other fruit, perhaps more than Eve." She laughed and turned the pages in her notebook. "Ah, here it is, only a line, but I might develop it into an essay on the senses: *the pure taste of the apple is as much a contact with the beauty of the universe as the contemplation of a picture by Cezanne.* Do you like it, Denis?"

"My God, Sabine. You're the last person on earth I would have expected to rhapsodize about the taste of an apple."

"My doctors don't know what to make of me. I eat like a stevedore and X-rays show my lung is healing."

"It's bloody incredible, is what it is. A miracle—if I believed in such things."

"You may have to make good on your promise."

"What promise was that?" He asked, half hoping she'd forgotten.

"Oh, don't look so worried, Denis. I knew you were lying, bribing me to eat, out of pity. You're much too sweet to have powerful friends."

"I meant what I said, Sabine. I know such people. But you must get stronger still—to leave here and be fit for hard work."

Sabine smiled, not believing a word, and bit into her beautiful apple.

When he got back to London, Colson began to make inquiries, while checking regularly on her condition. Part of him hoped her recovery would slow, to buy him time. His mathematician friend refused to pass Arnaud's name on to his superiors, because they might suspect he had talked to Colson about his work, which could get him "thrown in jail or shot." Other Cambridge contacts with ties to British intelligence were also discouraging. The old boys club was not welcoming to French nationals, especially those of Jewish origin.

Colson had no choice but to lean on Carlton Hays. They met in the bar of Colson's London club; his membership a perk from being the son of an earl. Hays had never set foot there before, or in any club reserved for the ruling elite. Though he had contempt for the Crown and the upper class, he loved the hushed calm of ancient privilege, the green-shaded lamps, and the dark leather of his wing-back chair. The single-malt scotch and aromatic cigar also served to put him in a generous mood. So he listened politely as Colson made his case.

"Denis, I sympathize with your dilemma, old chap. But one must be careful with promises. I try never to make them myself. Especially to women." He laughed. "Because they never, ever forget—no matter how much they had to drink the night before."

"There must be something," Colson insisted. "I know I'm not supposed to know. But SOE is a large operation. Surely you have desk jobs for women. Wireless operators, support staff, that sort of thing."

"Your Jewess, as I recall, can neither type nor cook nor sew nor even drive a car. I doubt she could be a decent file clerk."

"You don't know her as I do. She's brilliant, fearless, determined."

"And she wants to join the Resistance, of course. To fight and die for her countrymen."

"Yes, there is that, too."

Hays held up his crystal glass of scotch, admiring the caramel color. "In honor of this lovely drink, Denis, and your splendid cigar, I shall make you a *semi-promise*—for old times' sake. Next week I'll be near Ashford, on business, if I have time, I shall pay Miss Arnaud a visit. Perhaps I judged her too harshly the first time."

"She's different now. Strong. More sensible."

"Perhaps. And if, by some remote chance, I do find a job for her, even behind a desk, I won't tell you what, or where, and you can have no further contact with her. Understood? After all, Denis, my operations are top secret. I could have you arrested for what you know."

CHAPTER EIGHT

Craig caught the morning train back to London. He'd called
Rita the night before, after his dinner with Colson, but got
no answer. When she failed to pick up in the morning, he began to
worry—and he seldom worried about Rita. She could take care of
herself. Still, when he got off the train in Victoria Station, he found
himself jogging toward the hotel.

When he opened the door to their room, the first thing he saw
was the wheelchair by the bed. It looked ancient, with wide wheels
and a wicker chair. The next thing he noticed was the pistol on
Rita's lap. She was sitting up in bed, wrapped in a towel, her black
hair stringy wet.

"Hi, Marty. Like my chair? Got it at a thrift shop."

Craig stood by the bed and stared at the gun. It was an old
revolver, with the bluing worn off and the pistol grip cracked.

"Your professor spill his guts?" Rita asked brightly, ignoring his
glare. "No? A waste of time? Like I told you? Well, I've been busy,
I found out—"

"What the fuck is this? And where were you last night?"

"You scared of guns, Marty?"

"You want to go to jail? You moron—this isn't East LA. Where'd you get it?"

Rita picked up the gun, opened the cylinder, and dropped four live cartridges into her palm. "I was followed yesterday by an ugly bald guy. It's hard to tail a woman in a wheelchair. He stopped every half block to pretend he was window shopping. Not bright, but big. So I got me some protection. You should be happy."

"I asked where you got it. *How* you got it."

"You don't want to know."

"I asked how you got it."

"It don't matter."

"Who sold it to you? What did it cost me?"

"You? It cost nothing."

"You slept with some lowlife, didn't you? And I was up all night—worried sick about you because you didn't answer the phone. What was the price, an old pistol like this? A blow job? Or did you have to blow the whole fucking bar?"

Rita laughed, which made him angrier.

"You miserable cunt. What a fool I am—"

"So I'm a cunt now. What else? Let me have it, Marty. I'm a lowlife barrio slut, ex-con, ungrateful tramp?"

"That's a start."

"How about that word you invented for Alice? She's a *cuntundrum* you said, an inexplicably mean-spirited woman. Funny. But you got to admit, Marty, I'm understandably bitchy—because I'm pissed I have cancer, and I'm pissed about these assholes who think they can push us around. And I'm pissed that you're not more pissed."

"Go to hell."

"You ever wonder why you fall for difficult women with nice boobs."

"They remind me of my mother?"

"Well, come to Mama." Rita peeled off the towel. "I'm squeaky clean."

"Go fuck yourself."

"I wish I could."

Craig laughed, in spite of himself, and sat on the bed. He felt like crying.

"Come on. I want that big fat cock in me. Remember, I'm dying. I'll be out of your life soon." Rita gave him a pouty look. "You still like me, a little? Can I have a kiss? I'll tell you how I got the gun. I talked to this—"

"I don't give a shit." Craig covered her mouth with his, mainly to shut her up, and then relaxed into a lingering kiss.

Rita took his face in her hands. "You're a good man, Marty... the best." She helped out of his clothes. He was already hard. Craig got inside her and began to pound with violent thrusts, out of anger, at first, and then passion. It was over quickly. But the second time lasted until they were drenched in sweat and deliciously spent.

Rita lit a cigarette and took a long drag, blowing perfect smoke rings. "Little blow jobs," she said, laughing.

"Was I too rough the first time?" he asked, stroking her breast.

"I deserved punishment from your enormous cock."

"I think I'm falling in love."

"Not with me, you're not. You need a fine, educated lady. But just for the record, I'm no slut. I didn't screw nobody for the gun. The thrift shop guy, Leo, is a dude from Brooklyn who believes in the right of every Brit to own a gun—for a crazy price. It cost me a bundle of traveler's checks."

"My checks, you mean? That you stole from my suitcase and forged *my* signature on? And your pal Leo should go to jail for cashing, not to mention selling you a gun."

"Would you rather I blew him?"

Rita had done her homework. By searching old newspaper files and current phone books, she'd tracked down three surviving agents who were in training in the fall of 1943. Craig started with Blanche Charlet, who lived in the East End. Before calling her, he reviewed the published record of her exploits.

Born and raised in Paris, she fell for an officer on leave from the Royal Marines, married him in 1938, and followed him to London. When the Nazis invaded France in 1940, her husband was part of the British force sent to help the French repel the attack. He was killed in retreat on the beaches of Dunkirk. Not one to feel sorry for herself, Blanche joined the Civil Defense Corps, providing first aid to casualties during the London Blitz. She served with distinction, often risking her life to extract the wounded from burning buildings. Recruited by SOE, she began spy training in February 1943. Her fluency in French, courage, and street smarts made her an ideal recruit. In December 1943, she parachuted into France, serving as a wireless operator and courier between Resistance networks in and around Paris.

Shortly before D-day, she was arrested by the Gestapo, but stuck to her cover story—playing the role of a scatter-brained farm girl searching for her sister in the big city. After three days of brutal interrogation, she was released. Undeterred, she went back to her Resistance work. When the Allies marched into Paris in August 1944, Charlet was there on the Champs-Élysées to greet them. After the war, she returned to London, became a hairdresser, and lived an uneventful life. She remarried in 1951, this time to a bus driver. No children. Both Britain and France had honored her with their highest awards for bravery.

The more he read about the heroics of spies outwitting the Nazis, the more his own fears seemed manageable. After all, this was Britain, not a police state. And he had a moral duty to uncover the truth about a woman he had long revered—whether or not she was his birth mother.

When Craig got Charlet on the phone, he used Hollywood as an icebreaker, assuming she'd be impressed. Steven Spielberg had sent him to London to research a script he was writing about wartime espionage. Blanche had never heard of Spielberg, so he lied again and said David Lean was coproducing the project. Yes, she did remember *Lawrence of Arabia* and *Doctor Zhivago*, but hadn't seen either film. She liked musicals. And she had no time to talk because her husband was in the hospital.

Craig countered with perfunctory sympathy, then offered, in desperation: "Mr. Lean has *insisted* I interview at least one former SOE agent, no matter what, so I am prepared—if you are not offended—to offer you the sum of fifty pounds for thirty minutes of your time." There was a short silence before she responded, curtly: "For seventy-five, in cash, I will make time."

They agreed to meet at the hospital where her husband was recovering from surgery for lung cancer. It was easy to convince Rita to stay at the hotel when she heard the words "hospital" and "cancer." She continued to have spells of nausea, but Craig held his tongue about returning to LA for treatment.

After leaving the hotel, he circled the block twice before heading for the Tube station. No man, bald or otherwise, followed in his wake. Once on the train he noticed a stout woman near the back of the car that he might have seen near the hotel. He resolved not to look again, knowing that paranoia feeds on itself, but he did anyway. When he got off in the blighted East End, she remained on the train. Still, for the sake of caution, he lingered at a newsstand in the station until all the departing passengers had dispersed.

Craig was eager to meet Charlet, and nervous about what he might learn about Sabine. He wanted the truth, but he also longed for the safety and comfort of his former life. If Charlet knew nothing, he was that much closer to going home.

He found the hospital cafeteria, where she said she'd wait. It smelled of disinfectant, cigarettes, and fried fish. The white-tiled walls, none too clean, reminded Craig of a morgue. And it was cold. The National Health Service might offer free care to all, but it was stingy with the heat.

Charlet sat at one of the red plastic tables, cigarette burning. She stood and invited him to sit, without shaking hands. She was well-groomed, with curly gray hair and pink-framed glasses. But her brown coat was worn, skirt frayed, leather purse scarred by age. No wonder she'd accepted his crass offer of compensation; Blanche needed the money. Evidently, the Most Excellent Order of the British Empire, or MBE, which she'd won for exceptional valor and service to the Crown, did not preclude life in the under-class.

Blanche Charlet looked like any other sixtyish woman you might glance at on the street and dismiss as irrelevant. Except for the eyes. Behind those pink frames, her clear blue eyes were quick, shrewd—almost predatory.

"Did you bring the money?" she asked, with the hint of a French accent.

Craig handed her an envelope. She counted out the bills, put them in her purse, and tore up the envelope, leaving the pieces on the table.

"Now, then," Craig began.

"You seem like a nice young man. So let me give you some advice. Don't lie to people unless you are quite sure they are stupid."

"I beg your pardon."

"I know who Spielberg is. I've seen *Jaws*. I've also read that writers in Hollywood are treated like dirt. So I doubt he'd send you to London to research a script. Also, I know David Lean, though not well. He came to me five years ago when he *was* considering a film about the Resistance, but he decided the well was dry on that subject. I've been technical advisor as they say, on three British films made about SOE agents—all of which did well at the box office, though I was paid a pittance. So, now I have my pittance from you. Who are you and what do you want?"

Embarrassed, Craig stammered out his reply. "You're right. I lied. I'm sorry. But I was desperate to meet you. And I *am* a writer—comedy, TV stuff. But that's not why I'm here. Have you ever heard of Sabine Arnaud, the French philosopher?"

Charlet had not. And she didn't remember the face when he showed her photographs. She was certain that she hadn't seen Sabine at Wanborough, or at any other training site. "I have a good memory for faces, and I would not forget a face like that. She looks Jewish."

"She was."

"Then SOE would not have recruited her."

"But is it possible?"

"Unlikely. Not impossible. When Michael Foot was writing his SOE history, he complained to me about the lack of cooperation he got from Maurice Buckmaster, Carlton Hays, and the other higher-ups. They didn't want an official SOE history written at all. They considered the project secret and wanted to keep it that way. What I don't quite understand, young man, is why this woman is so important to you?"

When Craig explained his quest to discover if Sabine was his birth mother, Charlet softened, and stopped glancing at her watch. He left out Daudin's suicide, and other hints of a conspiracy. After what she'd endured, she might think him silly or paranoid.

"Ah, your mum," she beamed. "Or so you think. Now I understand. Every boy should know his mum. Be proud of her. Know who she was and what she did and how she died. Maybe I can help. You say you have names of other agents. Who are they? I know them all, of course. We are a small, pitiful group, we survivors."

"Pitiful?" Craig said. "You're heroes."

"The names, please."

He fumbled in his pockets to find the card where he'd written them down. He could feel her eyes on him. It made him fumble more. "Got it," he said, unfolding the index card and rattling off the names. "Yvonne Aisner, Cecily Lefort I have phone numbers for. No contact info for Pearl Beekman, Jeanne Bohec, and Aimee Corge."

"Cecily and Yvonne will meet with you—if I ask them to. And so will Jeanne—she lives in Liverpool. But Jeanne went through the same training cycle as me, so I doubt she saw your mum if I didn't. Pearl died last year of breast cancer. And Aimee will never talk to you about the war. She is too damaged, too fragile, even now.

"You see, I was lucky. I was arrested only once by the Gestapo, but they had no evidence. Just suspicion—because I was out after curfew. So they beat me, gave me the *baignoire*—dunked my head in a bathtub until I nearly downed. The usual Nazi tricks to force a confession. But I was a very good liar, unlike you, Mr. Martin," she smiled. "So they had their fun, and let me go. Aimee had it worse, much worse. She was caught red-handed with her wireless set, so they knew she was a British agent. They took her to Gestapo headquarters in Paris and tortured her for days, to extract the names of her Resistance contacts. I don't care what she told them, or who she betrayed. I would have told them everything. And so would you. She suffered things that no human being should have to endure."

"I can imagine."

"Can you, really?"

"I suppose not."

"Then don't say you can. It dishonors Aimee, and all those who truly suffered. You live in Hollywood, Mr. Martin, you write for TV. Maybe you've had a cruel boss, suffered a broken heart or two, or had your nose bloodied in the schoolyard. But have you ever been truly at the mercy of another human being? At the mercy of a person who has the power of life and death over you? A person who inflicts pain, unimaginable pain, without remorse, without pity, but perhaps with pleasure?" She looked hard into his eyes until he had to look away.

"This is all ancient history," Charlet continued. "But not to Aimee. She lives alone in Brighton with her seven cats. Her neighbors think she's crazy—and she may be. When I visit her we drink tea and watch the telly and never talk about the war. She's won all the medals I have, for bravery. She's a 'hero,' as you put it. And maybe she still is, for taking good care of her cats, when nobody gives a damn about her."

Charlet stood up. She offered her hand. "I must get back to my husband. The poor chap has been given less than six months to live. He's not taking it well. I'll have the girls call you. We still call each other girls, to this day. Because we were all so young back then."

"It was an honor to meet you," Craig said. He watched her walk away, briskly. Then she turned and came back to him.

"How stupid of me. You must also talk to the Doves."

"Doves?"

"Girls who flunked out of training or never got a mission. Their names do not appear in the record. Maybe your mum was one. We call them Doves because they never fought. I know some. They stick together and love to talk about the war—maybe because they never got into it. They are lucky ones, my little Doves. They don't know how lucky."

She embraced him and kissed his cheek. "You too are blessed with luck, Mr. Martin. Young and healthy in a time of peace."

CHAPTER NINE

Marguerite Whiting had a French mother and an English father of family wealth. She was born in London, but spent her youth in Swiss boarding schools, at the insistence of her mother, where she learned perfect French and the social graces. Recruited by SOE in July of 1943, she excelled in all aspects of training except one: learning Morse code. She could not attain the required speed for sending and receiving messages and was dropped from the course. Disqualified from going to France, she was retained by SOE as support staff. Marguerite was a "Dove." After the war she married well, divorced, and then married better, to a rich industrialist. Craig learned all this from Charlet, who called to say she'd arranged for him to meet Marguerite. She took the initiative because Marguerite was unlikely to make the arrangements herself, being a lady whose social calendar was always full. "She's not a snob," Charlet explained, "just a victim of her class."

They met in the lobby of the Savoy Hotel. Marguerite was dressed in a gray suit with matching hat and white gloves. Her formal bearing was offset by a lopsided grin that lit up the room. Rita took to her at once. Marguerite was fascinated by the antique wheelchair, inspecting it with glee, as Craig squirmed. The pistol was hidden in a zippered pouch beneath the seat. They'd fought bitterly over the gun, but Rita refused to give it up.

"My goodness," Marguerite enthused, "will you just look at these marvelous wood wheels and the bamboo thatching of the seat. Made in India, I suspect. Before the war."

Craig seized the handles of the chair, suggesting they chat in the tearoom next to the lobby. Marguerite readily agreed. "I'm famished," she beamed. "A mushroom omelet might be just the ticket." A handsome waiter in a monogramed blazer was instantly at their table, handing out menus tall enough to hide their faces. Rita flirted with him, to Craig's annoyance, asking about the origin of the word *bangers* with a coy smile. Unfazed, he dutifully explained that sausages used to burst, or "bang,"while cooking. So, of course, Rita ordered bangers, pronouncing it *bang-hers*, to Marguerite's amusement, along with mashed potatoes and onion gravy. Despite recurring bouts of nausea, Rita was not careful about what she ate. Small talk ensued about Rita's broken ankle, the car accident, and the cold and drizzly London weather.

"This is so much fun," Marguerite said. "I almost never meet people from Hollywood."

"Charlet told you that?"

"You write movies, she said, for Steven Spielberg. How exciting."

"She is too kind."

"And she said you want to find out what happened to your mum. How very sweet."

"I'm not sure she *is* my mother. The philosopher, Sabine Arnaud."

"The name is vaguely familiar. I've not read her work. You think she was recruited by SOE?"

As their food arrived, Craig told his story to Marguerite, recounting his mother's friendship with Sabine Arnaud, the clues that led him to believe Sabine was his birth mother. He mentioned the postcard mailed from Guildford and hinted at a government cover-up, but left out details that suggested he and Rita might be in danger for wanting to expose it.

Marguerite was enthralled. "I just love detective stories. You and your charming Rita are like Nick and Nora Charles, straight out of Agatha Christie."

"Dashiell Hammet, actually," Craig said. "But onward, Mrs. Whiting, to the exciting part of our conversation." He opened his portfolio, extracted the photographs, and placed them facedown on the table. "I'm going to show you a series of images of Sabine Arnaud. If you haven't read her work, it's unlikely you've ever seen her photograph. Some are original shots, taken in New York in 1942. Others I've copied from books, which include her passport photo from 1943. I know it's been more than thirty years, but I want you to study these images and think back. Was there any recruit you saw at Wanborough, or at any other training site, who looked like Arnaud?"

Marguerite set down her teacup, wrinkled her brow, and seized the photographs. It didn't take long for her to react.

"My God, I do believe it's Marie! Or the spitting image of her. Yes, I'm quite sure. The hair was shorter when I knew her. Cut like a boy's."

"Marie was her code name?" Craig said.

"Of course. We never used our real names and were forbidden to ask. Mine was Simone, I rather liked it." Marguerite put on her reading glasses, inspecting each photograph with a wistful smile.

93

"Ah, my dear, clumsy Marie. She was blind as a bat, you know, without her glasses, always bumping into something, tripping over her own feet. I thought her an odd recruit—"

"But *where*," Craig interrupted. "Where and when did you see her?"

"At Beaulieu, in the New Forest. The encryption and wireless school was there, in an old country house. I was there from mid-October through December of 1943. I wasn't good at Morse, and got put in a special class—for dumbbells. That's were I met Marie. There were only two of us in the room, with our earphones and practice sets. It was early November, I think, when I first saw Marie. She was there until about December, when she stopped coming to class. They flunked me out just before Christmas—I was heartbroken. But they were kind enough to keep me on, as stenographer. Anyway, Marie and I got to be friends, of sorts. We chatted on breaks, mostly in the loo. I only saw her in class. I don't know where she slept. She was kept isolated from the other girls, which I thought strange, but I knew better than to ask questions. I do remember, quite distinctly, coming out of the loo with her one day, talking and laughing, and Carlton Hays—second in command at SOE—was waiting in the corridor. He was furious that Marie and I were getting chummy. 'Stop wasting our bloody time and learn your goddamn lessons!' he shouted. I was quaking in my shoes, but Marie took it in stride. Nothing fazed her. Carlton could be a bully, but he was no coward. He went to France himself later, and was captured, and escaped from a Nazi prison. A brave, brave man. And now an MP, though I don't like his politics."

"I read about him," Rita broke in. "He helped recruit agents. If there is a dirty secret, he knows it."

"Not so fast, Rita. Are you certain, Mrs. Whiting?" Craig asked. "Dead sure that Marie was Sabine Arnaud?"

"You mean, would I swear to it in court? On a stack of Bibles? Bet my life on it? Certainly not. But, yes, I'm sure."

"Do you remember anything Marie told you—about herself? Did she mention New York, or hint at having had a child?"

"Well, she was older than the other girls, not frivolous. No talk of boys, romance. But her eyes were full of life, I remember that. Intense. But she wasn't stuffy—she could laugh. Still, she made an impression—that she was different somehow. Not like a normal person." Marguerite studied the photos again, and then looked hard at Craig. "I can't say, in good conscience, that she might have been your mother. I see no resemblance. And it's difficult to imagine the woman I knew as Marie having any man's child. But then, who am I to say?"

An awkward silence followed, pierced only by the sound of diffident forks on fine china. The folly of his mother quest descended on Craig's spirit with crushing finality. He was a fool for coming to Europe and sticking his nose into places where it didn't belong.

"Marguerite," Rita said, "what about your code teacher in that school? He might remember Marie."

"Old Cecil? He was half-dead then, in his sixties. I'm sure he's long gone. But there's an easy way to solve your mystery. Give me your photos and I'll get my husband to show them to Carlton. He's a member of my husband's club. They chat from time to time. I suspect this is all some dreadful clerical error."

"Mrs. Whiting," Craig said, "there's a stone in the Ashford cemetery with Sabine Arnaud's name on it. I was there. If she was learning code three months after she died, it's more than a clerical error. Please, don't say anything to your husband about our conversation. We have more ex-agents to interview—maybe we'll find somebody who also remembers Marie. Or maybe this is a case of mistaken identity. Isn't everyone supposed to have a double out there, a look-alike? But please, no mention of this to anyone, just yet. Agreed?"

Marguerite stiffened and handed back the photographs, offended. "As you wish. I thought you'd be eager for my help. You stand no chance on your own, of course, without access to the right sort of people."

They had to move fast. Marguerite, at the very least, was certain to tell her husband all the juicy details about her lunch with the inquisitive Americans. Worst case, she'd dig up photographs of Arnaud and insist her husband show them to Hays. *She*, not the uncouth Yanks, would solve the mystery of Marie's identity. It would not occur to Marguerite that the distinguished MP and war hero might be, in Rita's parlance, "a disciple of the Evil One."

Craig researched the London media and decided that Rodney Boyle of *The Sun* was the right man to pitch the story to. Boyle had a reputation for exposing greed, corruption, and immorality—so long as the culprit was a royal, business mogul, or a respected member of parliament. Craig called him, made his pitch, promising secrets he could not reveal over the phone. Boyle took the bait, instructing Craig to go the Roaring Lion, a pub near his office. "Sit in the booth next to the toilet. It's always empty—it stinks back there. I'll meet you in an hour or two or three. I'm on deadline. Wait."

Rita insisted on going along, staking out a table by the front window, where she had a view of the street. She swore daily they were being followed, and wanted to keep watch. Craig trusted Rita's instincts, but had yet to spot the tails she insisted were there.

It did stink in the booth, and the three pints of stout Craig downed while waiting didn't blunt his sense of smell. Boyle's entrance was announced by boozy shouts from the regulars. "The Rodman is here!" "*The Sun's* in bed, and Sheila's next!" He stopped at the bar to grab a schooner, locked eyes on Craig, and waved him to a less odiferous booth.

"Sheila's the hot bartender," Boyle explained. "Not my type, but I like the lothario image. In fact, I'm a faithful husband—but don't tell these blokes."

Except for broken capillaries in his generous nose, Boyle was decent-looking, with a black head of Byronic curls damp from the rain. Get-acquainted banter ensued, with Craig recounting his ups and downs writing for TV and film. Boyle was fascinated, sharing his own struggle to find a Hollywood agent for his screen-play—"a dynamite thriller" about a crusading tabloid reporter. Craig promised to help. Boyle was grateful and listened attentively as Craig pitched his scoop.

"I love it, but..." Boyle began. He explained that *The Sun*, despite its reputation, had high editorial standards. "We're a scandal sheet, but respected—*and* feared—because we don't print what we can't back up."

Boyle couldn't go after Carlton Hays without reliable witnesses who had seen Arnaud after her alleged death. The hints of a lethal conspiracy—Daudin's suicide, the dead cat—were intriguing, but unsupported by fact. "Could you get a member of Arnaud's family to exhume the body?" Boyle asked. "If her coffin is empty, it's a hell of a story. I'd run with it."

"Her parents are long dead. Her brother, André, died a year ago. So, no immediate family," Craig said.

"Well, my friend, get me another witness or two who'll talk to me—on the record. I'll call your Marguerite, but her husband is a business tycoon, so I doubt she'll want to be quoted in *The Sun*, especially on a story this explosive. Also, I should confess, Carlton

Hays is one of the few men in parliament I respect. He's pro labor, you know, always fights for the little guy. And a bloody war hero to boot. Here's my card, Craig. I'll drop off my screenplay at your hotel in the morning, if that's okay. I'd like your expert opinion on it. If it's crap, please tell me. If you love it—a big *if*—maybe you'll send it to your agent. And if it sells, I'll cut you in on the spoils. We scribes need to stick together, don't you think?" With a too hearty handshake, Rodney Boyle dashed off to get home in time for dinner.

Craig joined Rita by the window table and related his conversation with the ethical—or gutless—journalist. She told Craig to leave first and she'd lag behind a block or two to scan for tails. "Walk slow, Marty. I'll catch up when I'm sure it's safe."

It was cold outside, wet, spitting rain. He turned his collar up, jostled by men and women with heads down, clutching umbrellas, hurrying home. He lingered in front of lighted shops, letting the crowds flow past. When he looked back, Rita was nowhere in sight. Just a sea of black, bobbing umbrellas.

As he crossed the street at the light, somebody bumped him from behind.

"Sorry, mate," said the voice. "I could have hurt you."

"Forget it."

The man drew alongside, hat pulled low, and grabbed Craig's left arm at the bicep. The big hand surrounded his arm and squeezed tight.

"I want to apologize." The man's accent, Eastern European, sent a gut shot of fear through Craig.

"I said forget it. Get off me!" He tried to jerk free, but the man held tight, and grabbed Craig's left wrist with his other hand, finding the pressure point and crushing nerve on bone. "In here, mate." He pushed Craig into an alley and dragged him away from the light. Craig tried to shout for help, but the searing nerve pain in his wrist rendered him mute.

It was black in the narrow alley and stank of garbage. The stranger slammed Craig against the brick wall and punched him in the belly. Craig sank to his knees. The man yanked him to his feet and seized him by the throat. "You accept my apology? Speak up!" Craig could neither speak nor breathe, his vision going gray. He knew he was going to die. The man leaned in close, breath smelling of whisky. "Go home, you Hollywood faggot. We don't like your kind here. Go home or next time I won't be so nice."

The man released his grip, punched him twice more in the belly, and stepped back. Craig sank and pitched forward, facedown. He curled in a ball, retching, gasping for breath. He saw the man's black shoe near his face, and then the shoe moved away. He heard, dimly, through his pain: "You don't belong here, lady."

His senses returning, Craig blinked his eyes and saw the silhouette of Rita in her wheelchair, backlit from the streetlight. He tried to cry out through his pain to warn her, but it was too late.

There was a blinding flash, an echoing report. The man was on the ground, twisting, groaning. Craig watched in horror, his cheek on cold bricks, as a spreading pool of warm blood touched his forehead. "Oh God, no, please, Rita, no... Oh God, no...."

CHAPTER TEN

The steel door opened and Rita hobbled in on crutches, wearing jailbird denim, trailed by a matron in blue. The visiting room was empty at this early hour, and stone-cold. Rita eased into a chair opposite Craig at the long metal table. There was no barrier of glass or wire between them. He reached for her hands.

"Holding hands permitted," the matron told them, "but no kissing, or overt displays of affection."

"Thank God," Rita said. The matron stifled a smile and moved a discrete distance away. She pointed to a sign under the clock: *Inmate visits limited to 10 minutes.*

"I got you a defense lawyer," Martin said, "the best in London."

"She's sweet—giving us space. I like it here. Civilized."

"His name is Morris Scofield."

"Save your money."

"It was self-defense. We can beat this. "

"I told the cops I didn't mean to shoot him—or even fire a warning shot. I knew I'd be in deep shit if I shot a gun off in this town. I wanted to scare him, that's all, but he laughed at me—big mistake. Then he grabbed for the gun—bigger mistake. I aimed at his thigh and hit him in the pelvis. The cops told me he had no gun, no knife, no weapon. Just car keys and nail clippers. They shit themselves laughing over that one. Asked if I feared for my pretty purple nails. So, what's your best case, Marty? Your hot lawyer gets me a slap on the hand? Say, five to seven years for the gun and attempted murder? But I'm dead in one with this beach ball of cancer in my gut."

"You're not a doctor, Rita. You don't know."

"I'm done, Marty. You're the one I worry about."

"Me?"

"I'm safe here. I'll take the stand, sure. Say my piece in court. You do the same. Swear our lives are in danger, people in high places want us dead. Nobody will believe us. But you're on the outside, Marty, *free*. They can still get to you. And they will, believe me. Unless you get them first."

"We can subpoena Whiting. Force her to testify under oath."

"She'll lie."

"I'll go back to Boyle. We're page one news. He won't turn his back on us."

"Whatever you do, Marty, do it quick. You won't have me to watch your back. But get these cocksuckers. Bring them down. I don't mind dying, but I want to die happy. So do it for me, do it for us—do it for Sabine. Or do it because you're pissed and won't take no more shit, ever. From anybody. Even me. "

Rita smiled and squeezed his hand.

"Oh, don't look so sad, Marty. Maybe we can get married. You can screw in prison here, right, if you're married? The Feds had little rooms for it—even pictures on the wall to make it cozy. You made good love to me last time. Well, better. Ask the lawyer if we can marry and party soon."

"Funny. Ask him yourself. He promised to see you tomorrow. And do exactly what he tells you to do. His clients always walk."

In fact, Morris Scofield had promised nothing until his retainer was paid in full. Craig got on the phone to LA and offered his pristine turbo Porsche to a friend for low Blue Book, providing the money could be wired immediately to Scofield's bank. That covered the retainer, and then some, but he'd need more. So he called his agent, Saul, and pitched an action film, promising a treatment by the end of the week. "Think *Dirty Dozen* with a female lead," Craig enthused. "Think Barbra Streisand. Jewish refugee from Paris parachutes into France to free her husband from a Nazi prison—think Jean-Paul Belmondo. Jewish Joan of Arc meets Mission Impossible." Saul loved the idea. He'd get the treatment to an executive at Warner who was chummy with Streisand.

"I'm inspired, Saul. I've found my true calling: action—not comedy. If they option the treatment, I can deliver a full script in four weeks for an advance of twenty-five thousand—or more. And I know you'll get us more."

"I smell a deal," Saul gushed. "Get your ass back to LA."

After Scofield interviewed Rita, he met with Craig in his Mayfair office to talk defense strategy. Dubbed the "Savile Row Shark" by the media for his natty clothes, Scofield was a trim man with short gray hair. He wore a beautifully tailored gray suit, with a silk tie and French cuffs. Despite his flashy attire, the attorney exuded warmth and charm, and was blessed with kind eyes and an honest face. It was easy to see how he'd convinced many a jury to declare the guilty innocent.

Craig talked at length about why he believed that Carlton Hays, and perhaps others, wanted him and Rita dead. Scofield listened patiently, without comment, occasionally twisting his gold cuff links.

"The man Rita shot is the key," Craig said. "A hired killer—if we could connect him to Carlton Hays."

"Yes, that would be splendid. But the police investigated Sergey Koslov. I have their report. He's from Bulgaria, owns a limo—works some for the Soviet Embassy, because he speaks Russian. Does other odd jobs. No criminal record, though his wife says he's abusive and prone to getting into brawls. Koslov denies that he was following you, or Miss Gaona. He says you bumped him on the street, refused to apologize, and he lost his temper. A harmless scuffle ensued. Koslov is an unpleasant fellow, but not the sort of man an MP would know or hire to kill you, or rough you up. Besides, you're not dead—or even seriously injured, which presents a problem for the defense you suggest."

"I might be dead, if not for Rita."

"Of course, I believe you. But a jury would need broken limbs, a cracked skull, a once handsome face beaten to a pulp. Do you like basketball?"

"What?"

"The L.A. Lakers—Are you a fan?"

"Screw basketball. I'm here to—"

"You know the phrase 'slam dunk'? I think Chick Hearn coined it. I wish I could talk as fast as that man; I'd *never* lose a case. I spent three months in L.A. last year on a case, and became a Laker fan."

"And your point?"

"This case, Mr. Martin, is anything but a slam dunk. The only play I have is the sympathy angle. Vulnerable woman in a wheelchair, alarmed by the savage beating of her boyfriend, and fearing for her own life, guns down his assailant. But our helpless woman has spent six years in prison for dealing drugs, has an illegal firearm, for which there are stiff penalties, and shoots down an unarmed citizen—who may be crippled for life.

"As for the conspiracy defense, I contacted the woman Miss Gaona said you met with, Margaret Whiting. She swore over the phone that she did not identify Sabine Arnaud as a woman she knew as an SOE recruit. She saw only a vague resemblance, and would testify to that in court, along with the fact that she thought you were both rude and paranoid."

"She's a liar. There must be something."

"On the sympathy play, yes. Miss Gaona was examined by a prison physician. She has a mass, a tumor—perhaps cancerous—that will require surgery. If she has a short time to live, a judge might, and I say *might*, allow her to go home instead of dying in prison."

Craig felt helpless, his world collapsing.

Scofield continued: "There's another Chick Hearn phrase I love: *The mustard's off the hot dog.* You know, when a flashy player drives in for a spectacular play and gets the ball stolen, makes a fool out of himself."

"So?"

"So, that's what they'll say about me if I take this case to court—or words to that effect. *The mustard's off the hot hog.* My reputation, Mr. Martin—*and* my outrageous fees—are based on my track record of winning difficult, high-profile cases. Not on my skills as a negotiator, or pleading mercy for dying defendants. I don't win every case, of course, but I don't accept cases that *can't* be won. Which is why I'm returning your money and referring you to a barrister who will cost you considerably less."

An hour later, Craig had cornered Rodney Boyle at his favorite watering hole. Boyle had dubbed Rita the "Wheelchair Annie Oakley" in his feature story, playing up her criminal past and hinting that she and her writer boyfriend might be less than innocent tourists.

"You asshole," Craig said. "I give you the story of your sleaze-bag career, and you throw Rita under the bus."

"I'm sorry, man. But all the press took the same angle: American ex-con tourist guns down Londoner. That's the *story*. What else could I write: 'Brave Yank Foils MP's Hired Killer?'"

"Exactly that. If you had the balls."

Boyle said nothing and sipped his Guinness.

"The 'victim,' as you called Koslov, drove a limo for the Soviet Embassy. Did you know that?"

"No."

"Hays went to Cambridge. Trinity College. The same leftist hotbed that spawned the likes of Guy Burgess, Anthony Blunt, and Kim Philby."

"Oh, Christ," Boyle said. "Now you're telling me that Carlton Hays is a Soviet spy."

"Think about it. Hays has a dirty wartime secret involving Sabine Arnaud. Something that could sink his political career. And let's assume that, being a true believer in the Socialist cause, he passed on secrets to the Russians during the war, and does so today. Hays wants to protect his career at any cost, and his Soviet friends are happy to oblige—at the cost of two American lives. It makes perfect sense. And it's the story of the fucking decade if you had the guts to write it."

Boyle sighed, and pushed his beer aside. "If I had one or two hard facts, I'd have the guts. Believe me. Get me an eyewitness who'll talk on the record. Show me an empty tomb, as my Jewish colleagues say, and I'll write about the resurrection."

Craig zigzagged across London on the Tube, getting off at random stations, shopping for supplies, and reboarding the train in another direction. By the time he reached Victoria Station, he was lugging a black duffel and felt certain he had not been followed. Unless his pursuers were—as Rita suggested—emissaries of the Evil One, in which case their powers of surveillance might be supernatural. He was almost too tired to care. The hours of examining every face on every train as a potential threat had transformed his fear into numb exhaustion.

Craig boarded the 10:20 p.m. train to Folkestone, with stops in Maidstone and Ashford. He flopped into a seat and rested his head on the cold window. The car was empty except for a teenage girl and an elderly couple. He closed his eyes, praying silent prayers to calm his nerves. Arnaud's words drifted through his mind—words that seemed to rise out of the core of being with their hard truth: *We are the crucifixion of God.* There was no solace in the absent God of Arnaud. Each of us was destined to cry out from the cross that fate had nailed us to: *Father, father, why hast thou forsaken me…* And no answer would come, no glorious resurrection would follow. There was only the cross. That was the divine truth of Christianity for Sabine Arnaud.

Afraid to sleep and miss his stop, he watched the night fields gliding past, forlorn towns, factories, bare trees, a lighted cottage like a ship at sea. The sky was low, the clouds solid. If there was a moon tonight, its light would not touch the earth.

When he got off the train in Ashford, it was after midnight, the station deserted, and freezing cold. Each breath exploded in cloud. Out of the bag he pulled a heavy coat, gloves, and a knit cap. Inside were a shovel, pick, crowbar, flashlight, trowel, rubber boots, and a thermos of tea for the night ahead. What else did a grave robber need? He'd brought a camera and flash to record the dig and the empty grave. And if the grave included a body, he would photograph that, too, at close range: the skull, jaw, teeth, hair. Would there be hair? What did a corpse look like after thirty years in the ground? He had no idea—except for the zombies in horror films. He'd even thought of removing the head and taking it with him. But that was too creepy. If he took meticulous photos, forensic experts might determine the body was not that of Sabine Arnaud. He'd even brought a measuring tape to lay out beside the body when he photographed it.

Craig had no qualms about desecrating Arnaud's grave. He was certain she was not there. But could he pull it off without getting caught? How deep would he have to dig? Six feet? Deeper? That was a lot of dirt to move by himself before dawn. It wasn't too late to retreat. Take the train back to London, rethink his options. But he knew in his heart there were no options. He picked up the black bag, which rattled and clanked now, suspiciously, without the big coat inside.

The station was on the east end of town, the graveyard to the west. How far? A mile, two? He started walking, keeping to the shadows. The village was dark, except for streetlamps and the glow from one pub. Even the quaint police station, more like an ice-cream parlor than an arm of the law—was dark. He passed the tearoom, bakery, curio shop. A black cat with green eyes glared from behind the window of an antique shop. It startled him, but it wasn't real. A porcelain statue.

Once outside the village, he breathed easier. But it was darker, the night closed in. He stumbled—the bag clanked. He could see only a few yards ahead on the gravel siding of the road. Not a single car passed. Scattered cottages on one side, pasture and woods on the other. Up ahead, above the treetops, was the tip of the chapel spire, its cross dark against the clouds. Despite his fear, he kept flashing on black-and-white horror films. The colorless landscape of bare trees, dead leaves on wet ground, a Gothic church, a graveyard. What was most real was like a movie remembered. Not the real earth, not the earth where we lived and died.

As the chapel came into view, he quickened his pace. Somewhere off in the blackness a dog barked. Once he got off the road and into graveyard he felt safer. There was one cottage near with lights burning, probably where the vicar lived. What was a man of God doing at this hour? No doubt watching TV, like every other lonely insomniac. Maybe even Johnny Carson. *The Tonight Show* reruns on the BBC. He suddenly longed for the life he'd left behind. Being paid to do what he did best—care about nothing so he could make fun of everything.

Crouching low, flashlight held just off the dirt to illuminate his path, Craig worked his way to the back of the graveyard. He'd been here before, but everything looked different now. It took precious minutes to find Arnaud's flat stone. Like an archeologist before an excavation, he photographed the marker and the undisturbed grave. Then he quietly got out his tools and started to dig. The shovel slid in deep. The earth was soft, but got firmer as he went down. Soon he was using the pick to break up clods and cut roots.

After the first thirty minutes, the fear of being discovered abated and he concentrated on the task at hand. Sweating despite the cold, oblivious to his surroundings, he lost himself in the work. The next time he checked his watch, standing in a waist-deep hole, he felt proud that two hours had passed. He remembered Sabine's words: *Absolutely unmixed attention is prayer.*

By the time clouds on the eastern horizon showed traces of rose, he stood at the bottom of an unholy pit with the rim well above his head. How deep was deep enough to prove her grave was empty? China? He would dig another foot and then photograph the site.

The pick buried and hit something, hard but not stone. He used the trowel to scoop out the soil. Pieces of rotten wood came up, then more wood mixed with dirt. Now his heart began to pound with the horror of what he was uncovering. There was fabric tangled and torn in splinters of wood, and something else lower. Something long, yellowish and streaked with black. He was afraid to switch on the flashlight to look closer.

He didn't have to. Light suddenly flooded the grave, illuminating the hideous corpse. Craig turned and was blinded by two flashlights.

"There he is! The sick bloody ghoul... I told you! I told you, Dan!" shouted a hysterical voice. And then another voice, professional, calm: "Get your hands up, lad, where I can see them. *Right now.*"

CHAPTER ELEVEN

RAF Tempsford Airfield, England. January 1944

It was close to midnight when Hays finished briefing Marie Ducat. He was patient and thorough, as he was with every agent, though everything he told her was a lie. They were alone in the barn that served as the operations center for the secret airfield, nicknamed Gibraltar Farm. There were still bits of straw on the dirt floor and the lingering smell of livestock. It was a stable, a manger, Hays mused. A fit place from which to send a sacrificial lamb to slaughter. The RAF had commandeered the old farm because of its isolation and flat acreage suitable for grass runways.

On moonlit nights, single-engine Lysanders flew across the Channel from Tempsford, delivering agents to improvised landing fields in France. The field, typically a pasture or country road, was marked by flashlights of the Resistance cell, or "circuit," the agent was to join. If all went well, the pilot dropped off his passenger and flew back to England. If the Gestapo had been tipped about the rendezvous and lay in wait, the fate of those captured was imprisonment, torture, and death.

Larger aircraft, like the four-engine Halifax, also flew from Tempsford, dropping agents by parachute and caches of arms for the Resistance. The night drops were safer for the pilots, but more dangerous for the agents, who were helpless in the descent and easily spotted from the ground. If they missed the drop zone, as often happened in the dark, a bad landing on rocky ground could break bones. And a water landing in a lake or river could mean drowning. Because an agent's survival depended on mobility and stealth, an injury that caught the attention of the authorities was virtually a death sentence. Besides the Gestapo, SD, and SS to evade, there was the dreaded Milice, the French secret police, who served their Nazi masters with zeal.

Marie had taken the news well when told the day before that she'd have to parachute into France because a suitable landing field could not be found. It was a lie, of course, but Hays admired her aplomb. Marie had no parachute training, and would make her first jump at night, behind enemy lines. "It's a snap," Hays assured her. "The static line opens your chute. And the drop zone is a plowed field, soft as a pillow."

Marie asked intelligent questions about steering the chute to avoid obstacles, and the proper way to land to prevent injury. Hays demonstrated the PLF—parachute landing fall—by jumping from a table in the barn, landing with legs together, knees flexed, and rolling to absorb the impact. When Marie tried it, she landed flat-footed, stiff-legged, and pitched forward, bloodying her nose. It was ugly. In a real jump she might have dislocated both hips. Still, he let her practice until her technique improved. He owed her that much. But even the best PLF wouldn't help when she hit the ground at more than a hundred and fifty miles an hour. Hays was sure of that. After all, he'd packed her chute himself, away from the prying eyes of the professional riggers, wrapping the risers around the canopy so it would not fully inflate. Marie's mission was to die less than twenty seconds after exiting the aircraft, trailing a useless banner of silk.

Against his better judgment, Hays had grown fond of Marie Ducat. He seldom thought of her as Sabine Arnaud. After all, poor Sabine had died months ago. The woman who sat across from him now was lean, fit, hair cut short—like a black helmet—glasses held in place by an elastic cord. Behind the thick lenses, her dark eyes were luminous, rose-tinted in the glow of the lantern that hung above the table.

Hays pushed the maps aside and offered her an American cigarette, a Camel, which she adored. He lit it for her, then one for himself—though he much preferred a pipe. Smoking a last cigarette together was one of the unspoken rituals of sending off an agent to France. Marie took a deep drag, then coughed. She still had a smoker's hack, but all trace of infection had vanished from her lungs. The SOE doctor, a Catholic, thought it a miracle, but Hays knew better. He didn't believe in God, but he did believe in the power of the will, the power of purpose. He'd given her a reason to live, to fight for France, and her body had healed itself. There was nothing you could not achieve if you set your mind to it. Hadn't he come from nothing, a child of the slums, to win a scholarship to Cambridge?

With the exception of his doting mother, saddled with his worthless drunk of a father, Hays doubted that he'd ever truly love a woman. He loved the sport of chasing women, the thrill of conquest, but he preferred the company of ambitious men. Marie was different, of course, unlike any woman he had ever known. Since taking her under his wing, he'd come to both fear and love her.

The fear, which Hays could not admit to himself, arose from how small she made him feel when they talked philosophy, politics, or religion. He took pride in his education, his intelligence and wit, his skill in debate, but came away from every argument feeling exhausted and stupid. This made him fear confrontation, while his pride drove him to butt heads with her, hoping for the intellectual victory he could not achieve.

The love, which Hays could acknowledge, barely, arose out of admiration. He'd never met anyone—man or woman—so determined to succeed in the face of adversity, so impervious to pain and failure, or so comically inept.

Marie had struggled in every phase of agent training that required a modicum of strength or dexterity. On the rifle range, she nearly killed her weapons instructor when the recoil of a Sten gun caused her to spray bullets behind her. And she nearly killed herself on the obstacle course, getting tangled in the rope ladder and hanging upside down thirty feet above the ground. Refusing rescue, she managed to free herself—after an epic battle—and clambered over the wall, white chicken legs failing. When she collapsed across the finish line, utterly spent, her classmates gathered her up like a fallen hero. In hand-to-hand combat, Marie lacked the aggressiveness and agility to subdue a single opponent, and was cruelly mocked by her instructors. Still, she persevered without complaint. In almost every phase of training, her instructors wanted to drop her. "She's my girl," Hays told them. "She stays until I take her off your hands. I've got a special job for her, one she can handle. Trust me."

The only combat course in which Marie earned passing grades was explosives. She knew math and chemistry and grasped the science of bomb making, along with the physics behind the placement of charges to destroy a bridge or railway. Even so, with her poor eyesight and clumsy fingers, instructors kept their distance when she set fuses for practice demolitions.

Outside, the night silence was broken by the sound of an aircraft. The Halifax had landed, flown in from a base in Scotland. It grew louder as the plane taxied close to the barn, the engines backfiring as they shut down. They heard the sound of hatches opening, the good-natured voices of young men talking and laughing.

"Your chariot is here," Hays said, his voice cracking. He was surprised by the emotion that swept over him—a mixture of guilt and pity. "But we have time for another cigarette or two, at least. They have to take on fuel, load up. We're dropping an arms cache tonight, along with you. Small arms mostly, and *plastique*, your specialty."

Marie believed she was joining the Cyrus circuit, near Les Lagnys, as a demolition expert. In fact, Hays had known for some time that Cyrus had been compromised by the Gestapo. The circuit had dropped off the air for three weeks, then returned—blaming a faulty wireless set. The passwords and encryption protocols were correct, but the "fist" of the agent, his style of keying Morse code, was different. The "fist" was like an aural fingerprint to the ear of an expert. It became clear that the Gestapo had taken out the circuit and tortured the wireless man to reveal his codes and passwords.

So SOE traded messages with the Gestapo, as if it was Cyrus, feeding them dubious intelligence and dropping arms for the Resistance to keep up the charade. Now SOE would send an agent, dead on arrival, with microchips of sabotage targets sewn into the lining of her coat. Marie had no idea she was carrying them. And even Hays didn't know what the chips contained, only their purpose—to mislead the Nazis about the location of the Allied invasion that everyone expected in the spring. The Gestapo would find the chips when they thoroughly searched the dead agent, and pass on their intelligence coup to the Abwehr.

Hays had to admit it was a brilliant plan, hatched by his Cambridge pal, Freddie Basset of the Secret Intelligence Service. Freddie had approached him not long after he'd seen Arnaud at Grosvenor Sanitarium, as a favor to Denis Colson. Hays had been impressed by her improving health and determination to serve— but had no intention of accepting her for training. Her intellect, mysticism, and fanatical need for self-sacrifice troubled him. The best women agents were shrewd, street smart, liked men—and wanted to live, not die as martyrs.

Over drinks at the Dorchester, Freddie asked if Hays might have a SOE recruit who was "expendable," for a highly classified mission—the exact date of which had not been set. Hays knew better than to ask questions, but Freddie hinted that he was privy to advance planning for the long-awaited second front.

"Of course I can't tell you what I know, other than the obvious, that we'll play dirty tricks to confuse the krauts about when and where the invasion will come. If you choose to 'volunteer' somebody for this mission—and it's entirely up to you—understand that you are sentencing them to death. But for a grand purpose. The mission, if successful, could shorten the war and reduce our casualties substantially. The sacrifice of one life to save many. The sex and competence of this 'expendable' agent are irrelevant. Any breathing body will do nicely. It should be a relatively new recruit, someone who will be in training for the next four to six months. I won't know the exact date of the mission for some time. When I do—we shall move quickly.

"But I must warn you, Charlie, if you get onboard, this is strictly between you and me. Nobody else in SOE can know. This is the kind of dirty little secret—if it got out—that could hurt us later. And I know we both have big plans after the war, don't we, old chum?"

Hays thought immediately of Sabine Arnaud. And Freddie loved his idea of having her die *before* the mission. Only a code name would be used, and no records of her real identity kept by SOE. Once sequestered in training, Hays would ensure that she had no contact with the outside world. He would allow her to write one heavily censored letter per month to anyone she pleased, which he would post in the furnace for classified documents. The absence of return letters could be easily blamed on the vagaries of wartime.

So it was decided that Sabine Arnaud would die twice for her country. Of her first death, she was blissfully unaware. Two weeks after Hays removed her from the sanitarium for medical tests (she had to be fit enough to survive training), he notified the chief physician at Grosvenor, Dr. Charles Melton, that Arnaud was dead. The body, that of a homeless prostitute who died of exposure, was delivered in a sealed coffin, along with an autopsy report that Melton was instructed to sign—as a matter of national security. He was also told to notify the proper authorities of her death, from tuberculosis and self-starvation, and arrange for a prompt burial. The body was not to be viewed—by anyone. There was a war on, and Dr. Melton did as he was told.

Marie took a long drag and stubbed out her cigarette. She fixed Hays with her gaze until he wanted to look away.

"I must not forget to thank you," she said. "With all my heart."

"What on earth for?"

"For choosing me—for this mission. Others are more skilled, prepared. You know that."

"Thank me after the war—if we survive it. I'm going over myself soon. I feel like a fraud on the sidelines."

"I think you'll survive, Charlie," she said. "You're very clever. But I won't. I am quite certain of that. "

"Stop talking rot, Sabine."

"You called me Sabine. It sounds strange on your lips."

"Sorry—and me the stickler for security."

Hays fumbled with the cigarette pack. Angrily, he shook the remaining cigarettes out on the table.

"Marie, please. Smoke another with me. You won't get a decent cigarette in France. They smoke corn silk now, chestnut leaves—only the Germans get tobacco."

She shook her head, watching him strike three matches before getting one to flare. He cupped both hands around the flame, though the air was dead still in the barn.

"Sometimes I wish I wasn't an atheist," he said.

"I rather think God prefers the atheist to those who look to him only for consolation."

"Then why believe? If God can't help us."

"Because I know my love for God is *real*. But I also know that God cannot be anything like I imagine—and in that sense is *not* real. Don't you see the beauty, the truth in that contradiction? God exists; God does not exist. What's the problem?"

Hays managed a smile. "You lost me, professor."

"But you never answered *my* question, Charlie. Why me? I thought you might have taken me on as a favor to Denis. But then, you are not the kind of man to be swayed by sentiment. There must have been a better reason, a logical reason—for a man like you."

"Nobody wanted to serve as much as you did. Nobody. That's a fact."

"But that's not a *logical* reason."

"For Christ bloody sake what difference does it make? Maybe I was a fool, maybe I fell in love with your big brown eyes. Maybe I made the biggest bloody mistake of my bloody career. Which I may have. But time is short, my friend. You best get on your gear. I'll check your kit one more time."

Hays removed the heavy quilted jumpsuit from the wall. Marie stood. Like every agent bound for France, she'd been issued clothes that would not arouse suspicion. Her coat, pants, shoes—even her undergarments—had been manufactured in France. They were worn, dowdy clothes that matched her identity. Marie Ducat was the spinster daughter of a dairy farmer in Narbonne, recently deceased. She taught school and worked as a bookkeeper. She carried a work permit, ration cards, family photos, school papers, paper francs, and coins. In the weeks before, Marie had memorized a dossier on her fictitious history and been grilled mercilessly in mock interrogations to test her ability to lie convincingly under pressure.

Marie struggled into the jumpsuit. It was heavy with survival gear zipped into the pockets: a flashlight, canteen, food packets, knife and revolver. Hays had briefed her on every contingency—if she landed in a tree, or water, or far from the drop zone. He derived pleasure from his patient briefing, as Marie was steadied by it. There was no reason to send her off to her death with unanswered questions or needless anxiety.

Outside, the air was biting cold, the moon bright. Two men were under the aircraft, lifting metal canisters, the *parachutage*, into the bomb bay. The pilots stood by the barn, warming themselves by crackling flames from wood blazing in an oil drum. They smiled at Marie, and the younger pilot gave her a jaunty salute.

"This is Marie," Hays said. "Your guest tonight. I trust you've already been briefed on the coordinates for the drop."

"Yes sir," said the taller of the two men, with an Australian accent. "The weather is good. We should put you on target just fine, ma'am. No worries."

The four of them stood in silence, their hands extended, as if in prayer, around the comforting altar of light and warmth.

"We best get back to the cockpit, ma'am. Checklists to run and all that," said the tall pilot. "We'll get you onboard soon."

"Should I put on my parachute?" Marie asked.

"No need. At least two hours to target. Stevie, our jumpmaster, will get you hooked up when it's time. Not to worry."

When they had gone, Marie took deep breaths, stamping her feet against the cold.

"This is real," she said, glancing at the plane. "I'm going back to France. I can't believe it. I'm frightened."

"You'd be crazy if you weren't."

"Not so much of death—but that too. I'm afraid I won't measure up. That I will fail—that others may die because of me."

"You will *not* fail, Marie," Hays said with conviction. "I *promise* you. You will not fail."

She took comfort in his words. And when she mounted the stairs into the fuselage, clutching her parachute, her step was jaunty. She turned and waved at him, smiling, like a teenager about to take her first roller coaster ride.

Hays stood by the fire and watched as the Halifax taxied to the end of the grass runway and made its takeoff run past the barn, lifting off into the dark. He waited until the sound of the engines faded into silence.

"God exists," he said aloud, flicking his cigarette into the fire. "And God does not exist. So what's your bloody problem?"

Marie sat on webbed seats with her back to the cold metal of the fuselage. Stevie, a stocky kid, sat opposite. Whenever their eyes met, he grinned, gave her a thumbs-up. It was too noisy to talk, unless you shouted. The engines throbbed and groaned, sometimes changing pitch, as they climbed or descended. It was smooth at first, then rough when they crossed the Channel. The flight seemed endless. There were no windows to look out of: the Halifax was a bomber—not designed for passenger comfort.

In the floor was a round hatch, like a manhole cover. Stevie had shown it to her when she boarded. Close to target, he'd open the hatch and hook her up to the static line. She was to sit on the edge with her feet dangling and wait until he gave her the signal: three sharp taps on the shoulder, and then go. Marie felt her whole body go weak at the thought of falling through that hole into black space, but nodded gamely that she understood. She didn't dare tell him that this was her first jump. Or worse, her first flight in an airplane. Years ago, as a girl, her father had taken her aloft in a carnival balloon tethered to the ground. She had been too queasy to enjoy the bird's-eye view of Paris.

An hour into the flight, Stevie brought her tea from a thermos and a ham sandwich, which tasted like sawdust in her dry mouth. The motion of the plane, combined with gnawing fear, made her want to vomit. The tea was tasteless, but the warm cup felt good in her cold hands.

Stevie went to the cockpit for a while and then came back, standing over her. "Almost show time, ma'am. Time to gear up." He helped her slip on the parachute and secured the buckles. "Who packed this, ma'am? I don't see no tag. The riggers always leave a tag, with a number—to show who packed it."

"I'm sure it's fine, " Marie said. "Charlie gave it to me."

"Charlie, eh? Well, ma'am. Just to be on the safe side, you go with my chute. I won't need it. Not tonight, not on this milk run. I packed it myself—never had one let me down yet." He unbuckled her chute, got his from under his seat, and snapped her in, pulling the straps tight. "Snug as a bug, ma'am. You ready?"

A red light went on behind the cockpit doors. "That means we're close," Stevie shouted. "When the pilot sees the ground signal, the red goes to green, and we'll drop the cans from the bomb racks. Then I'll open the hatch and we'll make another pass. Red light, then green—and off you go!" He squeezed her shoulders, his lips brushing her ear—by design or accident, a farewell kiss.

The bomb bay doors opened with the sound of gears turning and the roar of onrushing air. The light turned to green and the aircraft rose, relieved of its cargo. Stevie lifted the hatch, cold air flooding into the fuselage. Below were patches of cloud, dark woods, the silver thread of a moonlit stream. He hooked up her static line and helped her sit, her legs pounded in the slipstream. He held her tight, like a lover who didn't want to say goodbye. The red light turned to flashing green. She felt two hard taps on her shoulder, and the third was a shove. She was gone.

CHAPTER TWELVE

Craig was a writer again. He sat on his bunk, back to the wall, and wrote in pencil on a yellow pad. When his fingers cramped, he jogged in place to warm up. It was always cold in the cell, except late at night, when somebody cranked the heat so high he sweated. He wrote eight to ten hours a day. There was no writer's block in jail, no fear of failure. His failure was complete in being where he was. Writing was the one freedom he had left. He'd forgotten the tactile pleasure of writing in longhand, sculpting each word, slowing the pace of his thoughts to match the crawl of his hand. Happily, his Ashford jailers were generous with paper and pencils, and even trusted him with a pencil sharpener. Perhaps it was a British tradition, dating back to Oscar Wilde, that incarcerated writers should not be denied the tools of their trade.

In the first week he finished the screenplay treatment he'd promised Saul. It ran to sixty pages with corrections and insertions, but it was a "fair" copy, as scribes used to say. Saul would bitch at the cost of getting it typed, but the story was solid. It should lead to a development deal to write the script. At his current rate of output, he might knock that out in two weeks. Why not? Every insecure, self-loathing writer ought to do a stretch in jail, Craig mused; it would lower the suicide rate. And there was another benefit to being behind bars—he felt safe.

The treatment done, he wrote notes for his defense, crafting eloquent closing arguments that would electrify the court. To the consternation of the authorities, Craig had refused to give a statement to the police, pleaded innocent to all charges, and demanded a jury trial, along with the right to defend himself. The magistrate refused to set a trial date until the defendant completed a psychiatric evaluation to determine his mental competency. That had yet to occur. So Craig waited. And while he waited, he wrote.

The *Ashford Gazette* followed the bizarre story of the "grave-robbing LA ghoul," the same man whose "pistol-packing paramour" was behind "steel London bars." A kindly guard shared his daily paper with Craig, who was delighted with the coverage and purple prose. Nothing much happened in Ashford, and the locals were buzzing with rumors of satanic cults, stolen bodies, and "unspeakable acts" with the dead. The London press had also picked up the story. Rodney Boyle sent him a craven note requesting an exclusive interview and promised to cover the trial. Craig was certain if he could defend himself in open court, the media coverage would pressure the authorities to investigate the fictitious death of Sabine Arnaud.

Craig had tried to call Rita, but rules prevented one jailbird from talking to another. So he wrote her letters, long and heartfelt, promising to secure the "justice and satisfaction" they deserved. He alluded to his courtroom strategy, but left out the details, assuming his letters would be screened by censors. He signed off every letter with "All my love, always," and meant it. Rita had yet to reply, which worried him.

On Monday morning, during the second week of his incarceration, Craig was escorted from his cell to a windowless room, where a balding man in a plaid sport coat and bow tie extended his hand.

"I'm Doctor Austin Clyde. Please, sit."

"Psychiatrist?"

"Forensic Psychologist."

"I'm all yours. How should we begin? This is the twentieth of December, nineteen hundred and seventy-seven. I'm a college-educated white male, American born. I've never been hospitalized for an illness, physical or mental. My medical history is available from my physician in LA, who has treated me since I was an adult. Like most human beings I am prone to occasional periods of sadness, which come and go—often because of the loss of a woman or a job, or simply a bad day, when life can seem a 'stale, unprofitable enterprise,' as Hamlet whined. I've never taken medication for anxiety, depression, schizophrenia, or paranoia. I've never had a visual or auditory hallucination. I have no thoughts of doing harm to myself or others—even *here*, in this hell hole, which might qualify me for sainthood. I've never taken hard drugs—opiates, cocaine, methamphetamines. I've smoked marijuana, but don't like the high. So I prefer a stiff drink, but seldom drink to excess. I've never experienced a blackout or been violent under the influence of alcohol. On the contrary, when mildly buzzed I'm more affable and amusing, or so I think, which is why most people drink. I am a writer by profession, TV mostly, comedy, and successful I might add. Which speaks to my sanity—if not my character. You can make it in Hollywood without scruples, but not without common sense and the social intelligence to work creatively with others—even if they're assholes. And most of the time, trust me, Doctor, they *are* assholes. If you check my personal effects, you'll find my Writers Guild of America card, along with the name of my agent at International Creative Management, Saul Litt, who can attest to my professional competence. Saul can also tell you, to the penny, how much money I've put in his pocket. That's a joke—but I'm not anti-Semitic."

Clyde smiled as he continued to make notes. "You're making my job very easy, Mr. Martin."

"That's my intent."

"But aren't we a bit flippant, considering your situation?"

"Oh, I'm very aware of my situation. I've never been in jail, and I don't like it one bit. My flippancy, as you call it, is partly a defense mechanism, because I'm nervous. And it also stems from my irritation at having my intelligence and sanity questioned. Hence, I'm eager to show you that I'm an educated, articulate man who can speak clearly and stand up for himself persuasively in court. I might also argue that my flippancy, my use of irony, my attempts at humor, are all evidence of my mental health. From what I've read, the world of the schizophrenic, psychotic, and the criminally insane is invariable *serious*. It is a world without irony, without the kind of benign absurdity that often provokes a knowing chuckle among rational, sophisticated adults such as you and me."

Clyde pulled a folder from his briefcase and flipped through it. "You express yourself well, but you must admit that your behavior of late has been far from ordinary. Three weeks ago you were engaged in a physical altercation in London, during which your lady friend shot your assailant. More recently, you were apprehended at the bottom of a grave, in rubber boots, with a pick and shovel, and a corpse at your feet. That of Sabine Arnaud, a philosopher of some note, I understand—though I've not read her. This is hardly the behavior of your typical American tourist."

"I have," Craig said.

"Beg your pardon?"

"Read Sabine Arnaud. She is the most profound spiritual thinker of the twentieth century. I revere her work. Even comedy writers need a god to believe in—maybe especially comedy writers. I also have a personal connection to Arnaud; she was the dear friend of my mother in New York, in 1942, the year of my birth. I have correspondence between them that speaks to that relationship. My purpose in coming to Europe was to research the depth of their friendship—and perhaps write about it. The last thing I would do is desecrate the grave of a woman my mother loved and that I admire."

"You dispute the accuracy of the police report?"

"One portion of it—which is the core of my defense strategy. And which I would prefer not to reveal, except in court. Certainly, I don't dispute the fact that I dug the hole where I was apprehended."

"But if you *are* a sensible man, as you seem to be, why not plead guilty to a lesser charge, pay a fine, throw yourself on the mercy of the court? And if you have the resources, which I suspect you do, why not hire a first-rate barrister? And why refuse bail? You don't have to be in jail waiting for trial."

"Again, Doctor Clyde, my reasons for wanting to stay in jail relate to my defense strategy—which is within my right to withhold until the trial. Otherwise I'd be helping the prosecution. I will tell you that my defense is based on evidence, albeit circumstantial, that proves my actions were without criminal intent."

"Really?"

"Oh, I expect to be found guilty of *something*. But intent is crucial in determining the severity of a crime. Wouldn't you agree? I'll give you an example. A man walks down a country road at night, minding his own business, when he passes a farmhouse. There are lights on, but the light is an odd color—reddish orange. Curious, he draws closer, and what he sees, quite clearly, are flames behind the windows. Alarmed, he runs toward the house and climbs the fence that surrounds it. An act of trespassing. Next he pounds on the door, but gets no answer. So he knocks the door down to find a phone to call for help. An act of breaking and entering. As he searches for the phone—"

Clyde interrupted: "I'm not stupid. In such a case, you would not be prosecuted."

"I know you're intelligent, which is why my parable gets more intriguing—if you'll hear me out. Our man, in searching for a phone, discovers a beautiful young woman, unresponsive, lying on a sofa. He picks her up and runs from the burning house. An act of kidnapping—but viewed in the proper context, of course, an act of heroism. Then a curious thing happens, our hero stumbles in the dark and pitches forward. He lands hard and the fair lady's head hits a rock, cracking her skull. Just then police and fire trucks arrive, having been summoned by an observant neighbor. The upshot is that the woman had been overcome by smoke, but recovers fully in the hospital. What she doesn't recover from is the blow to the head, which results in brain damage, limiting her ability to hold a job, as well as dimming her prospects for marriage, children, and a happy life. The police decline to charge the man with a crime—given his admirable intentions. But the woman files a lawsuit. She argues that our clumsy hero preempted the work of professionals, who would have rescued her without injury. The jury decides in her favor, with a hefty award for damages that bankrupts our hero, who later commits suicide. This is a true story by the way. It happened in Kansas some years back."

"I don't see your point," Clyde said impatiently

"I love the story because of its irony, its moral ambiguity. Was our hero deserving of blame by the woman he rescued? And was she to blame for *his* death? There is no simple answer. My point, which I will make to the jury, is that my intent on the night in question, when seen in the proper context, was admirable. As admirable, in fact, as a man who risks his life to save another. My actions may have been misguided, inept, and outside the law, but they served a higher purpose that the jury has a right to know. And the public as well—since my trial will have press in attendance."

"So why not pretend I'm the jury and state your case? Tell *me* why you dug up the grave of Arnaud."

"If I was your patient, Doctor Clyde, paying for psychotherapy, I would trust you to keep what I say in confidence. However, because the court is paying for your time, I must assume that anything I say is fair game for your report. So, under these circumstances, I prefer not to reveal my intentions that night. They are complicated and best understood in the context of the evidence I shall present at my trial."

Clyde looked as though he were about to ask a question, then lowered his eyes and made notes. Several minutes passed in silence, his pen scratching over the paper, the hint of a smile on his moist lips.

"I have all I need—and then some—for my evaluation. In the morning, my assistant will administer an intelligence test and a personality inventory. I will deliver my full report to the court within forty-eight hours."

That night Craig lay sweating in his bunk, wishing he'd been more deferential in the interview. *Fuck it. I'm not crazy*, he thought. *I may have been rude, but no way can he declare me a nutcase.* Still, he had trouble drifting off to sleep.

In the morning, he got a lift—a letter from Rita. It ran two pages, with words blacked out. By holding the thin paper to the light, he could decipher most of the expurgated material. Evidently, the prison censor was a prude. "Dear, dear Marty" it began, "bless your good, brave heart for what you done. You got balls, but smarts maybe not since you got caught. Welcome to my world, Marty— the proletariat, the underclass, the stepped on and forgotten. Now we both are royally fucked, but I am proud of you. SING OUR STORY LOUD. You got the words and the music. Get our justice. Get those evil pricks who fear and hate the TRUTH."

She went on to describe her boring days, the lousy food, and the kind guards. She was pleased with the news that the man she shot was expected to recover fully. "Just some slob doing his job—paid by big shots who don't want to get their hands dirty." The prison library sucked, but she'd just finished a classic: "Great Expectations (end in dogshit)." Her lawyer wanted to plea bargain; she wanted to testify in court. And promised she would.

Rita closed with: "Love you too, stud muffin," followed by the doodle of a heart pierced by an arrow dripping blood. Then a P.S. "I'm going to hospital for tests. Not my choice of course. But WE SHALL OVERCOME said Pancho Villa, or was it Emiliano Zapata?"

Two more days passed with anxious pacing and furious writing. The guard who usually brought him dinner showed up without a tray. He unlocked the door. "Follow me," he said. "You're a free man."

"What do you mean free?"

"I don't make the rules."

They went into the property room where he'd been booked. The constable set a paper bag on the counter. The clothes Craig had been wearing when he was arrested were piled on a chair.

"Check your valuables, sign for them. Change your clothes. We're keeping your tools and camera for evidence. Your trial is scheduled in twenty-two days."

"I didn't post bail."

"The court ordered your release. Just show up for trial. In the meantime, get out of Ashford. You're not wanted here. You might get beat to death by a local. We don't like our dead dug up by freaks."

"But I want to stay in jail."

The constable laughed: "This isn't a bloody hotel. Give us back our clothes and put on your own. Change in the loo. Do it, *now*."

CHAPTER THIRTEEN

Craig stood in front of the police station, unsure of his next move. It was six o'clock, dark and cold, shops closing, pedestrians hurrying home. How paranoid should he be? At least he'd felt safe in jail. Three weeks was a long time to wait for trial if somebody wanted you dead. He toyed with the idea of catching the next plane to LA and waiting there. It was inviting, the thought of sun, palm trees, friends, and favorite haunts—the safety of distance. But he'd feel like a shit for leaving Rita. So there was no choice, not really. He'd go back to London and try to help her. It was the right thing to do, but the decision didn't settle his nerves.

The timetable he'd picked up at Victoria Station was still in his coat pocket. The next train to London left at 8:45. Time to kill. He turned up his collar, hunched down, and walked fast. Every half block he glanced over his shoulder. He entered the Boar's Head pub and found a table in the rear where he could watch the front door. He ordered a stout from the pretty, buxom barmaid. It tasted good. The second one tasted even better. The blessed balm of alcohol was working its magic. He ordered corn beef and cabbage and wolfed it down. The barmaid's smile put him at ease. Her wink said she found him attractive. And no wonder. The other patrons were men in their fifties or sixties with red faces and soft bellies. Craig felt the whisper of lust in his loins, an encouraging sign. He began to feel like a man, instead of a terrified schoolgirl. He paid his tab, left her an obscene tip, and asked for her phone number. She was happy to oblige, but warned of her jealous husband. Craig laughed. Women with great tits always had jealous husbands. "Farewell, my lovely," he said, and kissed her hand gallantly.

He decided to jog the half mile to the station. If he set a brisk pace, it would be easy to spot a tail trying to keep up. It seemed like a foolproof tactic to expose a pursuer and shake his paranoia.

After covering three blocks, he heard his name. A woman's voice, from the street.

"Craig! Craig—is that you?"

He slowed, his ego telling him it might be the smitten barmaid. A silver Mercedes had pulled alongside. The woman at the wheel leaned out the window, waving, her face in shadow.

"It's me, Craig! Linda, from LA." He'd dated three or four Lindas, and fallen hard for one of them—a decade ago. He stepped closer. Close enough to see he didn't know the woman and she wasn't alone. Two shadowy forms stirred in the back seat. He froze, backed up, and felt a strong hand on his shoulder

"Don't turn around, Craig. If you see my face, you will die right here, right now." The man spoke with a thick Scottish accent.

"Get in the car, lad. I won't harm you. You have my word."

Craig felt something hard, pointed, press against his spine.

The rear door of the car swung open. Craig hesitated, mind racing. What if he cried for help, or spun and grabbed the knife or gun, like he'd seen heroes in the movies do. Was it better to end it now—escape or die trying? He was poked again, harder. He felt the point of a knife pushed through his jacket and prick his flesh. Craig flinched, but the hand kept him in place, pinching a nerve under his collarbone. His knees buckled. He wanted to run—but could barely stand.

"Die now," the Scot said. "Or we chat. Your call."

Craig got in the car, sick with fear. When he saw the two men in ski masks, he knew he was a dead man. He hated himself for not putting up a fight on the street. The man in the middle climbed over Craig and pushed him toward the center. The other held a small pistol. "Put this on," he said. It was a hood, with a hole for the mouth. Craig did as he was told.

It was hard to breathe under the hood. Craig fought for air, sucking cloth into his mouth. "Relax," the man to his right said. "It's a long drive." The hood was lifted over his mouth. Something stabbed his neck. He flinched, but the men grabbed his wrists so he couldn't touch the wound. Blood trickled down his neck. The last thing Craig heard was the cheerful voice of the Scot who had grabbed him on the street. "Good work, Sheila, I'll drive." And then his body filled with soothing warmth, and he drifted into oblivion.

Craig woke to blinding light. He was flat on his back, staring up at a bank of fluorescent lights. He was cold and felt naked, but couldn't move his head to look at his body. His arms and legs were spread and restrained. He smelled dog, like in a kennel, but heard nothing. As he fought panic, composing himself to cry out, a mirror swung into place above him.

Craig looked up at himself in terror. He was naked, on a metal table, as if in an operating room. His head was locked down by a metal band across his forehead. His legs were spread, ankles pinned by metal cuffs, arms wide in a crucifixion pose, bound at the wrists. By rolling his eyes left and right he could glimpse white tiled walls. And he felt the presence of someone behind his head.

"Who's there? Anybody? Am I hurt—in a hospital?"

A gloved hand appeared. "Fuck!" Craig screamed. "What is this? Where am I? Talk to me!"

"Easy, lad." It was the Scot, standing behind his head. Latex-sheathed fingers stroked his cheek. Craig struggled to breathe. He began to sweat. The hand used a tissue to dab beads of perspiration from his face. In the mirror, Craig saw the hand, arm clothed in surgical gown, but no face.

"I won't hurt you," the Scot said. "At least, not yet. It all depends on the bond we establish, the depth of trust—affection, even."

Something slid over the floor, perhaps a chair.

"Now, Craig, or should I call you Marty? Isn't that what your whore calls you?...Well, is it?"

"She's not a whore," Craig said, surprised by his courage. "Rita, yes... she calls me Marty." He was panting, chest heaving.

"Marty, you must breathe deeply. Can you do that for me? Breathe in through your nose, deep and slow, and exhale through your pretty mouth. We have all the time in the world. One can die of fright, you know. I've seen it happen. Calm yourself. I'm going to sit where you can't see my face—for obvious reasons—and ask you questions, fascinating questions, which you will answer at length, and with complete candor. I know you're uncomfortable, Marty, but that's really the point, isn't it? To demonstrate that you are no longer free, no longer a *man* in any meaningful sense of the word. You are, in point of fact, utterly powerless. As helpless as an infant. And I am your father—perhaps kind, or unspeakably cruel. It depends on you, Marty. Do you understand?"

Craig lost control of his bladder. Warm urine flowed down his bare legs.

"Oh, dear me. I fear you've messed yourself. And I'm out of diapers for a baby your size." A man in a white lab coat appeared, wearing a ski mask. He used a towel to wipe Craig dry, but the smell remained.

"Thanks, Billy," the Scot said. "Which isn't his name, by the way. Nor did Sheila drive the car. We're not amateurs, you know. But I digress. I was about to compare you to Christ on the cross. Crucifixion was the cruelest form of execution ever devised. Did you know that, Marty? The victims didn't die from blood loss—which would have been humane—but asphyxiation. They struggled to breathe for hours, sometimes days, gasping for each shallow, painful breath, until they gave up the ghost in pure agony. Indeed, I suspect that Jesus the man—for he *was* both *all man* and *all God* the story goes—also lost control of his bladder on that rugged cross of Calvary. But it wouldn't do to put that in the Gospels, now would it? That one embarrassing detail, understandable under the circumstances, might have doomed the spread of Christianity and changed the course of human history. 'Blood and water flowed from the wound in his side, and piss ran down his legs.' See what I mean? Would you like a glass of water before we begin?"

"Yes, water."

Craig heard a motor activated that tilted the table until he was nearly upright. He could see the far wall now. It was lined with empty animal cages. Billy brought a tall glass to his lips. Craig drank, then gagged, and coughed. Laughter filled the room.

"Wine-vinegar! Isn't that what Romans offered Jesus on the cross? A practical joke, Marty. Cruel, but funny. But most jokes have an element of cruelty, don't you agree? Can you forgive me? For having a bit of fun? Well, can you?...I asked you a question."

"What?" Craig coughed, trying to catch his breath.

His face was slapped, hard.

"I *said*, can you *forgive* me, for giving you vinegar instead of water?"

"Yes."

"Yes, what?"

"I forgive you."

"Excellent! I can't be your friend without forgiveness. Billy, fetch my boy some ice water." Another glass was brought to his lips. Craig tested it with his tongue, then gulped it down. The table was tilted back to horizontal.

"Shall we get started? No more practical jokes. You play fair with me and I play fair with you." The voice went silent. Craig heard a match struck, then caught the smell of a cigarette. "Why did you come to Britain?"

"What?"

"I'm going to lose my patience, Marty, if I have to repeat every bloody question. Why the bloody fuck did you come to Britain?"

"I'm sorry...I can't focus. It was a search, for my past. I thought Sabine Arnaud might be my birth mother. She knew my mother in New York, the year I was born. I wanted to talk to people who had known Arnaud—to see if it could be true."

"Sweet boy. You wanted to find your mum. Or should I say 'mummy'? There I go again—a bad pun! Get it? You dug her up. Proceed."

"That's why I came... research. I didn't want to cause trouble."

"Oh, but you have, my boy. Quite a lot of trouble. A scholar at the Sorbonne took her own life, your whore shot a man, and you desecrated the grave of Sabine Arnaud. You also met with a reporter and begged him to write lies about a distinguished member of parliament. That, in my mind, is your one *mortal* sin, Marty—the willful slander of a noble man. Oh, I left out a few peccadillos, like driving drunk, wrecking a car that didn't belong to you, and nearly killing your whore. Also, giving that poor scrub woman a fright. What was her name? Help me out here, Marty"

"Mavis."

"Yes, dear Mavis. We chatted in this very room. But I think she'll recover, and live out her pathetic life quite happily, along with her pathetic husband, who is thrilled with his new car. The dim-witted usually do, recover, that is. It's the bright ones, the educated, those born to privilege, who never quite recover from an encounter with a man like me. Like Professor Daudin. It wasn't my doing, you know, her suicide. She couldn't live with the psychic trauma of being in the position that you're in now. I rather liked Sophie, and I blame you, Marty, for her death. For arousing her curiosity. She stuck her ugly frog nose where it didn't belong. Oh, your intentions were innocent, even laudable, but the result was catastrophic for Sophie. Rather like a man who tries to save a woman from a burning house and ends up ruining her life. What guilt should such a man bear? What punishment does he deserve? You have an interest in such ethical questions, according to Dr. Clyde—whose report I have on my lap.

"Let's see …your scores on the Wechsler Adult Intelligence Scale are instructive. You're a bright boy, but not *that* bright. Less than one standard deviation above the mean. A man of superior intelligence would not find himself in your present predicament. He would be sitting where I am. Do you agree?"

"Yes."

"Good. Because we're engaged in a game of wits, Marty, that I will win. You must accept that. But onward, to your scores on the MMPI, the Minnesota Multiphasic Personality Inventory. Some indications of anxiety, depression, perhaps sexual deviance. You've never married, have you? Your body looks rather soft, girlish to me. And your whore dominates you, in my humble opinion. Does she use a strap-on? Ream you up the ass while you beg for more? But that's really none of my business, is it? In any case, the good doctor declared you competent to stand trial and defend yourself in court. And not a flight risk. Ha! You're certainly not a flight risk now. Are you following all this, Marty?"

"Yeah."

"Good. Stay alert. Because my next set of questions will determine your fate tonight. Whether you live or die. Tell me what you *think* you know about the death of Sabine Arnaud. If you hold anything back, I will not be your friend. I will make you beg for death, on this table, for a very long time. But I won't hear your pleas, because I only have ears for my friends, those whom I admire and trust. Do you understand?"

"Yes," Craig said miserably.

"When did Sabine Arnaud die?"

"I don't know. Not in August. She wrote to my mother in September."

"How often did Arnaud write your mother?"

"Just once. To my knowledge. A postcard."

"Perhaps I should ask your mother—if she has other correspondence."

"She died last year."

"Of course. Would this be the postcard?" The hand showed him the card. "We took the liberty of retrieving it from your hotel room in London. We thought it vital for your defense. That is, if you attempt to prove that Arnaud is not in the grave you dug up."

Billy produced a lighter and lit one corner of the card. The flame crawled upward, turning the card black.

"Now, in your opinion, Marty, where was Arnaud in September of 1943?"

"I think she was in training, at Wanborough Manor, in Guildford. How long she was in training, whether she was sent to France—I don't know. But a former recruit, Marguerite Whiting, told me she saw her in December 1943—or somebody who looked like her, with the code name of Marie. She also said that Carlton Hays seemed to take a special interest in Marie."

"Bravo, Marty! I'm proud of your detective work. You learned a lot more than Daudin. Have you ever worked for an agency of the U.S. government?"

"I was in the army."

"What time period? In what capacity?"

"1962 to '64. At Fort Sill. Artillery unit."

"Never worked in military intelligence?"

"No."

"Never worked for an intelligence agency?"

"No."

"Not even as an informant? Perhaps for the FBI? On subversive types in Hollywood, that sort of thing."

"Never."

"Excellent! Billy, give the boy another drink. Soon we'll break out the scotch and cigars. You'll have earned it."

The table tilted and Craig drank his fill of water. He was starting to feel a glimmer of hope that he wouldn't be tortured or killed.

"Now, my boy. I'm going to tell you what you don't know. Arnaud volunteered for a mission that remains secret to this day. She went to jump school in Scotland, in December 1943, where she died before her first jump, because the aircraft she was in, along with two other recruits, crashed shortly after takeoff. There were no survivors. And, of course, no official announcement. Arnaud's body was quietly returned to her grave in the Ashford cemetery—which had been empty.

"I won't tell anyone. I swear to God," Craig said.

"But you've already shot your mouth off. And written too much. Like these lies." The hand appeared, holding the yellow tablets on which he'd written his defense strategy. The tablets slammed down on his chest. "And this absurd idea for a film." The treatment Craig thought had been posted to Saul was added to the pile. "A Jewish Joan of Arc? Perfect for Streisand? You should stick to comedy, Marty. And Streisand should stick to singing. Don't you agree?"

"Yeah."

Craig was slapped, hard.

"I don't like slang. Say 'Yes,' or 'Yes, sir.'"

"Billy, take this trash and burn it." The stack of paper was removed from his chest. "Now, Marty, let's get down to business. You will not appear in court in February to defend yourself. Or be represented by an attorney. You will not stand trial. The press has a morbid fascination with your graveyard antics—which must cease. You will not appear in court for one of two reasons. I will leave it up to you to choose the more attractive option. Do you understand?"

"Yes."

"Option number one. I will open a bottle of scotch and you will drink until you are pleasantly buzzed. Then you will write a short suicide note—with persuasion, if need be. You will drink some more, no doubt maudlin with self-pity. Then we shall get you dressed and transport you to my favorite bridge. The bridge spans a stream, forty-five feet below, which is mostly dry in winter. Just a trickle through rocks worthy of Stonehenge. Hence, the bridge is a popular choice for suicides. If you're sober enough to walk, you may elect to jump, like a man. Or we can toss you. In any case, you will be soon forgotten, by the press and everyone else. Just another California freak who hated himself and chose to end his worthless existence. Do you understand option one?"

"Yes, sir." Craig was panting, fighting for air.

"Option two. Tomorrow you will board a flight to Los Angeles with a first-class seat and never set foot in Britain again. You will not be extradited—your crime was minor—and the charges will eventually be dropped. You will not write a screenplay about a Jewish heroine who is recruited by the Special Operations Executive. You will not write about World War II or the French Resistance. You will write comedy—what you're presumably good at. Within ninety days, your whore will also be flown back to LA. The court will show mercy and allow her to return home to die. The docs opened her up and removed a nasty tumor. She has ovarian cancer—with a life expectancy of six to nine months. Perhaps a year if God is merciful. Sorry to deliver the bad news, Marty—but at least you can hold your whore's hand when she expires. Do you understand option two?"

"Yes," Craig said, fighting back tears.

"Which option do you prefer?"

"Two."

"You're quite sure?"

"Yes." Craig said.

"Option two, I forgot to mention, comes with a souvenir, something to remember me by. In fact, I want you to think of me daily, like God. That you will never be truly free of me, of the thought of me, the fear of me—until death. My gift is a procedure. One I've performed countless times on dogs. And I will give you a local so you don't cry and moan like the neutered male you will become."

"Stop this…No! Stop it! I'll do what you want, please."

"After I give you a local, I'm going to make an incision in your scrotum and remove your testicles. Then I will sew you back up. The procedure will take about fifteen minutes. You will feel moderate discomfort."

Craig thrashed in his restraints."You fuckers! Kill me, kill me now! Do it! You sick mother-fuckers!" The man who had stood behind him was now at the end of the table. He wore a surgical mask and cap. Craig felt a hand touching his testicles.

"O God, O God…Stop! Please, God…stop! Please." Craig was sobbing.

"Oh, such language! This is best for you, Marty. You'll live a calmer, more peaceful life—no more women troubles, no rage, no thirst for revenge. Billy, hand me the scalpel. I've decided not to give him the local. This little shit insulted me—he deserves to suffer. I want to hear him squeal like a pig."

Craig felt searing pain in his scrotum. He bellowed, a bestial scream of agony and rage that came from the core of his being. He longed for death. But death was a dream. Only the pain was real—enduring and unendurable. Something hissed, and his balls felt suddenly cold and wet. He heard laughter and jeers.

"Show him, Billy." The mirror was positioned so Craig could see his groin. His penis and testicles were intact. There was no blood.

"I dipped a scalpel in liquid nitrogen and touched your scrotum. It caused a second degree burn—which I then treated with an aerosol disinfectant. Now I shall apply an ointment." Craig felt his balls massaged. "The wound will heal in a week or two and leave a scar. My calling card. Something to remember me by. Billy, get him up and dressed. You'll be spending the rest of the evening with us, Marty. But no more pain, no more fear, just a nightcap and a good sleep on clean sheets."

Craig was dressed and sat on the floor with his back to the door. It was locked from the outside. Billy told him he'd return in the morning and take him to the airport. Craig was utterly spent, but afraid to sleep. The room was small, with a bed, refrigerator, and bathroom. On the bed lay his suitcase, packed by his tormentors. All of his belongings were there—except for the pictures of Arnaud and his mother.

The refrigerator held fruit, sandwiches, and beer. How thoughtful. Craig was hungry but dared not eat; the food might be poisoned. Nothing would surprise him. He was tempted by the beer, but that might be tainted. Would he wake up on the table again? He'd drink when he got to the airport. Was he really going home? He held his knees tight to his chest and dared not hope.

In the morning he was hooded and driven a long distance. The car stopped and Billy helped him out. "Count to a hundred before you take the hood off. Give me your hand." Craig flinched. "It's your plane ticket, first class, and cash. My apologies for last night. A cab will arrive within ten minutes to take you to Heathrow."

Craig heard the car drive away as he counted slowly to one hundred. He pulled off the hood. He was at the intersection of two dirt roads. Around him stretched woods and farmland. There was not a soul in sight, just a distant farmhouse with smoke rising from the chimney. Craig sank to his knees, thanked God for his deliverance, and began to weep.

CHAPTER FOURTEEN

Above Orleans, Occupied France. January 1944

First came the roar and blast of icy wind. Then she was jerked upward, as if pulled back toward the aircraft. The canopy blossomed above her, like a beautiful white rose. She was safe, floating over the fields of France. Hundreds of feet below, off to her right, she saw flashlights—pinpricks bobbing over the ground—and white pale blotches where the *parachutage* had landed. Her countrymen, comrades in the Resistance, were there to welcome her, to take her in. Her fear was gone. At last, she was *home*.

But the lights on the ground were growing more distant. The earth was sliding away to her right. *There must be wind*, she thought, *strong wind*. Should she pull on the right risers, or the left? She'd forgotten which. And the ground was coming up fast now. She was over an orchard, bare trees packed close, branches waving in the wind.

She pressed her legs together and covered her face as she crashed down through a tangle of twigs and branches and suddenly came to a stop. Her forehead was bleeding but she could move her arms and legs. She had come to rest about five feet above the ground, tangled in lines and branches. It seemed hopeless to free herself. But she remembered the knife. It was razor sharp. She cut away the lines and dropped to the ground.

She heard distant voices, saw flashes of light. She began to move toward the light, but stopped. There was something wrong. The voices were too loud, too guttural. It was not French. They were Germans, shouting as they searched for her. Marie turned and ran through the shadows of the ghostly orchard toward the cover of thick woods.

She crashed through brush, stumbling, falling, banging her head on branches, running until she collapsed from exhaustion. Then she would hear the dogs again and glimpse the flicker of lights behind her in the trees. And struggle onward.

When she came to a creek, she remembered a lesson from training and ran upstream along the bank for one hundred meters, then reversed course and waded downstream the same distance, crossed to the other side, and angled off in a new direction. Each time she came to water she used the same tactic, and gradually pulled away from the Germans and no longer heard the terrifying howls of dogs in relentless pursuit of their prey.

Near dawn, utterly spent, freezing, her clothes soaked, she saw the light of a farmhouse.

Marie woke to the sound of bells. For a moment, she was in Paris, on a sleepy Sunday, church bells calling the faithful to Mass. Then came the smell of cows, the rough kiss of straw on her cheek, and panic. She was lying facedown in a hayloft. The hard object under her breast was a loaded pistol. Through gaps in the floorboards, she saw milk cows—bells clanging, udders swaying—ambling out of the barn toward green pasture, iridescent in the sun. An old man came into view, brandishing a stick. He swatted the rumps of the slow-moving cows. There was anger in the loud blows. She winced at his cruelty. When the cows were all outside, the farmer closed the door behind him. She was alone again. And it was dark—except for spindles of dusty light that fanned through cracks in the roof.

Marie Ducat was safe—for the moment. She lay back, reflecting on her narrow escape the night before. She weighed her limited options. Should she ask the old farmer for help? Perhaps he was a patriot, even active in the Resistance? Her SOE instructors had warned against blindly trusting her countrymen in occupied France. Collaboration was more common than defiance; cowardice, not courage, was the norm. Paid informants were everywhere. And even if the farmer was trustworthy, revealing her identity as a British agent would put his life and that of his family at risk.

She knew she was near Orleans, south of Paris. But that's all she knew. There was no backup plan to contact the Resistance if her "reception committee" turned out to be the Gestapo. "This is a milk run," Hays had assured her. "Maurice and his crew will be there on the ground to meet you. I guarantee it. They'll take good care of you."

Her mouth parched, Marie crept down the ladder to search the barn for water. She found a hand pump over a filthy trough. The water flowed brown at first, then clean. She drank her fill. For nourishment, she dipped into a metal canister of milk, scooping warm handfuls into her mouth. *A milk run*, she thought, amused by the irony. Her journey had taken her from the barn at Gibraltar Farm to another barn in France. And a dirty, foul-smelling one at that.

Back in the loft, she burrowed under the straw for warmth, her clothes still damp from the woods. She needed to plan her next move carefully, knowing the odds were stacked against her. There was Paris, of course, where she had old friends. But they were mostly intellectuals and rabble-rousing communists—the kind the Nazis often shot or sent to concentration camps. And if her friends were alive, could she elude capture long enough to find them? Paris was crawling with military and security was tight. It was also headquarters to the Gestapo, SD, and SS. It was far safer in the provinces.

Soissons came to mind, a quiet town on the Aisne River, north of Paris. She'd taught philosophy there in 1934, at a girl's lycée, until she was fired for her radical politics. She remembered her students as bright, idealistic, anti-fascist. A few had risked expulsion to march with her in communist rallies. Names and faces came rushing back to her, as well as the small white houses along the river where some of the girls had lived. Where she'd been invited after school to share a family meal. Her spirited girls were all young women now—strong-minded, she guessed, perhaps courageous. Some might have joined the Resistance. It was a long shot, but gave her hope of fighting for France. What she feared most was not death in battle, but torture and execution by the Gestapo.

Soissons was far to the north, but she had money, papers, and training to travel by train in occupied France. Always buy a third-class ticket, she'd been told; the Germans ride in first. Use small bills. Don't show a wad of cash. And keep your eyes unfocused, head down, as though you're exhausted, depressed. As though you're a Frenchwoman crushed under the Nazi boot.

Marie felt better with a plan. She'd wait until dark, then find her way to the train station. It was all right to rest now, even sleep. There was water and milk to drink, like a child. Her heart grieved for her mother and father in Montreal. How they must suffer with worry about her. Was it pure selfishness, her dream of fighting for

France? Did she seek glory for herself alone? Marie vowed to survive the war if she could, if only for the sake of her parents. What a miraculous reunion that would be—to hold her dear mother in her arms once more. She closed her eyes and imagined she was a child again, her mother reading at her bedside, until she relaxed into sleep.

Marie sat in the rear of the empty church. It was late afternoon, the gloomy silence broken by birdsong outside in the plane trees. It was spring. Three months had passed since Esme, one of her former students, had taken her in, using the cover story that Marie was a cousin from Lyon who'd come to help with the children. And Esme, a frail redhead, did need the help. Her husband had fallen in the first week of the German offensive; her twin daughters born shortly after the French surrender. On a part-time teacher's salary, Esme struggled to put food on the table. Marie proved a tireless companion for the girls and helped with chores—except for cooking, at which she was hopelessly inept. She also shared her supply of francs, so Esme could buy clothes for the children and milk on the black market when her ration coupons were exhausted. As always, Marie ate little, delighting in feeding the girls from her plate.

Luckily, Esme was the first of her former students that Marie managed to locate. Esme warned that two other students from Marie's class who still lived in Soissons could not be trusted. If they recognized Marie as their former teacher, Sabine Arnaud, they might also remember that she was a Jew and inform the police. Nazi persecution of the Jews was welcomed, even aided, by more than a few French citizens.

So Marie seldom left the house, except when she took the train to Creil to meet Jocquot, a *maquisard*. Esme had provided the introduction. The *maquis* were rural bands of guerillas, the outlaws of the Resistance. Many of the *maquisards* were men who'd fled their homes to avoid conscription by the *Service du travail obligatoire*, the labor draft that sent able-bodied Frenchmen to work in German armament factories. Others were rogues and career criminals, men used to living by their wits outside the law. And a few were women, motivated by patriotism or revenge for the Nazis' murder of a loved one.

Jocquot's *nom de guerre* was Picasso, because of his resemblance to the artist. Short and bald, with black eyes, he'd been a safecracker before the occupation. Now he was the wily chieftain of a *maquis*. He was suspicious of Marie at first, until she demonstrated both her courage and mastery of explosives by collapsing a railway bridge with less than a kilo of *plastique*.

Marie checked her watch. She'd been waiting more than an hour. The meeting protocol was for her to wait in the church on Thursday from three to five. If Picasso didn't show, she'd return the following day. This time, however, she was certain he'd come. Tonight's mission had been planned for weeks. If successful—a big if—it would destroy a munitions depot essential to the Wehrmacht's defense of the coast. Everyone expected an Allied invasion in May, at Pas-de-Calais or Normandy—the only two places where an amphibious assault could be mounted. The Germans had positioned troops and weapons to defend either location. They knew that if the Allies secured a strong foothold on the continent, opening up a second front, the war was lost. The invaders must be driven back into the sea.

While Marie waited, she whispered the Lord's Prayer in Greek, the language she thought most pure and beautiful. And while she prayed, she unconsciously fingered the lump in the seam of her coat, as if it were a rosary. She'd discovered the microchips soon after arriving in Soissons. With a magnifying glass, she saw that the four chips contained diagrams, possibly maps, and text too small to decipher. No doubt the Gestapo had the powerful optics necessary to reveal their secrets. It was then that Marie understood the true nature of her mission to France. And the depth of Hay's betrayal. Hays *knew* the Cyrus circuit had been compromised. Her job was to unwittingly deliver the chips to the Nazis. It explained why Hays had protected her from failure in training and hadn't bothered to send her to jump school. It didn't matter if she suffered injury or death parachuting into France. She was a carrier pigeon, nothing more. Expendable. Perhaps the parachute that Hays had given her, the one the Halifax jumpmaster had exchanged for his own, was not intended to bring her safely to earth. Hays might have considered that an act of mercy. He would spare her torture at the hands of the Gestapo by ensuring she was dead on arrival. It all made perfect sense, for a man as calculating as Carlton Hays.

Marie's first impulse was to destroy the chips, but she decided to sew them back into the coat seam. Hays would not have sent her to die unless it was vital to the war effort. Now, even if she was captured, her death would not be in vain. She would complete her mission.

As she prayed, she tried to find solace in the knowledge that God is infinitely good, and infinitely beyond our reach. But on this day, part of her wanted more—an imminent, loving God who heard and answered every prayer. Should she pray for deliverance from her enemies? Was it not obscene to ask God for victory in battle? It brought to mind the savage, vengeful God of the Old Testament, protecting only his chosen people—a God she rejected. As Marie struggled with the temptation to pray for her own survival, she heard footsteps on the stone floor.

Three hours later, Picasso and Marie, along with another maquisard named Leon, stood at the entrance to a limestone cave deep in the woods. It was dusk, bats streaming out of the cave in chaotic, black clouds that rose into the pale blue sky. Marie stood tall, refusing to duck as bats swarmed past, so close she could feel the air fanned by their wings. As a child, she'd been terrified of bats, believing them all tiny Draculas with rabid teeth. But it was time to cast aside such childish fears. She was a woman now, on the most important night of her life.

It was Leon, a wiry man in his fifties, who'd first shown Picasso the cave and where it led. Few knew it existed. Before the war, Leon had farmed mushrooms in the caverns under the Liverny plateau. The cave was a back door entrance to an area just below the largest cavern complex, which the Nazis had shrewdly chosen as an ideal storage depot for fuel and munitions. Above ground, the depot was protected by concrete bunkers and antiaircraft guns, as well as guarded by hundreds of troops. The Allies had bombed the depot, but to little effect. The prime target was deep underground.

Marie had devised a daring plan. They might destroy the largest cavern from below with a massive explosion, perhaps setting off secondary explosions from the stored munitions. The Germans might even think the blast was accidental—and spare the local citizens from the savage reprisals that always followed an act of sabotage. The usual calculus was ten innocents shot for every German killed.

The plan called for traversing a cave tunnel for nearly a kilometer until they were positioned under the center of the depot. They wore miner's lamps and shouldered sacks of explosives, wire, and detonators. Picasso would have preferred to leave Marie behind, because she was slow and clumsy, but she knew more than he did about positioning charges for maximum blast effect. And she was trained in the use of the new pencil detonators.

Leon led them into the cave. They turned their headlamps on and followed the bobbing circles of light into the blackness, assaulted by the stench of bat excrement. Marie followed Picasso, her boots crunching on small animal bones. In less than twenty meters, the cave narrowed, the ceiling lowered, and they crouched down, dragging the heavy sacks behind them.

Soon they were on all fours, their progress slow on aching knees. Beads of moisture seeped out of the limestone and soaked into their clothes. Marie wiped her glasses and checked her watch, knowing they would have to retreat by the same route once they set the timed explosives. It was important to complete the mission well before dawn to make their escape. Once the blast occurred, the woods surrounding the depot would be swarming with troops.

Marie focused on the illuminated swath of stone in front of her hands, inching forward to the pace of Picasso's sliding boots, sucking dead air that seemed devoid of oxygen, and fighting the panic of claustrophobia.

After more than a hundred meters of painful crawling, the passage opened up and they could walk upright again, heads low, picking their way over wet limestone slabs. Marie struggled to keep up, slipping and falling, banging her knees, but didn't protest the pace. When they reached their destination, they found themselves in a cavern at least ten meters across with a ceiling higher than their hands could reach. While the men sorted the equipment, Marie walked the circumference of the cavern, looking up, searching for holes where explosives could be placed.

As she examined the massive ceiling, it was clear that the charges must detonate simultaneously to collapse it. She'd hoped to use pencil detonators with a one-hour delay, but timed fuses were notoriously imprecise. So she checked the length of the wire they had brought, rolling the spool back into the tunnel until the wire ran out. About twenty meters. Not nearly enough. The shock wave from the main blast might kill or disable whoever stayed behind to detonate it. And at this distance, the explosion might also collapse the tunnel. She must be the one to stay behind—and give the others the best chance of escape.

Marie told the men why the ceiling demanded a simultaneous blast with a conventional detonator. But they would arm additional blocks of *plastique* with time pencils. If tons of fuel and munitions came down with the first blast, these secondary explosions might trigger a chain reaction that would destroy the entire depot. Marie expected Picasso to question her judgment, but he did not. There was something about the quiet resolve with which she spoke that caused both men to simply nod their heads.

Marie told them she would detonate the primary explosion. This was her plan and she must see it through to the end. "I will give you time to get safely away. I will not be in danger from the blast," she lied. "And if something goes wrong with the detonator, I know best how to fix it. I am the one who must stay."

Picasso knew she was lying about the danger. He placed his hand on her shoulder. "My brave, beautiful soldier," he said, and kissed her cheek. Marie stiffened, but accepted the comradely gesture of affection.

They set to work. Marie crimped blasting caps onto wire leads and inserted the caps into six blocks of *plastique*. Leon got on Picasso's shoulders, so he could place the explosives under the ceiling in the holes that Marie pointed out. The wire leads were then linked to a single wire that ran back into the tunnel and attached to the detonator.

Next, Marie inserted time pencils into four more blocks. The pencils were color-coded, red for thirty minutes, blue for one hour. She placed the charges low on the cavern walls, inserting blue-tipped pencils into each.

"When I activate the fuses, the clock's ticking," Marie said. "An hour, maybe less."

"Do it now," Picasso said.

Marie crimped the end of each detonator with pliers, crushing a vial of acid that would slowly work its way down the tube to trigger the explosion.

They retreated into the tunnel. Marie tripped and Picasso grabbed her arm. "Get on your way," she said. "I will wait fifteen minutes, then blow it and follow."

Picasso whispered something to Leon, and they began to pile large rocks in front of the detonator to help shield her from the blast. "Go!" Marie shouted. "You're wasting time. Leave me!" The men ignored her and continued to improvise a wall across the narrowest part of tunnel. They worked tirelessly until they exhausted the supply of loose rock.

Picasso flopped onto his belly beside Marie. "I'm too tired to leave now. I'll keep you company. Go on, old man," he said to Leon. "We'll be along soon."

"I need to rest," Leon said, wiping his brow. "Besides, I want to see the show." He lay down on the other side of Marie.

Picasso said, "No reason to delay now, comrades. Put your hands flat and tight against your ears. Otherwise your eardrums will burst. I can depress the plunger with my chest. The sooner we do this, the sooner we get out of this dungeon. Are you ready, my sister and brother?"

"*Liberté*," Marie said.

"*Liberté*," the men replied. Picasso covered his ears and leaned on the detonator.

CHAPTER FIFTEEN

"What the hell happened to you?" Saul studied him over the frosted rim of his iced tea and frowned. He'd always counseled Craig to "look like the million bucks you deserve to be paid." They were seated on the patio of the Ivy in Beverly Hills, surrounded by mostly beautiful people enjoying lunch in the sun. "In fact, you look like two ounces of cat piss."

Craig shrugged and picked at his free-range chicken. "Jet lag—no sleep."

"You've been home three goddamn weeks."

"We writers are sensitive souls." It was true he'd hardly slept, but it wasn't jet lag. Nightmares woke him an hour or two after he drank himself to sleep. And the fear of more nightmares kept him awake till dawn. The horrific dreams usually involved being naked, bound, helpless, at the mercy of merciless men. In one dream his throat was cut and he woke with the feeling of blood streaming down his chest. His psychiatrist prescribed Valium and said his symptoms resembled those of Vietnam vets traumatized by combat. But Craig refused to disclose the nature of his own trauma. His story was so bizarre the shrink might think him delusional. Besides, how could he be certain the shrink's office wasn't bugged? How long was the reach of those who demanded his silence? In the world where Craig found himself, nothing was too terrible to be true. It was safety, the ordinary, boredom even, that seemed like heavenly bliss.

"And what's with the coat?" Saul asked. "It's hot. Besides, it's ratty—you look like a hippie bum."

"Lay off, Saul. Writers are weird, right?" Craig wore his old army jacket because the big pockets concealed the Ruger .357 Magnum he'd bought the day after he landed at LAX. But Saul had a point, it was too hot for a jacket. And with warmer weather coming he needed a smaller weapon that was easier to conceal. Maybe that Colt .32 ladies' handbag special the clerk tried to sell him.

Nobody was going to take him by force—ever again. Death was preferable to the terror and humiliation he'd suffered on that metal table. How many times had he replayed the scene on the street in Ashford, when boldness was called for? He might have yelled for help, run, or at least fought to the death—like a man. Now he wasn't sure what he was, but it wasn't a man. Something had been taken from him that he could not name or replace. If it wasn't for Rita, he would dispatch the miserable suck of fear and pain he had become with a bullet to the head. He wrote to her daily, but she had yet to reply. Her attorney had sent a brief note that she was recovering from an operation and he was hopeful that he could secure her release from prison. He had also enclosed his bill.

"I need work, Saul. I'm sorry I let you down with the treatment. When I started to write it I knew I couldn't pull it off. It was a good idea, but I couldn't write the damn thing. I'm a comic—that's what I do."

"Warner loved the idea. They're pissed I didn't deliver."

"I'm sorry, really."

"It hurt my credibility, kiddo. I considered dumping you as a client."

"I've been good to you, Saul. I've put forty, fifty thou in your pocket the last few years. "

"More like thirty and change—and heartburn. It's not too late for Warner, Craig. Clean yourself up, dress sharp, and pitch them like you pitched me…Jewish Joan of Arc…distaff *Dirty Dozen*. You'll get a deal to write the script. I promise. Top dollar. You're not used to writing treatments—that was the problem."

"Get me sitcom work…whatever you can score. I'll even go back to Carson."

"Forget Johnny. That guy is an unforgiving prick—not like me."

"Ah, Saul—I knew I could count on you. One tiny favor—would you mind picking up the lunch tab, just this once?"

Over the next few weeks Craig made the rounds, pitching sitcom producers to write episodes, and the studios with movie concepts. He shaved, dressed casually hip, and left his arsenal at home. There wasn't much he could do about the bags under his eyes or his moist palms—which made a lousy first impression when he shook hands.

In pitch meetings, he tried to generate the faux enthusiasm required to sell himself and his story ideas. But his heart wasn't in it. His voice seemed no longer his; it was flat, distant, without affect. And he struggled for words in the presence of those he wanted to hire him to write them. It was embarrassing. In the end, everyone he pitched to got back to Saul with a pass. A woman producer for *Alice* had the gall to suggest that Craig write a spec script. "If he can capture the subtle character dynamics," she told Saul, "I'll give it a serious read." Saul was appalled by the suggestion—only chumps wrote on spec. But Craig took the bone offered. He asked the producer to send him sample scripts, so he could "study the wonderfully complex and quirky characters."

A letter arrived from Rita, projecting a release date in May. She had ovarian cancer; the prognosis was grim. "I took their deal. But I wish we'd fought the *(word blacked out)* in court. I can guess why you left London. Don't feel bad—at least you tried. Heroes win in fairy tales. EO rules here." EO he guessed was the "Evil One." Rita signed off not with "love," but "kiss, kiss." Which hurt.

With money tight, Craig moved out of his rental condo near Universal Studios to a one bedroom dump in Reseda. He kept a shotgun by the door and seldom went out—except to buy food and booze. He read the *Alice* scripts and watched the show on TV. It was sitcom subtle. Aspiring singer Alice Hyatt waits tables at Mel's Diner in Phoenix. Mel is a gruff male chauvinist, but soft at heart. Alice's fellow waitresses are Flo, a man-hungry redhead, and lovable but ditzy Vera. For pathos, Alice is widowed with a teenage son. *I get it*, Craig thought. He took a deep breath and sat down at the kitchen table in front of his typewriter. Nothing came, except a revenge plot that wasn't particularly amusing: Alice is raped by a truck driver and gets even by slicing his balls off with a butcher knife. The reformed rapist, now a mincing eunuch, joins the show as a quirky regular. Maybe not.

After another week of false starts, he gave up. He couldn't write cute. Not anymore. Gone was the smug, bemused irony that had allowed him to write for an audience that he held in contempt. His career as a TV writer was over. And he was broke.

Craig had worked at Lockheed during his first year in college, so he dumbed down his resume and applied for an opening in the machine shop. He landed a job as a punch-press operator on the graveyard shift. The mind-numbing repetition of the work was comforting. And he felt a kinship with Sabine, who'd done similar work at a Renault plant until she got fired for being too slow. Craig even liked the hours. When he got home at dawn he was so exhausted that he fell asleep without liquor or pills. And the nightmares were fewer when he slept in daylight.

In the evenings before work, he read Sabine for inspiration. He was drawn to the New York notebooks because he liked to imagine himself safe in her womb as she penned the words. The eclectic notes, never intended for publication, revealed her encyclopedic knowledge of history, philosophy, religion, and science. Her insights, seldom clarified by exposition, were often mystifying. She found precursors of Christ in the myths of Osiris, Odin, Dionysus, and Prometheus—and divinity in the number theories of Pythagoras. Craig lacked the erudition to follow most of her thought, but her oracular epigrams often struck a nerve. Though he couldn't grasp their logic, he *felt* the truth of them: *Humility is attentive patience...Pantheism is true only for saints who have reached the state of perfection...Suffering is to move either towards the Nothingness above or towards the Nothingness below.*

One of the longer entries in the New York notebooks was a terrifying prayer—a prayer that Arnaud scholars often cited as evidence of her perverse hatred of her own body, typical of anorexics.

Father, in the name of Christ, grant me this.

That I may be unable to will any bodily movement...like a total paralytic. That I may be incapable of receiving any sensation, like someone who is completely blind, deaf and deprived of all the senses. That I may be unable to make the slightest connection between two thoughts, even the simplest, like one of those total idiots who not only cannot count or read but have never learned to speak. That I may be insensible to every kind of grief and joy, and incapable of any love for any being or thing, and not even for myself, like old people in the last stage of decrepitude.

Father, in the name of Christ grant me all this in reality.

When Craig read the prayer, he flashed back to the horror of being bound and helpless, at the mercy of a sadist. But he knew that the prayer, chilling as it was, reflected Sabine's conviction that the Self separated us from God. Thus, we must surrender that which we fear losing the most—our individual existence—to be one with God. For Arnaud, our sin consisted in our desire to *be*.

Craig also speculated that—if Sabine was his mother—her pregnancy might have tempted her to embrace the life of an ordinary woman, with its joys and demands of motherhood. But it was a life opposed to her ascetic, spiritual quest. One she could not accept. Her pregnancy was also the reason she had to flee France, and the source of her guilt for abandoning her countrymen. Did the prayer arise, in part, from resentment, even hatred of her unborn child? If she had hated him, he didn't blame her. He was worth hating. He wished he'd never been born.

Craig started to attend AA meetings. There was one that met in a church basement near his apartment. He had no intention of quitting drinking, but it was a companionable group of lost souls. He was never compelled to speak, but he found inspiration in the horrific tales of those who had hit bottom, lost everything, and clawed their way back to sobriety and self-respect. One of the regulars, Pete, invited Craig to join the men's group at his church that met for breakfast every Saturday at Denny's. Why not? Craig was lonely and the men were good guys, if devout Christians. One morning, Craig made the mistake of talking about how much he admired the spiritual writing of Sabine Arnaud.

"I believe, as I think she did," Craig said, "that doubt goes hand in hand with true faith…that God wants each of us to wrestle constantly with the mystery of whether or not he exists. I think Arnaud even said that Christ wants us to prefer the truth to Himself, because before being Christ, He is truth."

From the stunned, perplexed, and hostile looks he got from the other six men at the table, Craig surmised, correctly, that he'd enjoyed his last Grand Slam breakfast with his brothers in Christ.

Rita didn't get back until late May. Craig met her at LAX, arriving early and pacing the international terminal until she cleared customs. He'd shaved, put on Armani slacks and a linen shirt, his pitch-meeting outfit, and left his gun at home.

When he spotted her among the disembarking passengers, dragging her suitcase, it was not the Rita he remembered. She was pale, gaunt, and walked with a cane. Craig wrapped her in his arms, burying his face in the warmth of her neck. He began to cry.

"Easy, Marty. It's over. I'm home."

"God, I missed you."

She held him until he stopped shaking. "Let me look at you." Gently pushing him back, she took his hands and studied his face. "You look sick. And what's with the dirty fingernails?"

"Sorry. It's grease, oil. My job."

"You're a writer."

"Not anymore. I'll tell you about it in the car. And you're staying with me. No arguments. I need you."

"Nobody needs a sick bitch. But your place—for a while. I want to sit on the balcony, look at the Hollywood Hills, and feel the sun on my face."

"I live in a one bedroom in the Valley. No balcony, no view— except a Burger King. And you'll hate my car."

"You sold the Porsche?"

"It paid for your lawyer."

"That tool? You know what their game was? They say I'm too sick to stand trial and cut me up and make damn sure I am too sick. So I knew it was die there or die here. You know what those cocksuckers did—what the topper was? They flew me back first class! I never been up there with the fat cats. Barrio Rita eating off fancy plates with silver knives and forks. *Real* silver. Except I am too sick to enjoy it. One bite and I barfed. And the stew, the little snot, was soooo nice about wiping up my puke, because she thinks I'm a rich bitch in first class. Well, screw her. And screw you too, Marty, for running out on me."

Rita pushed past him, refusing to let him carry her suitcase. "So what kind of loser car do you drive now, college boy?"

"A 67 Bug with a bad trans."

"Jeeez, Marty—your life is more screwed than mine."

Rita fell asleep in the car, so it wasn't until the next day, after he got home from work in the morning, that he told his story. They sat at the kitchen table, Rita in her bathrobe, Craig in his greasy coveralls. He was exhausted, but it was better to get it all out. He expected her to interrupt, ask questions, but she didn't. At several points in the story he choked up. She offered no sympathy, but was patient. She would listen as long as it took.

"I'm so sorry," he said finally. "Sorry I left you."

"So you're not a hero. They scared the piss out of you and you ran for your life. Most people would."

Craig took her hand. "I want us to get married."

"I can't fix you, Marty."

"I still pay my writer's guild dues. Their health insurance is better than Lockheed's. No clause about preexisting conditions. We get married and you can see the top cancer specialists—go the

Mayo Clinic if you want."

"There's no cure."

"There's a doc I found at Cedars, experimental drugs—five, seven years survival with ovarian cancer patients."

"Wash up, grease monkey. Get some sleep. I'll watch TV on the couch—maybe Jack LaLanne can get me in shape."

After showering, he put on a clean undershirt and boxers. Rita wasn't on the couch; she was sitting on the bed. She'd been crying.

"Come here. I want to tell you something. It won't take long. I know you're tired." He sat beside her and put his hand on her shoulder. "None of that—just listen."

"All right. I will."

"You know me, Marty—but there's stuff I hold back. You asked me once about when I was raped. I didn't want to tell you—because what's the point? You were just curious—like people slow down to gawk at a car wreck. What's the fancy word—*prurient*? Your interest was prurient. Now there's reason to tell you. Because of what you went through. Don't say one word until I finish. Promise me?"

"I promise."

"I was raped when I was fifteen, by a rival gang. I was hot-looking, but still a virgin—believe it or not. Anyway, I was pulled off the street, kidnapped. They took me to a chop shop—a garage. The floor was greasy—why I hate the sight of your greasy clothes and fingernails. So, one guy sits on my face, others pin my arms and legs. And they have their fun. For hours. Taking turns. Laughing. I was half-dead, naked, covered with piss and shit and cum and you name it when they finally dumped me on a street corner. I was in the hospital for two weeks. I made the front page of the *L.A. Times*. Savage gang rape…blah blah blah. You get the picture. I told the cops they all wore masks, so I couldn't finger nobody in a lineup.

It was suicide to testify. These were evil dudes, *pure evil*. So I let my homies get even. They killed three of them—but it cost my older brother his life."

"God…"

"I only told you because I *know* how you feel, Marty. Maybe you wasn't raped. But it's the same. When evil men—and they're *always* men—hurt you so bad you beg for mercy, or death, and they laugh at you, I swear to God your soul leaves the body. Like the devil himself ripped it out of you. Sometimes you get it back, or part of it. Sometimes you don't. And then you're dead inside— for good. So you kill yourself—or kill somebody else. Because life don't matter—it's hell. I see that in your eyes, Marty. And it breaks my fucking heart. You never had nothing bad happen to you."

"Not really. I was spoiled."

"After the rape, I didn't want nobody to touch me—except my mom. I was twenty before I let another man inside me. And I didn't like man sex at first. So I tried women. But that was worse. It was years before I felt whole again, like I was somebody. Like I had a soul."

"I'm so sorry, Rita."

"I want to see what they done to you."

"I told you."

"Stand up. They burned your balls. Show me."

"You think I lied?"

"I want to help you, Marty. Show me. Pretend I'm a doctor. I won't touch."

"This is crazy." He stood, pulled down his shorts, and cupped his scrotum so she could see the small scar.

"It's nothing, baby. You're fine. You're afraid somebody will come back and finish the job, that's all. But they won't. Because these people are very, very smart. They think they own you now.

And they do. You'd be better off if they *had* cut your balls off—don't you see that? You might be *more* of a man—not so scared all the time. Sorry, but it's true. Now I'll show you what they done to me."

Rita stood and spread her robe, exposing an angry red welt across her belly. "Touch it." Craig hesitated. "I said, touch it."

He ran his finger gently over the length of the scar.

"So," Rita said. "You showed me yours. I showed you mine. Feel better?"

"A little."

"Good. Now go to sleep. I'll watch out for the boogieman."

CHAPTER SIXTEEN

Craig's rebirth began in the back row of the Azteca Theater with *Deep Throat* on the screen. He'd dropped Rita off at a discount dentist in East LA to get her wisdom teeth pulled. Since returning home, she'd refused to be examined by a cancer specialist, or any medical doctor, but her aching jaw demanded attention. It was June, insanely hot, the sky bleached white, sun blasting off concrete, glass, and metal, his shirt sweat-stuck to the seat.

Searching for a cool, safe place to wait in East LA, he spotted the sleazy movie house and pulled over. Why not? The fat man in the ticket booth swore the AC inside was "primo." And Craig hadn't seen the film. Porn was mainstream now—almost hip. Besides, it might be therapeutic. Maybe the notorious Ms. Linda Lovelace could revive his moribund libido. During the week that Rita had shared his bed, before moving to her brother Raul's place in Boyle Heights, she'd offered him sex—out of pity, he guessed—but he couldn't perform. "Don't worry, Marty," she'd told him. "You're still a man. The dick's got a mind of its own. You can't order no dick to stand tall. Or beg. He gets nasty in his own sweet time." Ironically, Craig's most sturdy erections continued to appear upon waking from a nightmare. The more horrific the nightmare, the stiffer his prick, though it always deflated with the returning consciousness of his sorry self.

He took a seat in the empty back row, wishing the lights were down. He was early. Did they show porn trailers before the porn feature? Porn cartoons? He and a handful of other solitary males waited stoically, their gaze fixed on the sagging white screen—stained and patched—avoiding eye contact with their fellow cinephiles.

When the film started, Craig was pleasantly surprised. There was a plot of sorts, almost cute, about a frigid woman who discovers her clitoris is in her throat. No wonder she didn't enjoy sex. She'd never given her boyfriends a proper blow job.

Once the hard-core action started, Craig found himself shockingly aroused. He had no intention of pleasuring himself in a public place, but his swelling member forced him to reposition the small Colt in his pants pocket. His hand felt good there, so he left it. What the hell? That's what the movie was for—a jerk-off fairy tale for men who dream of kneeling women worshipping their holy cocks with succulent, silent mouths.

And then something very strange occurred. As he watched Ms. Lovelace writhing in pleasure from a swallowed prick, her eyes spoke to him, touched the very core of his being. She was *acting*, emoting, not just relaxing her gag reflex. She was doing her level best to *be* the character she was hired to play, displaying all of her modest, but God-given talents as an actress. An honest day's work for a day's pay. The protestant work ethic of our founding fathers still lived—though we'd cast off forever the shackles of sexual restraint. His arousal turned to compassion for the leading lady.

With the obligatory "money shot," to prove that no male orgasm was faked, Craig closed his eyes as poor Linda licked cum off her lips. He covered both ears against the bestial grunts of pleasure. He wanted to leave, but couldn't move. His body shivered, as if he were freezing, and then shook, convulsing in great, heaving sobs.

Craig wept uncontrollably, but he could not have said exactly why, or for whom, the tears flowed. Maybe he wept for Linda Lovelace and her schoolgirl dreams of Hollywood stardom. He wept for the unloved men in the audience who sought relief from their sorrow in porn. He wept for brave, dying Rita. He wept for the noble soul of Sabine Arnaud. And surely he wept for himself and his broken spirit and lost ideals, for the depths to which he had fallen, for the pathetic excuse of a man he had become.

When the tears stopped, he felt numb, but cleansed. He heard nothing, saw nothing, for a moment he was not sure who or where he was. He uncurled his back and stood. There was not one thought in his head. He took his first step as a new man, like Adam. And moved toward the light. He wanted to be in the sun, under the white LA sky, thanking God. But he found himself in front of the screen, his shadow comically cast over the hard-core action. Craig laughed and waved his arms playfully. He heard shouts, men cursing. "Move it, asshole!" somebody yelled. "Go home to mommy!"

Blinded by the light, Craig shouted back at the darkness. "*You* go home! All of you! Be the men your mothers wanted you to be!"

The crowd erupted in a chorus of jeers and laughter. Craig saw a flashlight moving down the aisle toward him. He pulled out the pistol and fired two quick shots in the air, then ran out the side door and down an alley, hurdling over piles of trash and one sleeping bum, tossing the pistol in a dumpster. It was insane to fire the gun. So why was he laughing hysterically? After zigzagging down a series of alleys, he stopped to catch his breath, drenched in sweat. He listened for sirens but heard none. Maybe the cops didn't turn out for shootings in East LA without a body count. No harm, no foul. He entered a discount TV store to cool off and realized he was hungry. Famished, in fact. The taqueria across the street beckoned. The orange pop and three beef tacos he downed were glorious.

When he picked up Rita he was still grinning. He took her arm as they left the dentist's office and helped her into the car. She was alert, but unsteady on her feet from the anesthetic.

"What the hell happened to you?" Rita said. "You look dumb and happy." Her cheeks were puffed out from cotton wads to stop the bleeding. She slurred her words.

"I *am* happy. Happy as Francis Macomber, just before his wife shot him."

"So you was chasing buffalo, and something happened, like a dam busting inside?"

"Exactly! You know your Hem like no nobody. God, I love you, Rita. I love you like crazy."

"Isn't it pretty to think so," Rita mumbled, not missing a beat.

Craig laughed so hard he felt tears flow again. "And I'm taking you to the best cancer doctor money can buy—whether you like it or not. We can beat this—there's always hope."

Rita fingered the rosary she always wore now. She'd returned to her Catholic roots, attending Mass on Sunday, confessing her sins before taking the sacraments.

"If you want to help, Marty, pray for me."

"I do, sweetheart."

"Then pray harder. I need a miracle. Pray to the Blessed Virgin. She's kinder than God, kinder maybe than Jesus. She was a mother.

An unwed, *unwanted* mother. She spoke to me once, when I was a girl." Rita didn't elaborate, and Craig didn't ask her to. Nor did he want to tell her about his porn-induced renewal, afraid it would break the spell. Afraid she would laugh at him.

Raul was Rita's younger brother, an ex-gangbanger turned family man. His house in the barrio was surrounded by an eight-foot chain-link fence topped by razor wire. Two pit bulls roamed the dirt yard littered with toys and rusted car parts. Raul was an auto-body man who worked out of his garage and under the table. Most of his customers were honest and poor; the others were thieves who paid him top dollar to strip stolen cars. Raul's wife, Lupe, was a nurse's aid who could comfort Rita as her disease progressed. And the Raul household was well-stocked with a variety of legal and illegal painkillers.

Craig signaled his arrival with three short honks. Lupe, pregnant with her second child, came out of the steel front door and met them at the padlocked fence. When the dogs saw Rita, their tails wagged like puppies'.

Craig rushed home, called in sick to work, and sat at his typewriter. It was hot in the apartment, so he stripped down to his shorts, got a pitcher of ice water, and started to write. He wrote through the night and into the next afternoon. When he was done he had the polished draft of a screenplay treatment he titled "Breakout." He drove to Beverly Hills and dropped it off at Saul's office with a two-word note: "I'm back."

Two weeks later, after pitching an exec at Warner, he got a deal to write the script and a hefty advance. He put the money in the bank and kept his night job. Everything he made from writing was to help Rita. He'd take her to the goddamn Mayo Clinic if need be. She was not going to die.

Craig secured an appointment with the oncologist at Cedars-

Sinai he'd read about, Harvey Zarem, who was considered the top specialist in ovarian cancer in LA. Rita reluctantly agreed to be examined. Since coming home she was pain free and feeling stronger. She'd even gained a few pounds. "Maybe you don't have a year to live," Craig said. "Maybe it's five years, or seven, or ten. This doc is the best."

They went together to Zarem's office in Beverly Hills. He'd requested medical records, but she had only the name of the local doctor who'd told her she had a tumor that might be cancerous. She'd been released from prison without her medical file and didn't remember the names of the doctors who'd treated her.

After Rita filled out a lengthy health questionnaire, a nurse escorted them to Zarem's spacious office. He was late forties, trim, affable, and looked at you with genuine interest.

"My patients are normally referred by another physician, often an oncologist. So your case, Miss Gaona, is rather unique. As I understand it, the situation is this. While you were incarcerated in the UK, a surgical team removed a tumor from your abdomen and you were told you have late-stage ovarian cancer. Did they put a number on stage—stage three, stage four?"

"They said I'd be dead in a year. What stage is that—eighty-six?"

Zarem laughed. "Four is the worst. I shall request your records from the penal institution that arranged for your medical care. In the meantime, I'll run a serious of tests. Blood work, CT scan, nothing invasive or uncomfortable. It will take several days to get the results. You're not in pain at the moment?"

"No."

"Ovarian cancer is a nasty disease. We must accept that. I don't believe in aggressive, debilitating treatments for this type of cancer. Our goal, Miss Gaona, is to give you periods of relatively good health while the disease runs its course."

"Do you have cancer?" Rita asked.

"I beg your pardon."

"Do you have ovarian cancer? You said 'we' must accept the disease."

Zarem waved off the question. "A mere figure of speech. I meant no offense."

"Are you Jewish? Isn't this a Jewish hospital?"

The doctor stiffened. "We treat people of all faiths here, from all walks of life. It's not a *Jewish* hospital. Now if you would see the nurse—"

"I'm not done. And I'm no bigot. I want to know if you're Jewish? I have a good reason for asking. In fact, my life depends on it."

"Yes, I am of Jewish heritage. But I don't see—"

"So you had a bar mitzvah, studied the Torah, all that?"

"Where is this going, Miss Gaona, I have other patients—"

"I want to know if Jews believe in miracles. I'm Catholic. And I believe in miracles. I never seen one—but I believe they can happen. Do you?"

"Ah, I see. No, I'm not a religious man. But I have witnessed one—a spontaneous remission we call them. A woman with stage four-ovarian cancer. Over the course of two weeks, every cancer cell in her body died—*poof.* She was suddenly cancer free—and on the road to recovery. It was beyond my power as a man of science to explain. So call it a miracle—a case of supernatural good fortune."

"Was she a Catholic," Rita asked, "or Jewish?"

Zarem smiled. "She was a devout atheist—and one of the most unpleasant patients I've had the misfortune to treat."

Rita smiled. "Perhaps the Evil One still had need of her on earth."

"*That* I can believe. Let's hope you don't a need miracle, Miss Gaona, from God or Satan."

Three days later, Craig was at the kitchen table in his shorts, working on the screenplay in the late afternoon. He'd adjusted to working nights and sleeping days and wrote for at least four hours as soon as he woke up. It was hot in the small apartment, but he kept a fan by the typewriter and a wet towel around his neck.

Somebody knocked hard on the door. He jumped up, heart pounding. Craig rarely had visitors, and never unannounced. He grabbed the shotgun and looked through the peephole. It was Rita.

"Holy shit!" she said, pushing past him with an open bottle of champagne. She was dressed in a halter top and tight jeans. She took a long pull and handed the bottle to him. "Drink up, Marty. I don't have cancer. I'm healthy as a fucking horse!"

"The tests came back?"

"You're damn right. I never had cancer. Those assholes concocted a story to get me out of jail and out of the country. So I wouldn't make no trouble."

"Or you had bad doctors who misdiagnosed you. Or you got the miracle you were praying for. So why are you pissed?"

"Because for months I thought I was dying. I went through hell for nothing. God, it's hot in here, Marty. I'm sweating. I'm hot. I'm a sexy, hot, healthy woman. Let's make love." Without waiting for a response, she peeled off her top and unzipped her jeans.

Craig picked up the phone and stepped out of his shorts.

"Who the hell are you calling at a time like this?"

"Lockheed. I'm quitting my night job."

Craig was making good progress on *Breakout*. He'd promised Saul a complete draft in two weeks. Since Rita had gotten her clean bill of health, he was less paranoid and no longer carried a gun when he went out. They were probably safe in LA. The men who'd terrorized him in England assumed he was suitably cowed and no longer a threat. And Rita was not about to go back to London, proclaim her health, and demand punishment.

Craig chose his favorite coffee shop, Patys in Toluca Lake, to write the climactic scene for *Breakout*. He sat on the patio under an umbrella, oblivious to the chatter of the lunch crowd. The "distaff dirty six," led by his Jewish heroine, Sabine Audry, were assaulting a prison near Paris to rescue her lover. It was one hell of a scene. Daring women with Sten guns mowing down Nazis and running to waiting getaway cars driven by Resistance fighters. This script was *not* going to die in development hell. It was too good. Or maybe too bad. It was good and bad in the way a blockbuster film had to be. It would get produced and be a huge hit. Craig was sure of it. And he'd tell every reporter in town what inspired the story. When the film opened in London, he'd be there too—talking to the media. The Brits would launch an investigation and heads would roll in high places.

"Excuse me, sir?"

Craig looked up to see a big guy, blond, in an Aloha shirt.

"Would you mind very much if I sat here? All the tables are full and I'd love to sit outside. I see you're working—I promise not to say one word. Just eat and run."

Craig reluctantly nodded his assent and went back to work. But the big guy made him nervous. After a while, Craig looked up and saw the man had a stack of paper on the table, in a manila folder. The same folder he'd left by his typewriter.

"Don't shit your pants, Craig. I just want to chat. I have some notes. Isn't that what they call them in Hollywood, 'notes,' when the studio weighs in on your script?"

Heart pounding, Craig glanced left and right, assessing his options. To run, cause a ruckus, shout for the police. Instinctively, he felt his empty pocket for a gun. He was surrounded by people—in a public place. There was safety in numbers.

"First off," the man beamed, enjoying himself, "I think you're one terrific writer, a real talent, so don't take this personally. I hate the name 'Sabine.' Call the heroine Bridget, something sexy. And don't make her a philosopher. What actress wants to play an egghead with glasses? And scrap the whole Jewish angle. SOE not wanting Jews? It makes our British friends look like schmucks. *Schmucks*, get it? That's funny. Or maybe it isn't. I could be dead serious. After all, buddy, you broke a solemn promise to some people across the pond."

The man picked up the folder and stood.

"If you don't mind, Craig, I'll keep this. I want to read it again. I'll be in touch if I have more notes. Okay with you? ...Cat got your tongue?"

"Fine," Craig said, shaky.

After a few minutes, debating his next move, Craig asked the waitress for a phone. He called Rita and explained what had happened. She told him to stay put. Thirty minutes later Raul showed up in his lowrider Camaro with two homies in the back seat, and plenty of firepower.

They drove to Craig's apartment and found what he'd expected. The front door was ajar, the locks drilled. Earlier drafts of the script that he'd kept in a drawer, along with handwritten notes, were all gone. So were his shotgun and pistol. There was a note taped to the fridge: "If you play with guns, you'll kill yourself." Raul and his friends helped him pack. Craig was moving to the barrio.

CHAPTER SEVENTEEN

Paris, Occupied France. April 1944

Carlton Hays was having lunch with Sturmbannführer Hans Goetz at the headquarters of the Sicherheitsdienst, or SD, at 84 Avenue Foch. The SD was often mistakenly referred to as the Gestapo, but it was a separate organization—the counter intelligence branch of the SS. Goetz was charged with hunting down spies sent to aid the Resistance. Anyone suspected of being a foreign agent was brought to Avenue Foch for interrogation. Goetz regarded the Gestapo with disdain, calling them thugs and amateurs. In particular, he disapproved of their brutish interrogation methods.

When Hays was first brought to Avenue Foch, after two days in the hands of the Gestapo, his face was badly bruised and two of his front teeth had been knocked out. He'd also been subjected to the *baignoire*. Hays was proud that he'd revealed nothing to his tormentors beyond the details of his fake identity. But his university French, devoid of slang, betrayed him as a probable British agent. When he arrived at Avenue Foch, Goetz summoned a doctor to treat his wounds. After several days alone in his cell, Hays was brought to Goetz's office, which was decorated with Louis IV furniture, on the top floor of the magnificent eighteenth-century villa that served as SD headquarters. The villa was set back from bustling Avenue Foch, offering privacy. And it was close to two of the best restaurants in Paris, the Place des Ternes and L'Étoile— where the portly Goetz habitually dined.

Hays was offered tea and an omelet garnished with foie gras— courtesy of L'Étoile. He drank the tea, but didn't eat, as a matter of honor. He would not be seduced by the promise of special treatment.

After a few pleasantries, with Goetz speaking English and Hays pretending not to understand, he was escorted to a back room. The walls were covered with maps and organization charts. Hays was shocked to see his picture, and title—deputy director F-section operations. Above him were the names of Colin Gubbins, Guy Atkins, and other SOE brass—along with dotted lines to some of their counterparts in the Secret Intelligence Service. There was even a map of London with a circle around SOE's secret head-quarters in Baker Street. And maps of France with the location of Resistance cells, some of which Hays had never heard of. "Bloody Christ," Hays said in English, "you know more than I do." Goetz laughed until he was beet red.

So Hays made a pact with the devil. He would cooperate, providing Goetz tried to protect captured British agents, including himself, from execution. Besides, he knew there was little he could tell Goetz that he didn't already know.

"I'll do what I can to save your people," Goetz had promised. He had a soft spot for the British, whom he considered his Aryan equals. "The execution orders come from Berlin. But I can rec-ommend prison, for those who cooperate. Sometimes Himmler's people even listen to me." By getting cozy with Goetz, Hays also hoped to improve his chances of escape. He was careful, however, never to let other prisoners held at Avenue Foch see him fraternizing with Goetz. They might conclude he was a traitor, instead of their advocate—which is how he saw himself.

On this particular afternoon, some three weeks after Hays arrived at Avenue Foch, the two men were sitting on the terrace, with a view of the Arc de Triomphe, enjoying steak and *pomme frites*. Often there was a sentry present, but today they were alone.

Goetz was an anglophile and never tired of asking Hays about life at Cambridge and the habits of the ruling class. As Hays fielded the inane questions, he thought how easily he could lunge across the table and bury his steak knife in Goetz's fat neck. But then what? He was clad in prison stripes with four floors of Nazis between him and the street.

"A new guest arrived yesterday," Goetz said. "Courtesy of the Gestapo. Half dead, of course. Marie Ducat. Is she one of yours?"

Hays froze. "I don't recognize the name. But it would be a code name."

"She was carrying microchips. Claims no knowledge of their contents. She told the Gestapo she was given the chips by a British agent just before he died of injuries from a parachute jump. He told her to give the chips only to a member of the Resistance who was in wireless contact with British intelligence. She did not have such a contact, but kept the chips, knowing they were important."

"Maybe she's telling the truth."

"Our Gestapo friends worked her over some more and she gave them an address—but it was phony. That's the problem with torture, people tell you anything to stop the pain. The Abwehr believes the chips contain vital military intelligence. They're sending over Dr. Freud to interrogate her."

"Freud?"

"Dr. Heim, an SS psychiatrist. He can make stones sing Wagner. His methods are brilliant, diabolical. Sometimes I call him Dr. *Schadenfreude*. You know this German word?"

"I went to Cambridge, remember. May I ask a small favor?"

"Perhaps."

"Is this Marie Ducat on my cell block?"

"She is."

"Could I look—to see if she's one of mine?"

"Even if she is, my friend, I can't save her. She and two *maquisards* blew up the Wehrmacht's most secure arms depot. A brilliant operation, I must concede. They were caught the same night. The men have been shot. The only thing keeping her alive is what she knows about the chips."

"Which makes me even more curious—to see this daring saboteur."

After lunch, Goetz and a guard escorted Hays to the third floor. Marie's cell was at the end of the corridor. The guard opened a peep-hole in the steel door. Hays saw a woman lying on a cot against the far wall, her face beaten to a pulp. He knew it was Marie from the helmet of black curly hair. She looked asleep or dead.

"I can't tell from here."

Goetz motioned for the guard to open the cell door. Hays moved quietly to the cot and knelt down. In addition to the battered face, several of her fingernails had been removed. Her eyes opened, dark slits behind swollen lids. He could hear Goetz and the guard chatting and laughing in the corridor.

"Marie," he whispered. "It's Charlie. I'm a prisoner too. Listen carefully. Sixteen rue Bonaparte is where you were told to deliver the chips, to a man called Pommera. Say that and they won't hurt you anymore. I promise."

Marie opened her eyes wider, startled. Hays whispered the same instructions again, close to her ear. "It's me, Sabine. It's Charlie—"

"That's enough," Goetz barked. "Is she yours?"

"No," Hays said. "Not mine. Just a French patriot."

Marie watched the man in prison stripes leave her cell. An SS officer in the corridor slapped him on the back, like a friend. Was it really Charlie? She had awakened from a dream, frightened by the man's face close to hers, speaking softly, urgently. It looked and sounded like Charlie. Was he really a prisoner? And if he was, why was he allowed to speak to her? Perhaps he was an imposter, trying to trick her into revealing the secrets the Germans were convinced she knew. The man had whispered something about an address and a man's name that meant nothing to her.

Marie rolled on her side and closed her eyes. She had lied before, to stop the torture. But she would not lie again. She prayed for the strength to suffer unto death. Her body could not take much more punishment. When the Gestapo was beating her, she had felt her soul leave her body for one blessed moment, only to return to the prison of tortured flesh. She had never known true suffering, not until now. Her misery had been of her own making, out of pride, in quest of some absurd ascetic ideal. And what egotistical nonsense she had written as a young philosopher: *When I think of Christ on the cross, I commit the sin of envy.*

She must try to rest now. She would need all her strength to endure what was coming.

The war was killing him. And the war was lost. Of that Dr. Karl Heim was certain. He needed pills to sleep, pills to carry out his ghastly duties, and was drunk more often than sober. The Russians were winning in the east, and soon the Allies would invade from the west. The fatherland would be destroyed. And with it, any hope of practicing medicine in civilian life. He was certain that the victors would show no mercy to members of the SS, those complicit in the worst of Hitler's crimes. He would be imprisoned or shot. That he had resisted the Nazi regime as a young physician, refusing to sterilize schizophrenics in the interest of "racial hygiene" would carry no weight. That he had been conscripted by the Waffen-SS and sent to Mauthausen as camp physician, against his will, would also be ignored. That he had followed orders to stay alive would be no defense. He was a participant, however reluctantly, in horrors that the victors would surely avenge—if only to expiate their own guilt for the mass murder of civilians by aerial bombardment. His father and mother, as well as his beloved maiden aunt, had all been obliterated in the merciless bombing of Frankfurt.

After securing a transfer to military intelligence, Heim had tried to bring science and a measure of humanity to the black art of interrogation. He experimented with drugs, both stimulants and sedatives, and psychological manipulation. Physical torture would be used only as a last result. In the end, he settled on a version of the good cop/bad cop routine he'd read about in American detective novels. Most of the time his subjects gave up their secrets without the need to inflict pain.

Heim stood in the corridor outside Ducat's cell. He heard his assistant, Sergeant Klemp, shouting threats and obscenities at the poor woman. He would make his entrance as her savior. Heim was an SS major, but never wore his uniform to interrogate prisoners. Instead, he dressed in a rumpled suit with a stethoscope around his neck, like a country doctor, and carried a black satchel with tongue-loosening drugs—along with several instruments of torture.

Heim checked his watch. He would enter at the prearranged time, when the prisoner was thoroughly demoralized. While he paced, Heim thought of his French mistress, Simone. She was the only thing that stood between him and putting a bullet in his head. In her arms, he could remember the man he was before the war: a man of learning, culture, and taste. In fact, the lovers spent far more time discussing books and music and art than they did in the throes of passion. Heim had told no one of his affair with the wealthy divorcee, eight years his senior, as Simone's brother was a Resistance fighter wanted by the Gestapo. Simone, too, had kept the affair secret from her friends and family, not wanting to be branded a traitor for sleeping with the enemy. She only met Heim at her secluded country estate in La Hauteville, far from prying eyes.

Heim noted the time and entered the cell. Klemp snapped to attention. Ducat was naked and tied to a chair. Her pale, thin body was discolored with purple bruises, both eyes blackened from beatings by the Gestapo. Klemp had been instructed to threaten and humiliate—but not to touch her.

"What have you done!" Heim shouted. "These were not my orders. Get out. Now!"

Heim took a blanket off the cot and covered her. Then he untied her and helped her to the cot. Like a father putting his daughter to bed, he tucked the blanket around her gently and put a pillow under her head. From his bag he removed a thermos and poured a cup of tea, which he brought gently to her lips. She sipped the tea, looking at him, but her eyes showed neither fear nor relief—and not the gratitude he expected.

"I'm so sorry for what you've suffered," Heim said. "You are a brave woman, and a patriot. I can help you, if you let me." He put the cup of tea in her hands, moved a chair near the cot, and sat quietly—her protector.

Heim saw her lips moving. He listened. It was not French. He heard the word "*abba*" repeated again and again. He remembered from his Catholic schooling that it meant "father" in Aramaic, the language of Jesus. This woman believed in God. She asked for God to save her. That was good. The devout were often the easiest to break, to manipulate. Only the weak needed the fantasy of a loving God.

"The Bible says the truth will set you free," Heim said. "Do you believe that, Marie? There is no secret you can tell me that will help Germany win the war. The war is lost. You've shown such courage, my dear, it's pointless to suffer. Please don't make us hurt you any more."

"I have no secrets."

"Please, Marie. I don't want to hurt you."

"I know. But you must."

"Just talk to me. Tell me what you know."

"I lied before—to stop the pain. I have no secrets."

"It is in my power, Marie, to save you," Heim lied. "But only for a short time. Tell me what you know and I can spare you from execution. I can ensure that you will be treated well for the duration of the war. No more pain, or hunger, or threats. But time to sleep and rest and heal. A prison cell, yes, but not a concentration camp. But we must do this together, right now. You and me. "

Marie closed her eyes and continued to pray.

"Do you not wish to live, Marie?"

"I am a saboteur and will be shot, like my brothers. But it is not just to torture me for secrets I do not possess. I have told you the truth."

"Why would you keep the chips this man gave you if you didn't know what to do with them? You are not a stupid woman. It was dangerous to keep them. You must know something more."

"I do not."

"I don't believe you."

"I have no secrets to save you."

"Save me?"

Marie said nothing.

"Save me from what? I am not the one in prison."

She looked at him without fear or hatred. But perhaps pity.

"From your duty…your terrible duty."

"My God, Marie, please. I don't want to see you hurt. I'm a good doctor—a healer."

"You should do your duty."

Foolish bitch!

Heim opened his black bag and removed the bone saw, a terrifying instrument of polished steel. Often just the sight of it would break a prisoner's spirit.

"This is what Sergeant Klemp will use to loosen your tongue— if you choose not to talk to me. Please, Marie."

She glanced at the saw, and returned her eyes to his. Heim held her gaze, heart pounding. He wanted to look away, but he could not. She looked at him from a place of infinite and tender sorrow. Transfixed by her luminous eyes that seemed lit from within, by the tear sliding down her cheek, a tear that he knew in his heart, beyond all reason, was shed for him, Heim felt something shift inside him, give way, collapse from the sheer weight of the horror it had been forced to bear for so long. He could not harm this woman, nor allow others to. She had told the truth. *I have no secrets to save you*. He had done his job; let the Abwehr do its job and decipher the chips.

189

Heim touched her hand. "I believe you now, Marie. I know the truth. No harm will come to you. I promise."

He could not save her from execution, but perhaps he could grant her a merciful death. Heim dug in his bag, removed a box of morphine and counted the ampules. There was enough.

"I want you to sleep now, Marie. I will give you peace. There will be no more questions—no more pain. Ever. Do you understand?"

She nodded. "Yes," she whispered.

Heim injected an ampule of morphine and watched as she drifted into sleep. He readied another ampule, knowing it would take at least four to kill her. And then he paused, thinking through the consequences of what he was about to do. If she died on his watch, the Abwehr would be furious. He could say that her heart failed during the stress of torture, as sometimes happened. But it had never happened to him. And he had not tortured her. If the Abwehr suspected that he'd euthanized a potential source of vital intelligence, he'd be shot, or sent to the eastern front—which amounted to the same fate.

Heim lit a cigarette and considered his next move. He should scar the body now, spill blood while she lived—and only then inject a fatal dose of morphine. Cutting off one finger would suffice. He had pruning shears in his bag for the task. Blood stains on his clothes, a severed finger on the floor. That was enough to back up his cover story.

He got the sheers and laid the index finger of Marie's left hand between the blades. The finger was limp and warm—and slightly moist. He watched her chest rise and fall, safe in his care. The pain would probably shock her back to consciousness. She might moan or scream. The thought of her waking in agony and knowing that he had lied to her was more than Heim could bear. *No harm will come to you. I promise.*

He lit another cigarette. He could hear Klemp pacing in the corridor, jackboots clicking on the stone floor, waiting for the sounds of human misery that he seemed to relish. It was suicide not to inflict a wound while Marie lived. Heim sat quietly, thinking it through, before he made an irrevocable decision that might cost him his life.

There was another form of suicide that he'd considered of late, but lacked the will to implement. He'd even discussed it with Simone. Perhaps this was the moment to act. He once believed in providence, in destiny. If there was ever a good time to discard your past and abandon hope of a future, this might be it. Heim took a deep breath, stubbed out his cigarette, and injected Marie with another ampule of morphine. He needed her comatose for another hour or two.

"Klemp!" Heim shouted. "Get in here! I'm losing her. She was starting to talk. Carry her to my car. I'm taking her to the officer's hospital."

"I'll get an ambulance."

"There isn't time. My car is faster. General Meier will have us both shot if she dies without talking."

Klemp carried the limp body down the stairs as Heim barked orders for the soldiers on duty to clear a path. The big Mercedes town car was parked at the curb. They laid the unconscious Marie on the back seat and Heim took the wheel. He roared off down Ave Foch, swung around the Arc de Triomphe, and went down boulevard Haussmann. He stopped in front of Abwher headquarters and ordered Klemp out of the car.

"Tell the general to come to the hospital in exactly two hours. She's agreed to talk. Don't tell him she's in a coma. I'll bring her back with an IV and adrenaline. Trust me."

Klemp hesitated, then got out and ran into the building draped with swastikas.

Heim knew where he was going, but it wasn't the officer's hospital. In two hours he'd be in La Hauteville, with Simone. She would declare him a hero, and not a coward, for deserting. Simone had money, connections, perhaps she could get him across the border to Spain. And she would hide Marie until she regained her strength. In any case, his war was over. Marie Ducat's was not—until France was liberated. But when Marie woke she would know that he had not lied to her, that she was in the care of a good doctor, a *healer*.

CHAPTER EIGHTEEN

Craig slept in the baby's room. Lupe wanted a boy this time, so Raul had painted the walls blue for luck. Craig slept by the big crib on a bare mattress, standing it upright in the morning to unfold a card table for his typewriter. He wrote happily, facing the window covered by iron bars. The house was built like a prison to keep the criminals on the outside. Nobody could touch him here. And he wasn't leaving until the script was done. Raul said he could bunk in the toolshed when the baby came, which was fine with Craig. He'd never felt more secure.

Saul was furious when Craig called with the story that his VW had been stolen with the nearly completed script inside. "Who would steal that piece of shit car!" he shrieked. "My Bug was a classic, Saul—but don't worry, I'm working off an early draft. I'll get a clean copy to Warner in two weeks. You can take that to the bank. I've moved to a friend's house ideal for writing. If somebody answers the phone in Spanish, don't panic, just ask for me."

Craig had never written a 120-page screenplay in two weeks,

but he would now. His life depended on it. He wouldn't be truly
safe until those who wanted him silenced were exposed. With a
hit movie, he'd leverage the media to shout his story to the world.
And if Streisand starred, he'd enlist her as an ally. Nobody would
mess with that diva. He could see her on *60 Minutes* with Mike
Wallace: "I've told the prime minister, Mike—*and* the queen—that
I will *not* attend the London premier of *Breakout*, nor perform a
Royal benefit concert, unless there's a full investigation into Sabine
Arnaud's wartime service as a British spy. And I want the men
who threatened my courageous screenwriter, the talented Craig
Martin, exposed and punished. Without Craig, who's become a
dear friend, I would never have learned about Arnaud—whom I
think of now as my soul-sister."

Okay, it was an absurd fantasy, but this was Hollywood—anything could happen, or nothing, which was usually the case. In
any event, he'd get paid for the script, move to a high-security
apartment, and plan his next move. Maybe he'd learn to forgive
the cocksuckers who'd ruined his life and go back to writing funny.
Anything could happen in Hollywood—even your worst sellout
nightmare of defeat.

Rita shared a bedroom with three-year-old Carmen. No longer
condemned to premature death, Rita became health obsessed.
She worked out with Jack LaLanne on TV, jogged at the park, and
played racquetball. At night, she often dressed up and went out
dancing with friends. Craig didn't ask where she went or who she
was with. If she was getting laid he didn't want to know. After what
she'd been through, she had a right to party.

On this particular evening, Rita had not gone out. They sat on
the patio, ate pizza, and drank beer. It was hot, but quiet for the
barrio. No blasting music from the neighbors, no sirens, no police
helicopters, just the lavender sky and a quarter moon rising above

the razor wire. Two pit bulls lay curled at their feet.

"You don't wear a crucifix now," Craig said.

"Should I?"

"You prayed to the Virgin and you got your miracle."

"I never had cancer."

"You don't know that."

"When Dr. Zarem gets my medical records I will."

"I doubt he'll get your file. Which means—"

"What?"

"It will stay a mystery. So why abandon your faith?"

"I'm enjoying life. You should try it, college boy, come out of your hole and live a little. Why don't *you* pray for a miracle? Like having the guts to move out of my brother's house."

"Ouch."

"Sorry. You made me feel like a selfish, ungrateful bitch. It takes guts to write that script. You're still my hero."

"Really? You're not around much."

"I like going out. I won't lie to you. I met somebody."

"Oh, please."

"I haven't slept with him. He likes to dance and treats me nice. He works for the gas company. He's a meter reader."

"A meter reader."

"I don't want to hide nothing from you, Marty. You're my best friend."

"And you're pretty goddamn precious yourself," Craig said, with all the sarcasm he could muster, turning away so she couldn't see the hurt in his eyes.

The script was blockbuster perfect. A brainy heroine called to action to save her man. A rogue's gallery of original but familiar characters. Smart dialogue, but not too smart. When Craig read it through for the last time there was not one scene that didn't snap. He called Darren, the studio exec, and said a messenger would hand deliver *Breakout* that afternoon. Raul obliged in his candy-apple red Impala, probably the only lowrider ever admitted to the Warner lot, and then delivered a copy to Saul—who called Craig that night with effusive praise.

Two days later, Darren called with more praise—not the usual nit-picky notes that called for a major rewrite. The script had been sent to Streisand, who loved the premise and promised to read it quickly. Then days of unbearable silence. The baby came, another girl, and Craig was exiled to the toolshed.

Then the long-awaited call came.

"Barbra loves the script," Darren enthused, "absolutely loves it. And the Sabine character is marvelous. Barbra thinks you're one hell of a writer. She'd like to meet you sometime."

"That's wonderful," Craig said, waiting for the other shoe to drop.

"She'd love to play Sabine, but doesn't feel in the right place, you know, *emotionally*, to take it on right now. She wants to do something lighter for her next film, maybe a romantic comedy. If you have such a script, she'd love to read it."

"So, Darren, did she have notes? Can I tweak *Breakout* to make it better for Barbra—make Sabine a less emotionally demanding role?"

"She thinks it's perfect for her, Craig. Absolutely perfect. We're putting the project on hold, just temporarily. I know you're disappointed. I'm bummed too. But six months from now, a year maybe, I think she'll come around."

"Can you think of another actress, Darren, who might like the script?"

"This is perfect for Barbra—no one else could play it."

So *Breakout* was on hold, temporarily, which meant—in Hollywood—that it was dead for the projected life of the known universe. And Craig couldn't pitch the idea to another studio because Warner owned the story. What now?

"So write funny for Streisand," Rita suggested.

"I can't. Come to Puerto Vallarta with me. We can sun, surf. Just relax."

"Lupe needs my help with the baby. Find a nice pad somewhere. You got to move anyway. I'll come visit."

Craig bought a used Mustang convertible with his movie money and looked for an apartment. When he ventured out, he didn't bother to check the rearview mirror; who the hell would follow him now? He was no threat to anybody but himself. Suicide was never far from his thoughts, but it generally lifted his spirits. If he had the guts to end it all, why not soldier on for a while? Find an apartment in Santa Monica, walk on the beach, write whatever he felt like, or write nothing at all. He could live for six months without making a dime. And he still had his good looks. Why not get in shape, swim, meditate, take a yoga class, play volleyball, and find a hot new girlfriend? A fun-loving girl, not too bright, with a sweet disposition—the kind he'd never dated.

Life was full of amusing pastimes to distract you from the black hole of Self. Didn't Pascal write that all of man's strivings, however noble, were simply diversions—to keep us from confronting the meaninglessness of existence and the inevitability of death? And if you chose to quit the losing game with a few chips left on the table, who could fault the logic, or the ethics, of your decision?

One morning, as he scanned the *L.A. Times*, looking for apartments, feeling low, he thought of something Rita had said to him years ago. They were drinking in a bar, and he was depressed, complaining about his life as a B-list comedy writer. He confessed, perhaps to shock her, or to elicit sympathy, that he'd considered suicide. "Why not?" Rita said, unhelpfully. "But let me know before you do it. I'll give you a list of assholes to take with you."

Why not indeed? And what royal asshole might be in reach? Last December, Denis Colson said he'd accepted a temporary post at Stanford to escape the English winter. It was August now, but Craig felt the wind of providence at his back.

He called the philosophy department at Stanford and got the answer his gut had told him he might. The eminent scholar had extended his stay and was teaching a summer seminar on Wittgenstein. It was also no secret where Colson lived: visiting philosophy professors of the highest rank were always nested in the "historic Waverly Cottage" near campus.

"Give me one full day, Rita, before I move out."

"What for?"

"Drive up the coast with me. Take a break from Meter Reader."

"Don't be a snob. His name is Mario. Why there?"

"I want to see that cocksucker Denis Colson. He's still at Stanford."

"You already talked to him."

"This time I'll get the truth. I can't let this go, Rita. You're better at reading people than me. I want you with me, just like we started out—the A-team. One day, maybe two. We can stop in Carmel and stay in a posh hotel."

"How posh?"

CHAPTER NINETEEN

With Craig at the wheel of the Mustang, the top down, and Rita in scarf and sunglasses, they left the barrio and headed north. After passing through San Luis Obispo, they jogged west and headed up the coast toward Big Sur. After an early dinner in Carmel, Rita selected the most expensive hotel with the best view of the ocean.

Craig hadn't asked about Mario, and Rita—perhaps grateful— suggested they make love with the veranda doors open to get the salt smell of the sea and the sound of the surf. The sex, with the orchestra of wind and waves and gulls, was romance novel perfect. Rita dozed off happily in his arms. Maybe they did have a future together.

They arrived in Palo Alto the next evening, parking near the Waverly Cottage, which looked more like a mansion. All the lights were on. There were three cars in the driveway, people moving around inside, some holding drinks—a cocktail party. An hour later, a group of young men and women, probably students, left in two cars. Then an older woman and a bearded man emerged, pausing to chat with a man in the doorway: Denis Colson. He looked tan and happy, dressed California casual in white pants and a flowered shirt. He waved as they drove off and went back inside.

Craig got the 9mm from under the seat.

"What the hell is that?" Rita said

"It's not loaded. I got it from Raul."

"Put it away. I'm not going back to jail."

"I just want to scare him."

"You enter a man's home and hold a gun on him it's kidnapping, stupid. Life in prison. If you threaten him, I'm leaving. I don't want no trouble. You can be pushy, but nice. He was friends with your Saint Sabine—appeal to his noble soul."

"That was my plan, actually. I brought the gun to impress you."

They approached the house and saw Colson through the kitchen window cleaning up. Craig rang the doorbell and stood in the shadows. As the door swung open, Craig grabbed it and Rita slid inside. Craig followed and closed the door.

"What is this?" Colson said, slurring his words. And then his eyes locked on Craig. "Oh, it's you. I thought you were bandits. Please leave." He reached for the door and Craig grabbed his hand and shook it warmly.

"Don't look so worried, Denis. I won't hurt you. This is Rita— you must have read about her in the tabloids, the wheelchair Annie Oakley? You're not armed, are you, Rita?"

"It's late. You should have called."

"One drink. We can catch up."

"Look, I'm a bit tipsy. I need to sober up. Maybe if you—"

"So make coffee, Denis. We got time."

They went into the kitchen and Colson fumbled with the coffeemaker.

"Do you mind, Denis?" Craig and Rita helped themselves to

wine from open bottles. They sat in silence until Colson got his mug of coffee and joined them at the kitchen table. He was probably too drunk to be scared, but he looked uneasy.

"Pay attention now, Denis. I'm going to tell you one hell of a tale. It's a Gothic horror story. So I'll start in a cemetery, with a shovel in my hands, digging up the grave of a woman we both admire."

Craig told him about being kidnapped and terrorized, and that Sophie Daudin had gotten the same treatment before she killed herself—or was murdered. He recounted Rita's "merciful" release from prison to die at home from cancer, the script deal and being followed and harassed in L A. By the time he finished, Colson was half-way through his second cup of coffee.

"I had no idea what you've suffered," Colson said. "I believe I know the man who kidnapped you, the Scot. His name is Alester Fraser. I've met him socially, at Charlie Hays' garden parties. He has some shadowy government post, and also fancies himself a dog breeder. Champion Fox hounds as I recall, much sought after by the royals."

"You lied to me in Cambridge. You knew Hays recruited Arnaud."

"I was afraid *not* to lie."

"So why should the intelligence agencies on two continents worry about me stirring up dirt on your friend Hays?"

"I have a theory, but let's start at the beginning, in 1943. I'll tell you what I know—"

"Don't look at me when you talk," Craig said. "Look at Rita. She knows when people lie. I don't know how, but she does."

Rita grinned at Colson and gave him the peace sign.

"Christ, this is like some bloody awful film. Right, I'll look at Rita. Yes, I lied when you came to Cambridge. I was the one who asked Charlie Hays to recruit Sabine. He rejected her at first—as I thought he would. But I had to try. Sabine was heartbroken, wasting away, because she couldn't get into the war. But while she was in the sanitarium she had a mystical experience and started to eat again, gain weight. The infection in her lungs began to heal; it was nothing short of miraculous.

"I urged Charlie to reconsider—and he did. He removed Sabine from the sanitarium for medical and psychological screening. Two weeks later he told me her heart gave out during a physical fitness test. For security reasons, her death was reported as having occurred at the sanitarium. And that was that. She wasn't well known then. Her death was a nonevent. Except for me—I loved Sabine.

"After the war, I began to edit and coordinate the publication of her work—mainly from the notebooks she'd given me. But I also wrote to her friends in France to locate more of her manuscripts. In 1947, or '48, I received a package from Nairobi—no return address. It contained about twenty loose pages of Sabine's writing, undated, with a typewritten note and a scribbled signature I couldn't decipher. I don't remember the exact words, something like 'our mutual friend Sabine would want you to have these notes, on the nature of evil.' I thought it odd, coming from Africa, but assumed it was a friend of hers in the French diplomatic corps. In any case, I was thrilled to get the additional material—which was published in *Gravity and Grace*. The pages were in Sabine's handwriting—but somewhat messy, words crossed out, that sort of thing. And her writing was not as fluid and graceful as was typical of her. It never occurred to me that the pages might have been written after the war, or sent by Sabine herself. Not until Sophie Daudin came to see me last November—"

"Another thing you lied about," Craig said.

"Because I feared for my own life. After Sophie told me about your postcard, I thought anything was possible. Maybe Sabine *had* been sent to France—or even survived the war. So I confronted Charlie. A mistake, obviously, in retrospect. He got angry and said the details of Sabine Arnaud's death remained classified. I should keep my mouth shut. He reminded me that I had my own wartime secret to protect—that I'd shared intelligence with the Russians. I was a socialist then, so was Charlie, and Russia was an ally. But if the press got wind of it now, it could destroy my reputation—put me in the same camp with Philby and other traitors. So, my old Cambridge chum threatened me—which gave me pause.

"When I learned of Sophie's suicide, I was shocked. She was an ebullient person—not given to despair. A short time later, another man came to see me, well-dressed, polite, nameless, who told me what an asset to the nation Hays was. He said it was my patriotic duty to protect him from slander—and also essential to my continued good health. When I complained to Charlie about the threat, he said there were issues of national security involved. No harm would come to me if I kept quiet. So, when you came to Cambridge, I did my best to discourage you from pursuing your inquiry—for your own safety. And for mine."

"You have a theory about Hays?" Rita asked.

"I think Charlie, like me, passed secrets to the Russians during the war. And later—just a hunch—he continued to spy for the Soviets and then switched sides—became a double agent. Or, he was caught spying by MI6 and was recruited to become a double agent—which is the best kind of agent there is. That would make him an invaluable Cold War asset, to Britain and the US. And he's rumored to be the next foreign secretary. It would explain the interest in protecting his career, on both sides of the Atlantic."

Colson got up and opened another bottle of wine. "I'm sober

now. Sober enough to want another glass of this excellent Cabernet."

"If Hays is so important," Craig asked, "why not eliminate me and Rita, and you too for that matter?"

"Because I think we're dealing with honorable men, who kill reluctantly. No doubt you and Rita have tried their patience. But here you are. And I have more to tell you. Since coming to Stanford, I've used the excellent library here to research Charlie's war record to discover what he might be hiding. In particular, I focused on Allied interrogations of captured SS men who'd served in Paris. When Charlie won the MBE and the Croix de Guerre, there were rumors—never proven—that he might have collaborated with the Nazis while he was in prison.

"I tracked down source documents, statements given to investigators. No hard proof, but several captured soldiers who'd served at SD headquarters noted that Hays was often in the Commandant's office alone, without a sentry present—which they thought odd. And I came across a fascinating interview with a sergeant who assisted an SS doctor, Karl Heim, with interrogations. Heim deserted, and took a female prisoner with him—a woman held at Avenue Foch. This occurred during the time that Charlie was incarcerated at the same location. A coincidence perhaps, but—"

"Rita doesn't believe in coincidences, do you, baby? She believes everything happens for a reason—it reflects the hand of God or Satan."

Colson smiled, refilling their glasses with wine. "In this case, my dear Rita, it is surely the hand of God. Because the desertion of an SS officer was simply unheard of. And he fled with a Frenchwoman he was charged with torturing. The sergeant claimed that Heim must have felt sorry for her—and not had a romantic interest—because the woman was ugly. I'm sure he wanted to make the point, probably to save his own skin, that not every member of the SS was a monster. Could the Frenchwoman have been Sabine? She had the power to change people with the sheer force of her personality. Had she and Charlie been on a mission together? Unlikely—but possible."

"So what happened to Heim?" Rita asked.

"No record the Nazis found him. The desertion of an SS officer was scandalous—and probably hushed up. I've checked with the authorities who hunt down war criminals and there is no record of Heim's death. Just after the war, there was an unconfirmed report that he was living in Cairo, but nothing since."

They continued to speculate on Sabine's fate until after midnight. Had she died in training, been sent to France and died there—or had she survived the war? And if she had survived, why didn't she come forward?

In lieu of facts, one theory was as probable, or improbable, as any other. Colson promised to keep digging into source documents from the war pertaining to British agents in France, the SS, and the mysterious Dr. Karl Heim.

"No secret is ever truly hidden," Colson assured them, "if it's been hidden on purpose."

CHAPTER TWENTY

Craig was energized by the encounter with Colson and wanted to drive straight back to LA. Pleasantly buzzed, he cracked the window to jet cold air on his face and sober up. They were quiet for a while, settling into the rhythm of the road. Craig couldn't stop thinking about the possibility, however remote, that Sabine was alive.

"She'd only be sixty-seven," Craig said. "Not so old. Wouldn't that be a resurrection story? Saint Sabine rises from the dead. I could ask her point-blank: Did I emerge from your virgin loins or not? I wouldn't care what her answer was. Only that I could look her in the eye and ask. And then get her story and tell it to the world—with a great photo spread. Heads would roll in high places."

"Maybe it's time for you move on, Marty. Figure out what you want from life. Do you know what you want?"

"First off, I want to move to a nice apartment in Santa Monica and walk on the beach and just daydream and muse for about a month. I'll decide if I want to keep writing—or find another way to make a living. Maybe teach. I'd be a good teacher. And I want us to be a couple. I want us to share a life, and share a bed. I was never jealous of guys you slept with before. But now I am. And I want to be better man too—for you, sweetheart."

He glanced at Rita for a response. "I know," she said, unhelpfully, and touched his arm. Then she leaned her head against the window and closed her eyes.

Near dawn, Craig was too sleepy to drive and stopped in Santa Barbara to rest on the beach. Fog was rolling in off the Pacific and they snuggled under a blanket.

"Don't you have an uncle who's a Jesus freak, a missionary or something?" Rita asked, playfully touching his crotch to get a reaction.

"My father's older brother," Craig said, pushing her hand away. "I never met my uncle Bob. He died when I was a boy."

"So how'd he die?"

"Some tropical disease. Why do you care?"

"When we cleaned out your mom's stuff, there was letters with exotic stamps…lions, elephants, I think. You save them?"

"I don't remember."

"Lions live in Africa, college boy. Colson got a package from Nairobi."

"Christ, another theory."

"Maybe she met your uncle in New York. Knew where he was going in Africa, figured it was a good place to hide after the war. Maybe they were best buds, how the hell do you know?"

"Well, it's possible my uncle met Sabine. But he lived in Georgia. And I think he was off saving souls the year I was born. I'll look into it. Right now I want to close my eyes."

"So where's the box of stuff you saved of your mom?"

"In the toolshed, sitting on a case of Pennzoil."

There was one packet of letters, bound with string. Most were from his father, love letters written to Alice from the South Pacific. In one, he begged for more photos of "baby Craig," praying he would live to "hold my son in my arms." In another, written in 1944, he wondered if Alice had news of Bob in "savage Africa," and praised his brother's "devotion to our Lord." And there were several letters Craig had written to his father from the army, bitching about military life and the heat in Oklahoma. But no letters from his uncle Bob.

So Craig and Rita searched the family photo albums. There were snapshots of his father and uncle growing up in Atlanta, and one of Bob being ordained a minister. And then they saw it. A black-and-white photo with the caption: *Elmolo Clinic, 1953.* Uncle Bob and his wife and daughter stood proudly in front of a whitewashed structure with a metal roof. Africans in tribal dress, many holding infants, some carrying spears, were lined up outside. In the background was desert and one scrawny tree.

Craig slid the photo out of the album and flipped it over. His uncle had penned a note: *Our happy African family, except for Dr. Rolf and wife Greta, always camera shy.* German names. It was too fantastic to believe, yet too coincidental to ignore. A Nazi war criminal and his Jewish wife living under assumed names? And camera shy?

"Well, college boy, is it worth checking out?"

Craig started with the LA Methodist diocese and a dozen phone calls later reached the director of Global Ministries in New York. Craig introduced himself as a journalist and devout Methodist who wanted to write a book about his uncle's missionary work in Africa. The Right Reverend Theodore ("call me Ted") Chambers was delighted to expound on the Elmolo mission. It was the second-oldest Methodist outpost in Africa, founded in 1927 by the "intrepid Scotsman, Waldo Balfour," on the shores of what was then called Lake Rudolf. After Kenya broke free of British rule, the lake was given an indigenous name: Lake Turkana. In 1939 Balfour was murdered by a tribal chief for reasons lost to history, and the mission lay dormant until the Reverend Robert Martin and his wife, Sarah, arrived in 1943. They established a clinic, school, and "a thriving community of believers." Martin died of dysentery in 1959, but his wife soldiered on until she too succumbed to the "rigors of missionary life," in 1973. Their daughter, Carol, and her African pastor husband, now ran the mission. "It's remote, of course, but also quite beautiful by the lake, or so I hear. I've never been to Africa, but its call is strong for many drawn to service."

The Reverend Ted knew nothing of a Dr. Rolf or Greta, but urged Craig to write his cousin (unreachable by phone), as Carol could answer his questions. "I'm sure she'd love to hear from you," he enthused, "but don't expect a prompt reply. I allow three weeks for a letter to reach Lake Turkana, and four weeks for a reply. Also, if you're ever in New York, we have archives with correspondence from our worldwide missions going back to 1928. Sadly, our records are in disarray. But you'd be more than welcome to browse. The history of our missions in Africa is a grand tale indeed."

Craig told Rita what he'd learned. "Come to New York with me. We'll stay at the Plaza. See a Broadway show. Two or three days. What do you say?"

"You go, Marty. Lupe needs my help. This is your show, Lancelot—bring me the Grail."

Craig took the red eye to New York. He couldn't sleep on the flight, his mind racing. What if Sabine was still alive, in possession of hundreds of pages of unpublished work? Finding them would be the philosophical equivalent of discovering the Dead Sea Scrolls. Craig imagined himself a modern-day Stanley, coming face-to-face with the great philosopher on the shores of Lake Turkana: "Dr. Arnaud, I presume?"

Putting aside this fantasy, he returned to the book on his lap: *Selected Essays of Sabine Arnaud*. He kept re-reading Sabine's reflections on evil. If the words were penned after she had suffered at the hands of the Nazis, they took on a richer meaning.

Imaginary evil is romantic and varied; real evil is gloomy, monotonous, barren, boring...Evil when we are in its power is not felt as evil, but as a necessity, or even a duty...We must ask that all the evil we do may fall solely and directly on ourselves. That is the cross.

Craig dozed, then woke as the plane began its descent into New York. He returned to the book, his attention drawn to a line that hadn't registered before—eight words that struck his core. *Two ways of killing ourselves: suicide or detachment.* He had thought often enough about the first method of self-elimination, but had always chosen the latter. Craig the aloof ironist. Craig the fair-weather friend, the uncommitted lover. Impregnable. Until he awoke bound to a metal table in a room stinking of dog, and his carapace was finally crushed, exposing the soft invertebrate. *It is the innocent victim who can feel hell.*

Craig took a cab from JFK to the Interchurch Center near Harlem, a nineteen-story building the cabbie called the "God Box." It was filled with an alphabet soup of Christian denominations in the spirit of enlightened ecumenicalism. When Craig marched into Methodist Global Ministries, Reverend Ted was shocked by his sudden arrival.

"Sorry to barge in on you, Reverend," Craig apologized. "I should have called first. But I can't wait to start researching my book. I'm hooked on Africa! On telling the 'grand tale,' as you put it, of our brave Methodist missionaries."

Impressed by Craig's drive, the reverend took him to the basement, which was sectioned off in wire cages assigned to various denominations. The Methodists were sandwiched between Lutherans and Pentecostals. The cage was about twenty-feet square, packed floor to ceiling with cardboard boxes. The boxes were labeled by country, or continent. Some had dates; others did not. There were no boxes marked Kenya, just Africa, twenty-six of them. "My apologies, Craig, for the mess. We desperately need an archivist—which we can't afford. I'll have a table brought down to give you a place to work."

"I'm eager to plunge in, Ted."

"You're welcome to take notes, of course, but please don't remove documents unless you check with me. I'm in the office all day, pop up later and we'll do lunch. I know a great Jewish deli around the corner. You're not anti-Semitic, I trust?" Ted laughed at his ecumenical wit.

Craig began by stacking the Africa boxes outside the cage, arranging them in chronological order as best he could. Some of the oldest-looking boxes were undated. He'd start with those and flip through every document, searching for correspondence from the Elmolo mission. Lunch time came and he wolfed down a corned beef sandwich with Reverend Ted, and then got back to work.

In the afternoon, he found photos taken at the mission in 1939, when the intrepid Waldo Balfour was still above ground. In one shot, a doctor in a white coat—lean, handsome—examined an infant. The mysterious Dr. Rolf? Perhaps he'd been a fixture at the mission before the arrival of his uncle Bob. In a report from that year, Balfour wrote of a Dr. Walter Mueller from Baltimore, "a Godsend for the mission and God's children we serve." Craig put the box aside.

Photos from the mission were sparse after his uncle took over in 1943. But Bob had written regularly to his superiors with mission news. Craig started with the earliest letter, penned just before Bob sailed for Africa.

August 24, 1943
Dear Reverend Stafford:

I am honored by your confidence in me to take on this assignment. I am stepping into the shoes of Waldo Balfour, a man whom I have long admired—and can never equal. But I shall do my best, with God's help, to be worthy of your trust. I know the journey will be arduous, and the challenges great, but Sarah is as eager as I am to serve the Lord in Africa. I am thrilled that our son, William, whom we were blessed to adopt last fall, will grow up with our mission family. Sarah is worried about his safety, of course, as any mother would be. But little Will is a sturdy lad, already taking his first bold steps! He should thrive in the vigorous, outdoor life we shall lead on Lake Rudolf....

Heart pounding, Craig struggled to breathe. *His uncle had adopted a son.* Hands trembling, he scanned the subsequent letters. In 1948: "Dr. Karl Rolf and his wife Greta have joined our mission family. They couldn't have arrived at a better time! Sarah has her hands full with baby Carol and young William is a terror. Only six but running wild and strong as any native lad." Not a word about where the new arrivals came from, or why they volunteered at the mission.

Dr. Rolf and Greta were mentioned in glowing terms in every letter his uncle wrote. And then, in 1956, tragedy struck. William drowned while fishing with a native boy in a boat on the lake. "A fierce storm came up suddenly, we are all heartbroken...shattered by the loss. Sarah is inconsolable, as is Greta—she loved the boy so. I know we must accept God's will. Please pray for us..."

After his uncle died in 1959, Sarah wrote of Greta "helping me endure my grief and carry on, as Bob would have wanted me to, for the sake of God's children we serve. Greta is a true saint. And what a marvelous teacher! The native boys and girls are learning Plato, if you can believe it, and the mysteries of geometry." And then, from 1963 on, there was no mention of Greta and Dr. Rolf. They ceased to exist.

Well, it was clear now why Sabine had gone to Africa: *She wanted to see her son.* Craig wept angry tears over his foolish quest to prove Arnaud was his birth mother. What misery it had brought to Rita and him! And all because he longed for a mother he could love and admire and worship like a saint.

And what now? He sat there debating his next move. At this point, he wasn't about to write his cousin and wait two months for a reply. He had to go to Kenya. Carol was about thirty now. She'd grown up with "Greta" and would know where Sabine was—if she was still alive. And Carol would surely have photographs of the "camera-shy" Greta taken during her years at the mission. And his cousin could swear—on a stack of Bibles—that Sabine Arnaud had lived at the mission for more than a decade under the name of Greta Rolf.

Craig went upstairs and announced his plans to go to Kenya. Reverend Ted counseled him on the inoculations required and the difficulties of transport to Lake Turkana. If Craig could afford it, it was best to hire a bushtruck and driver. He thanked the reverend for his kindness and checked into a hotel, utterly spent.

He called Rita with the news.

"You're doing the right thing, Marty."

"I know. I just miss you. "

"I'm worth missing."

"I love you, Rita."

"Don't go soft on me, Marty. You need to bring these pricks down and get your self-respect back."

"I'm worried about being gone so long. About you and Meter Reader. "

"His name is Mario. I can't promise I won't see him."

"I'll try not to think about it."

"Don't. I'll be here when you get back."

An awkward silence ensued. "Well," Craig sighed, "I guess this is it—"

"I'm sorry, Marty, about your mom. I mean finding out Sabine's not your mom. That must have hurt you real bad."

"Yeah, it hurt. I cried when I found out."

Another silence.

"Well, try and look on the bright side, Marty," Rita said. "You're still a WASP—the world loves you. Bring me home a scalp, Lancelot. Be my hero."

CHAPTER TWENTY-ONE

Cairo, Egypt. February 1947

She wrote in a back corner of the café, smoking Turkish cigarettes and drinking endless cups of bitter coffee. Her once elegant hand, the letters rounded and graceful, had become flattened and ugly—like a bombed-out city. Another casualty of the war. She struggled at times to read her own words, using a glass to magnify the scribble.

Sabine reminded herself constantly to slow the pace of her writing, to honor each idea, however flawed, by drawing out the words with loving attention. But her pencil skittered across the coarse paper, racing to match the urgent flow of her thought and leaving its sketchy tracks behind.

The other patrons of Kishawi's at this afternoon hour, exclusively male, played backgammon, smoked *shishas*—the tobacco soaked in molasses—and idled away the day like princes of poverty. Most wore filthy *djellabas*, talked too loudly, and gestured with habitual aggression. The regulars were used to the foreign woman at the corner table and no longer cast baleful looks in her direction. The proprietor, Ahmed, said she was the wife of the German doctor who treated the poor and was not to be disturbed. She was also his best customer—buying cigarettes, coffee, the occasional plate of figs or dates, and always leaving *bakshish*, a tip. Ahmed wondered how the handsome doctor could have chosen such an ugly wife.

Sabine worked on yet another draft of the letter to her brother that Karl had urged her for months to write. "He has a right to know you're alive, even if the rest of the world does not. Swear him to secrecy if you must, but write! Make him a happy man." She knew André was now a professor at the University of Montreal because his papers appeared regularly in the journals of mathematics she found in Cairo's public library. In fact, her brother was acquiring an international reputation for his seminal work in algebraic geometry and number theory—topics she could barely grasp.

Sabine delighted in her brother's success and longed to know more of his life. Was he married, a father? Perhaps she was an aunt! And André would have news of Papa. Had he survived the trauma of Mama's death? He'd be seventy-two now. Not so old for a man of his sturdy constitution. But how to tell André she was alive? Was it not more merciful to let him cherish the joyful days they'd spent as a family in Paris before the war? She read the draft of her much-revised letter yet again.

My Dearest André-

I am so ashamed for the suffering I have caused you. I should be dead. In many ways, I wish I was. But here I am. Where to begin my darling brother? I went to England with dreams, unforgivably selfish dreams to fight for France. I should have stayed in New York and found a way to join you and Mama and Papa in Montreal. But I chose to follow my own path at the expense of those I hold most dear.

And what an absurd dream I had! To join the Resistance and fight the Nazis! I was a sickly Jew, without physical prowess or psychological cunning. When I got to London and asked to join the Free French Forces they thought I was mad. And perhaps I was. Mad with my schoolgirl dreams of heroic sacrifice! But I soon learned that there is nothing noble about the business of killing and dying in war, though I do not dispute the necessity of armed conflict to defeat Hitler. It is only now, of course, that we know the full extent of Hitler's crimes—in particular the wholesale extermination of millions of Jews.

"Love your enemies" has nothing to do with pacifism or the problems of war. I was prepared to kill Germans because of military necessity, not because I had suffered personally from their acts, but because they were the enemies of every country in the world, including my own.

You see, my darling brother, your headstrong sister did realize her dream of fighting for France—to my eternal remorse. In the summer of 1943 I was recruited as a British agent, despite my obvious shortcomings, for reasons that I only fully understood later. While sequestered in training—utterly sealed off from the world—my fictitious death was announced, without my knowledge or complicity. You and Mama and Papa were notified of my sad demise from tuberculosis. Obituaries were written. A burial took place, my headstone carved. During this time, I continued to write you letters that went unposted by my British captors, who were preparing your recently deceased sister for a mission to occupied France: a suicide mission for which I did not volunteer, but was thought exceptionally well-qualified to perform—since I was already dead! I'll spare you the details. But survive I did—a failure even at death!

In France, near Soissons, I joined a band of maquisards and engaged in acts of sabotage in which arms were destroyed and German soldiers killed. And for every German who fell, the Nazis took ten French hostages, including women and children, and shot them in reprisal. It was a cruel calculus, but brutally effective in discouraging acts of rebellion. So you see, dear brother, my wartime exploits—driven by ideals and ego—resulted in the deaths of only a few Germans, but many more of our innocent, oppressed countrymen. If there is indeed a fiery hell for sinners, it is there I shall reside for eternity.

When Paris was liberated, still unaware that I was officially deceased, I went to our old apartment on rue A. Comte. During the occupation, sweet addled Agnes had been forced to cook and clean for the German officer who had confiscated our home. I cannot tell you how happy I was to embrace her. But the poor woman nearly fainted when she saw me. And it was from Agnes, of course, that I learned that I was dead. And that poor Mama had taken her own life not long after hearing the news. I was devastated, as you can imagine, and blamed myself for Mama's death. I swore Agnes to secrecy and left, resolved to live out the rest of my life in the shadows. As much as I longed to see you and Papa, I could not bear the shame of reappearing and asking for your love, knowing the grief I had already caused.

So, my darling brother, I am writing to you on the condition that you will not try to find me, nor tell anyone that I am alive. Please reply to the name and address on the envelope, that of Mrs. G. Heim, a dear friend who does not know my real identity (nor the place where I actually reside in Cairo). Write me a long letter—pages and pages! Give me news of Papa (I pray daily that he is in robust health), and tell me everything (no detail is too trivial!) about your life, as well as your theoretical work in mathematics. (Yes, I want to understand number theory!)

As children, you were the person I trusted most with my secrets, and now I come to you on my knees, full of shame and regret, to ask for your silence once again.

Sabine wanted to sign the letter, slide it into the stamped envelope, and post it before she could reconsider. But she could not. She knew the letter was not yet complete. There was one more confession she had to make, out of respect for her brother—and the truth.

But how to tell André that she was with child when she sailed from Marseille in 1942, and that she had left her own son behind in New York? And all because of her foolish quest to die a glorious death for France! André might not blame her for Mama's suicide, but what would he think of his sister as an unwed mother who had callously abandoned her child?

She wanted to explain it to André, every bit of it, without excuses, but the pencil refused to form the words. It was if she was in a dream trying to run and her legs would not move. After a while she put her head in her arms and wept bitterly.

When no more tears came, she tore up the letter and walked out of the café. She could not write to André until she first found her son. She needed to know that he was alive, that his adopted parents were kind and loving and nurturing his character and intellect.

Sabine had been making discrete inquiries ever since she'd arrived in Egypt with forged papers, identifying her as Greta Heim. But she had only the unremarkable name—Robert Martin—a missionary presumably in Africa. But where on this vast continent? She didn't know if he was Catholic or Protestant—and if Protestant, what denomination. She dared not write Alice for more details about her brother-in-law—doubting she would guard the secret of her survival. And besides, Alice might refuse to say where the boy was—fearing Sabine might want to take him back.

Two months later, the *khamsin*, a hot wind from the desert, was blowing through the streets of Cairo, covering the city in clouds of dust. *Khamsin* meant "fifty" in Arabic, and the wind was said to blow for as many days in April and May.

Sabine had taken refuge from the foul air in the Coptic Museum, not far from the flat she shared with Karl. She would have preferred to pose as his sister, which reflected the true character of their relationship, but of course they looked nothing alike. Karl never betrayed discomfort in introducing her as his wife, or doting on her as if she was, but Sabine was often embarrassed for him. The tall, handsome doctor, blue-eyed and athletic, married to the bony woman with thick glasses and an ugly nose.

Karl kept his distance from the other German expatriates in Cairo. Some were still sympathetic to Hitler, and a few were ex-Nazis on the run, fearing prosecution. The Nuremberg trials had concluded in the fall, with Hitler's notable henchmen executed, except for Goering—who escaped the hangman's noose by suicide. Other tribunals would follow. Karl had been paying an orderly at the hospital with connections to Cairo's underworld to establish a new identity for him. He needed to put his Nazi past behind—and quickly. He also wanted papers to go to British East Africa, where they believed Sabine's son was, courtesy of the same orderly—who could find out anything you wanted to know, for a ridiculous price.

From her table in the museum's reading room, Sabine could hear the wind rattling the glass of the high windows and see the reddish, smoky sky—as if the whole city was ablaze. Since learning that the Reverend Robert Martin was in a remote corner of Kenya, on a beautiful lake, she'd had trouble sleeping, fearing that Karl could not get them the necessary papers to travel there.

Still, as weary as she was from lack of sleep, her eyes gritty as if the *khamsin* had filled them with sand, she tried to write. She continued to wrestle with her rejection of church dogma, but still longed to believe in the possibility of a loving God, of redemption and forgiveness. She had always rejected the notion of a tyrannical, jealous, punishing God, but perhaps there was a day of reckoning, of judgment, when one's life ended on earth.

But what would it be like? Maybe the Last Judgment will be like this, she wrote: *The soul which has just passed through what men call death becomes suddenly, irresistibly convinced beyond all possibility of doubt that all the ends to which all of its actions were directed during life were illusions, including God. Entirely penetrated by this certainty, it re-lives in thought all the actions of its life. After which, in most cases, it is seized with horror, desires to be annihilated, and disappears.*

Engrossed in what she was writing, she only glanced at the man in uniform who opened the heavy door at the far end of the reading room. Light flared from the street, along with the noise of crowds and traffic, and then the quiet and soft gloom returned. She didn't look up again until the man stood very close to her table.

"Mrs. Heim, I presume?"

Startled, she looked up to see the stout British officer smiling down at her. It took her a moment before she realized it was Carlton Hays. She had never seen him in uniform before, and he had put on weight. He took off his hat and sat down. His face was red from the sun, skin peeling.

"I thought I'd find you here, surrounded by books."

"You've changed."

"You thought I was dead, I suspect."

"I didn't know."

"But you wished I was?"

"I guess I didn't care."

"In any case, you and your Nazi husband were not hard to find. Much too easy, in fact."

"He's not my husband."

"Yes, I rather doubted you shared a bed with that sadistic pig. I'm attached to the war crimes tribunal now, tracking down Nazis. Karl Heim is not high on my list, but I wanted to find him first—because I thought I mind find you. I don't want to hurt you, Sabine. You've suffered enough because of me. I know Heim helped you escape. But I also know you believe in justice. I have the power to arrest him and send him back to Germany for trial. But I will do as you wish."

"Then leave us alone. Please. "

"I shall. But I suggest Herr Heim does a better job of covering his tracks. If I can find him, so can others. And they will, believe me. He deserves to hang, like the rest of the Nazi scum."

"Karl is a good man."

"Just following orders, no doubt."

"Like you did, Charlie? Dropping me in France, where you knew I'd be captured and tortured."

"You were supposed to be dead on arrival."

"The parachute you packed—just for me."

"There was a war on and we had to win it. I sent you to die, Sabine, that many others might live. But I didn't want you to suffer. "

"Should I thank you?"

"It was a goddamn miracle you landed safely. But why the bloody hell didn't you notice that lump in your coat seam before April, when you were captured?"

"Oh, I found the microchips."

"Why didn't you destroy them? If you were captured—"

"The Germans would find the chips. Wasn't that the point? I wanted to complete the mission on which I was sent. If tortured, I could tell them nothing. And my silence would convince the Germans that I would rather die in agony than reveal my secrets. And thus the chips must be of enormous strategic value. Surely, Charlie, you can see the logic of my decision to keep them."

"Logic?...Dear God, Sabine."

Hays sat there in silence, stunned. Sabine thought she saw tears in his eyes.

"Ironically," Sabine added, "the chips saved my life. Because Karl was assigned to interrogate me."

"Another bloody miracle," Hays said. "Your SS savior. I only found out after the war what was on the chips. Sabotage targets, to convince the krauts the invasion would come at Pas de Calais. Of course, there were other deceptions, besides yours. But Hitler held back two Panzer divisions in reserve on D-day, which ensured our success at Normandy. And saved thousands of lives."

Hays fumbled in his pockets, removed a gold medallion, and set it on the table.

"Do you know what this is?"

Sabine said nothing.

"The Victoria Cross, Britain's highest award for valor. I won it for my exploits in France. But I wouldn't have had the courage—if not for you. I want you to have it." He pushed the medal across the table.

"The dead have no use for medals."

"You don't have to play dead. Why not come forward? It would destroy my career, of course, and perhaps a few others in his Majesty's service, but what's that to you? Why not claim the honors that would certainly be showered upon you? You are a great hero of the war."

"I prefer the anonymity of death—for reasons of my own."

"Then dead you shall remain."

Hays stood and put on his cap. He left the medal on the table.

"When I file my report, I shall state that Karl Heim lived in Cairo for a short time and fled the country—perhaps to Argentina. For what it's worth, I'm sorry I sent you to France as a sacrificial lamb. I could have sent you on a real mission, and you would have performed admirably. I wish you well, Sabine, I do. With all my heart."

She watched him walk away, heels clicking on the stone floor.

CHAPTER TWENTY-TWO

N airobi was cooler than LA, and the air fresher. After two
hectic days arranging transport north, Craig relaxed on the
veranda of the Norfolk Hotel, drinking gin and tonic and eating
fried Nile perch. The night smelled of jasmine, palms rustled in
the breeze, and black waiters attended cheerfully to the needs
of their all-white patrons. Craig felt—guiltily—like a plantation
owner doted on by contented slaves.

Hemingway had stayed at the Norfolk, as had Clark Gable, Ava
Gardner, Gregory Peck, and other Hollywood stars while shooting
safari films. There were old photos in the bar; celebrity trophies
lined up under the trophy heads of big game.

Craig read a book for company, a gift from Reverend Ted: *Journey
to the Jade Sea*, by John Hillaby. It recounted the British adventurer's
camel trek across the Chalbi desert to what was then called Lake
Rudolf. This was in the 1950s, before enlightened Europeans felt
obliged to extol the virtues of every indigenous people.

> At midday we reached the drab huts of the Elmolo, a race of
> lakeside fisherfolk … They live in huts like untidy birds' nests,

made of grass and bits of driftwood. Rotting fish remains littered the ground; naked babies snatched at the flies; a few sticks upheld tattered nets. The impression was Neolithic. I felt as if we had stumbled on a race that had survived simply because Time had forgotten to finish them off.

Craig laughed, skimming the pages, hoping the author might mention the Elmolo mission. He did not. Still, it was instructive to learn what lay ahead, some three hundred miles to the north. Lake Turkana was the largest desert lake on the planet, stretching from northern Kenya into Ethiopia, surrounded by a moonscape of volcanic rock. Its color famously changed with the weather. In strong winds, the lake was blue; in calm air, algae rose to the surface and the lake turned to pea soup. Or *jade*, if you were a romantic Brit.

Craig had tried repeatedly to call Rita, but the Nairobi phone system wasn't up to reaching LA. So he sent a telegram: "Here safe, unreachable when I leave Nairobi—at least a week. Reply care of my hotel here. Miss you. Love and hugs. Wait for me." He was worried about Meter Reader. Rita was impulsive. She might marry the jerk before he got home.

Craig paid the check, tipping grandly to expiate his white guilt. The waiter refused to accept it. Perhaps he feared losing his job by taking advantage of a tourist who didn't understand the value of Kenyan banknotes. So Craig retracted half the bills and the waiter nodded his approval.

Back in the room, he undressed and got in bed, cocooned by mosquito nets. He didn't expect to sleep. Jet lag told him it was morning, and his gut churned with anticipation over what he might find at the mission. So he looked up at the swooshing blades of the ceiling fan and waited for his wake-up call.

Karo, his driver-guide, wanted a predawn start to escape Nairobi before gridlock. Karo was pricey, but came highly recommended by the Methodist Church of Kenya. He spoke Kiswahili, the national language, along with Arabic and four or five tribal dialects, including Samburu and Turkana—used on the northern frontier. His armored car of a bush truck, a cast-off military vehicle, had enormous tires and wrist-thick steel bars up front to pulverize game or livestock stupid enough to cross an African road at night.

Karo was also reportedly adept at cajoling, bribing, or threatening local officials who might impede his progress through the bush. And he carried an arsenal of weapons, including a sawed-off shotgun, to discourage bandits. He was part Kikuyu, part Arab, and moved with the furtive grace of a dancer wanted for murder. When Craig had asked how many hours it would take to reach Lake Turkana, Karo laughed and slapped him on the back. "How *hours*? You funny, mon. Two, four day. Bad road. Bad peoples. I get you there. No worry. *Hakuna wasiwasi.*"

Two days out the truck, along with its passengers, was covered in red dust. Green savannah had given way to desert scrub and howling winds. "Fooking *upepo*," Karo spit. His English was a mixture of vulgar slang and Kiswahili words he assumed every foreigner knew. Like *upepo*: wind. On the horizon, orange clouds signaled the approach of a dust storm. Karo had hoped to reach the lake before dark, but now he veered off the track and bounced over the scrub until he found an outcropping of volcanic rock. He positioned the truck close behind it. "*Upepo* strip paint, fook motor, mon. We wait."

Craig read; Karo dozed. Two hours passed. The rocks shielded them from the worst of the storm, but outside the visibility was near zero. When Craig got out to piss, aiming carefully downwind, sand stung the back of his neck. As the afternoon wore on, the wind abated, no longer a gale.

Craig was impatient to get moving. He'd already spent one miserable night sleeping in the truck. "We go now?" he asked. "I tell you when, mon." Another hour passed and the wind died with the sun low. "Let's move, Karo. How about it?" "No, mon. Not safe drive in dark. Too hard find *barra-barra m'zuri*… the good road."

Karo could not be swayed, so they ate bananas and antelope jerky and settled in for the night. Minutes after sunset it was dark, stars glittering in the black sky. "Be careful pee in night," Karo warned. "Lion here—pee quick."

Later, with Karo snoring, Craig thought of Rita, and had a premonition that he would never see her again. Hyenas wailed outside. A lion roared, perhaps scaring the hyenas off, because the night went silent. Strangely, his thoughts turned to Alice. He remembered that she'd loved the Tarzan books when she was a girl, growing up poor on a Virginia farm. When he was a boy, she'd read him Tarzan stories, displaying her acting chops—giving each character a distinct voice, mimicking the sounds of apes and jungle birds. And he remembered the sack lunches she'd packed for him in grade school: sandwiches wrapped in wax paper, an apple for health, Oreo cookies—his favorite. The word he'd once coined to describe Alice, *cuntundrum*—an inexplicably mean woman—didn't sound so clever in the African night; it just sounded *mean*. Meaner than she was. She deserved his respect, if not his gratitude. Alice was the only mother he was ever going to have. And Earl, brave but broken, the only father.

He wished he could have known his father before the war, when he was a dashing young man about town, handsome and happy. Earl had been in sales, the kind of guy—his mother said—that everyone wanted for a friend. He was witty, generous, the life of every party. And he was a man you could trust. After the war, and many months of painful skin grafts in a VA hospital, his face was a mass of red scar tissue, his mouth twisted into a grimace. His father scared people when they first met him. So Earl chose a life in the shadows, working as a bookkeeper or night auditor, jobs he mostly hated. But he did his duty, earning a living as best he could, though Alice berated him for his meager paychecks and averted her face when he aimed a goodbye kiss at her lips.

Craig knew what it meant to be broken now, unable to cope. As for raw courage, the kind Earl had displayed in battle, Craig knew nothing—unless shooting up a porn movie counted as heroism. He could have done worse for a father. Earl was never mean or violent—and he often came to Craig's defense if Alice was verbally abusive. He was a better father than Craig had been a son, growing up with his nose in a book—or in the air.

When the horizon showed pink, they were off again. The dirt track often split, without a marker, offering two routes through the rugged desert hills. Karo seldom hesitated; he guided on a distant peak that bordered the lake. When they neared Turkana's south shore, Karo stopped the truck and scanned the horizon. "Samburu women," he said. "Samburu beautiful." Craig took the binoculars and saw shapes in tribal dress, shimmering in the heat, moving with a herd of goats.

"They look like men to me." Craig said.

"Sparkle, sparkle. Many trinket."

As they got closer, Craig saw the sparkles in the sun. They *were* all women, six of them, adorned with silver armbands, neck rings, and disk earrings. Karo waved and shouted something in Samburu. They giggled and waved back. They wore loose-fitting blue robes and sandals made of tire treads. And they were beautiful.

The lake suddenly came into view. It was green, jade—the wind calm. They passed through Loiyangalani, a desolate fishing camp, and soon had the mission in sight: low concrete buildings with corrugated iron roofs, one topped by a metal cross. Dotting the hills were the round, thatched huts of the Elmolo.

Karo leaned on the horn as the truck skidded to a stop. A black man in shorts and flip-flops appeared, then ran toward them, waving and grinning. He seized Karo in a bear hug, and they laughed and wrestled playfully. The man introduced himself as Reverend Ashura Maina; he was Carol's husband.

When Craig explained who he was, Ashura was dumbfounded. He didn't know his wife had a cousin. "This way, please. This way!" He led them to a small concrete building, the door propped open. Inside was an empty classroom and a thin woman in a faded pink dress painting the walls white. Carol was five years younger than Craig, but looked older. The desert had not been kind to her skin.

"Yes, your cousin!" Craig repeated. "Your father was my uncle Bob, whom I never had the pleasure of meeting."

Carol stood there, mouth open, brush raised, paint sliding down her wrist. Ashura seized the drippy brush. His cousin's gaunt face broke into a lovely smile, except for one gold tooth. "How wonderful," she said. "How wonderful you have come."

She invited Craig up to the house for tea. Ashura and Karo were eager to get out on the lake. It was a good day to fish. The house was perched on a hill, built stone by stone by his uncle in the 1940s. Inside, it was cool, windows open to catch the breeze. Antelope horns adorned the walls, zebra skins covered the floor; her husband was an avid hunter, as well as fisherman. The couple had a daughter, Mary, who lived with Ashura's mother in Nairobi during the school year. Carol had spent much of her youth in Nairobi as well, at boarding school.

She wanted to know of Craig's life and family history, and he obliged—without mention of his TV career, which might elicit questions. He was a magazine journalist, writing a book about the missionary experience in Africa. The Methodist archives in New York had supplied facts, but he needed the personal stories of those who braved the wilderness to spread the word of God. And he wanted photographs. He'd brought a camera, of course, but he needed historical photos of the Elmolo mission.

"Oh, I *love* photography," Carol enthused. She produced a stack of albums with pictures taken in recent years. He feigned interest in the shots of new construction, colorful sunsets, and beaming black faces. "You're an excellent photographer, Carol. But I'd love to see some *older* photos, when my uncle ran the mission."

In the bookcase was a slim, leather-bound album, the binding torn. "My father did not like taking pictures. This is all I have." Craig snatched it from her hand. "Sorry," he said. "That was rude."

He lifted the fragile cover, exposing the first page of photographs. They were all black- and-white, with serrated edges that reminded him of the pictures he took as a child with his Kodak Brownie. Some of the photos were out of focus, others marred by sun flares. His uncle was no Edward Weston. Each year got one page, never more. The pictures were captioned in white ink on the black paper. In 1945, a shot of Uncle Bob, wife Sarah, and toddler Will, standing on the lakeshore. Will held a toy shovel; his hair dark, unruly as Arnaud's.

"I read your father's reports. Will was adopted, wasn't he? Do you know where they got Will, who the mother was?"

"No. They just said what a blessing he was. My mother didn't think she could have children at the time. I guess Africa fixed that, or I wouldn't be here. Ha! I didn't know Will was adopted until after he had passed. I don't think Will knew. You can see in the picture, he didn't look like Mom or Dad. He was darker."

"You're telling me."

"Yes, I just did."

"Of course you did. And I thank you." Carol was oblivious to irony. Her unrelenting sincerity was both refreshing and tedious.

Craig turned the pages slowly, trying not to rush. He'd come a long way for this moment of truth. In 1951, the shot of a handsome doctor vaccinating a child. In the background a woman with black hair, face shadowed, glasses catching the sun.

"My uncle Karl," Carol said brightly.

"Your uncle?"

"That's what I called Doctor Rolf. He was German, but very sweet, and kind—like an uncle."

"Germans are always kind," Craig said, knowing his cousin would miss the sarcasm. "Might that be Mrs. Rolf in the background?"

"Yes, Karl and Greta," Carol said. "You should tell their story."

"I fucking want to tell it."

Carol jumped as if poked with a cattle prod.

"Sorry—forgive my foul mouth. I've spent three days with Karo—he swears like a sailor."

"Oh, was he a sailor?"

"Indeed he was. On six of the seven seas. You must ask him."

Craig returned to the album. He examined all the years when Sabine had worked at the mission. There were two more shots of Karl, and one that showed Sabine in profile, at a distance. The hair and glasses identified her in his mind, but wouldn't to a skeptic.

"Are there other photos of Karl and Greta—that show their faces clearly?"

"Oh, yes. I have a splendid one!" On the kitchen wall was a

framed photo of grinning Karl with his arm around Carol when she was a gawky teen. But no Greta.

Craig caught himself before shouting *fuck fuck fuck* and pounding the wall. Instead, he took a deep breath, and asked: "Do you know where the Rolfs are now? I'd like to meet them, get their story."

She said that Karl and Greta had left when she was sixteen, away at boarding school. Karl wrote her a wonderful farewell letter. He said they were headed to Addis Ababa, to work at a hospital there. Her mother was always vague about why they'd left suddenly, but hinted at a religious dispute with Greta. In any case, Karl continued to write, encouraging her to stay in school, which she disliked.

Later, when she fell in love with Ashura, Karl told her to follow her heart and ignore the bigots, including her mother, who didn't want her to marry a black African.

"What a super guy, that Dr. Rolf," Craig said. The SS sadist was probably short-listed for the Nobel Peace Prize: he'd married a Jew and championed racial equality.

"Karl stopped writing about four years ago, when they left Addis Abba and went to another city to work there."

"What city—in Ethiopia?" Craig asked.

"Tigray, I think, a town in the north."

"So how would I find them?"

"You'd have to go to Tigray—ask people there."

"Why didn't I think of that?"

"Oh, I'm sure would have. You're very smart."

There was something missing in his cousin's brain, besides a sense of humor.

"I have a book in the truck, Carol. With pictures I want to show you. Will you come outside with me?"

On the way, he concocted a fairy tale about the Rolfs that might

235

appeal to Carol. He removed the book from the front seat. The sun was hot now, the air still. They moved to the shady side of the big truck.

"Have you heard of a French philosopher named Sabine Arnaud?"

"No. I wasn't smart at school."

"Don't feel bad. Most college graduates haven't heard of her either. During the war, she was a hero of the French Resistance, fighting the Nazis. And then she disappeared. Nobody knew where she went, or why. Some people even thought she was dead. But I believe Arnaud changed her name and felt a call to come to Africa and serve the Lord. She's a big reason I came here—because I want to tell her story as one of the most inspiring missionaries of our time. So, please, Carol, look carefully at these pictures and tell me. Is this the woman you knew as Greta Rolf?"

He opened the book to photographs of Arnaud taken in London in 1943.

"Yes, that's Greta. She was older when I knew her. Not so thin. And her hair was shorter."

"But it's her. You'd swear to it?"

"Why would I swear? You don't believe me?"

"I *do* believe you, Carol, with all my heart. And now my book will include an inspiring chapter on Arnaud and Dr. Rolf—sacrificial servants of our Lord in Africa."

Later that day, when Carol returned to her painting, Craig shot a close-up with his Nikon of Rolf on the kitchen wall and lifted two photos from the old leather album.

CHAPTER TWENTY-THREE

Dan Robbins was the *New York Times* bureau chief in Nairobi. He resembled a young Norman Mailer—short, intense, pugnacious. Diplomas from Princeton and the Columbia School of Journalism hung proudly behind his desk. His bureau consisted of one reporter, himself, to cover all of sub-Saharan Africa. Craig had pitched the Arnaud story for more than an hour and fielded the reporter's tough questions. It was hot in the cramped office, both men soaked in sweat, like boxers in the last round of a fight— in this case a fierce battle of wits.

Dan squinted through a loop to examine the Turkana photographs yet again.

"I agree, there's a resemblance to Arnaud. And you've got an eye witness who'll swear that Greta Rolf was Arnaud. That's good. But your cousin, by your own admission, is not bright—which hurts her credibility. You also have good shots of the doctor, whom you say is Karl Heim, an ex-Nazi, without proof. My files on war criminals don't list his name. That doesn't mean he isn't one, it just means he's a second-tier fugitive at best. I'll wire my colleagues in

New York for background on Heim. If they produce a wartime photo, proof he was an SS doctor, then we can start to build—"

"Dan, I'm giving you the scoop of a lifetime. It's on your desk, under your nose. You can win the Pulitzer, be the next Bob Woodward, get the corner office in New York with a view of Central Park. Trust your gut, man—stick your neck out a little. That's what great reporters do. Run with what you've got."

"I *love* this story, Craig. It's a mind blower. If you had proof the Rolfs were alive, which you don't, and knew where to find them, which you don't, I'd be on the next plane to Addis Ababa. Your cousin said they went to Tigray four years ago. Tigray isn't a city, it's a *province*. It's huge. It's also home to rebels fighting the Derg regime. I need the last piece of the puzzle before I set foot in Ethiopia. Have you heard about the purges, reporters jailed, dissidents murdered? I'll risk my life for a great story—and have—but not for a wild-goose chase. Go back and talk to your cousin. Dig deeper. Sometimes the second or third interview with a source is more productive. Maybe she'll remember the name of the city the Rolfs went to. Maybe her husband—"

"I got another idea, Dan."

"Yeah?"

"I take my story to the *London Times*. The Brits have a nose for news."

"In that case, you can go fuck yourself."

"The f-word. How clever. You're a wordsmith."

"Get out of my goddamn office."

"You're right. It is a goddamn excuse for an office. Get used to Nairobi, Dan. Your career has peaked."

Of course Craig had pitched the *London Times* bureau first and gotten a similar response. An incredible story, he was told, but irresponsible to print without proof that long-dead Arnaud was the same woman as Greta Rolf. What now? Craig went out on the crowded street. The air was hot, but oddly refreshing. *Fuck you, Dan, and forgive the unoriginal expletive. I can write my own damn story.* He hailed a taxi.

At the Ethiopian embassy, he was met by a grim guard in uniform with beautiful coffee-colored skin. When Craig asked for tourist information, he was directed to a room across the hall. Inside was a young man in a white shirt with the same beautiful skin, smoking a hand-rolled cigarette. The ash tray, in need of emptying, was packed with brown stubs. He stood, and smiled with a slight bow.

"Welcome, sir, to the Ministry of Tourism. I am Samson. Would you like to visit Ethiopia wonders?" He handed Craig a black-and-white brochure, ruins on the faded cover.

"I wish to see your beautiful country. But only if I can find my dear uncle." Craig explained that his uncle had practiced medicine in Addis Ababa for some years, but since moved to the province of Tigray. "Surely, all foreign doctors are licensed. So records must be kept."

"Of course, sir. The Ministry of Health in Addis Ababa will have these records, most accurately and precisely kept for the benefit of the people."

"Just as I thought! But my stay in Africa is short. I won't go unless I am certain I can find my uncle. I will write his name for you. Surely, the embassy can communicate with the Ministry of Health. If you could check by this time tomorrow, I would be most grateful." Craig placed a hundred-dollar bill on the desk. "This is for your trouble. And the same amount tomorrow—whether or not you find my uncle. And should you locate where he now practices medicine for the people of Ethiopia, I shall double this—in humble appreciation. Is this fair?"

"Most excellently fair, sir."

The next morning, as Craig had coffee on the hotel veranda, the concierge brought him a telegram on a silver plate: "Big fight with Raul. Moved out. Now at Mario's. It's not what you think. Don't worry." She supplied a phone and address in Pasadena, and closed with: "Stay as long as it takes, my Lancelot. Bring me the Grail. I love you of course." He wished she hadn't added "of course." She could have saved the price of those two lousy words and just said "I love you." Or, for a few pennies more, too much to hope for: "I love you with all my heart." Whatever their relationship was, it was never going to be a tender romance. *Fuck you Rita, and Mario too. I also love you lots.* He tore up the telegram.

One more visit to the Ethiopian embassy, where he expected nothing, and he could go back to LA. He had more than enough to pitch the story to the *National Enquirer*, or another sleazy American tabloid, whose journalistic standards were less pristine than the mainstream press. And if they all passed, then what? Maybe he'd go to Mexico, live on the beach and write a novel about his foolish quest. Call it *The Red Virgin*. Or feed himself to the sharks if he got bored, or ever wanted to fall in love again.

Samson got up from his desk, beaming, when Craig walked into the tourist office. "The Ministry of Health has met your request with speedy service." He handed Craig a single sheet of paper, embossed with the seal of Ethiopia, with two words in bold type: Sekota, Tigray. "Sekota is town where Red Cross has clinic. There you will find uncle doctor."

Craig forked over the two-hundred-dollar bonus, knowing Samson could have chosen the town at random. But something in Samson's eyes spoke of patriotic pride: the Ministry of Health actually *did* keep accurate records and had responded promptly to his unusual request.

"Does the clinic have a phone?" Craig said, knowing the answer.

"Telephone not now, sir. But people's bus speedy from Addis Ababa. I give you tourist visa, at no charge?"

Well, what's your play, Lancelot? No guts, no Grail.

Right up until he was mugged and beaten, Craig's first impression of Ethiopia was favorable. The national airline delivered him on time to Addis Ababa, he breezed through customs, the taxi driver swore he loved Americans, and the Taitu Hotel ("tell them Samson sent you") was clean and comfortable.

After a late hotel dinner of *doro wot*, chicken stew, he went for a walk to locate the bus station. The night was warm, shops dark, pedestrians few. Out of the shadows a boy emerged, skeletal, cheeks sunken, teeth yellow. He fell on his knees, palms raised in supplication, hungry eyes imploring. Craig dug in his pocket and was struck from behind, hard. It felt like a brick. Dazed, he was on the ground, hands pulling at his clothes. He kicked at somebody yanking on his boots and was hit again in the head. There were shouts, chaos. Then quiet.

He struggled to one knee. A kind soul helped him stand. As he gathered himself, Craig looked down at his bare feet. His boots and socks were gone, along with his jacket, belt, watch, wallet, and passport. Blood slid down his face from a gash on his scalp. He limped slowly back to the hotel, unsteady. People steered around him, avoiding eye contact. A barefoot, bleeding *faranji*, holding up pants, could only mean trouble.

The hotel concierge stopped the bleeding, skilled at first aid. He cleaned the wound and wrapped the bandage tight. "My apology, sir. This no longer city I love, when our king rule. Please not go hospital with wound. Police ask many question."

The next morning, Craig retrieved the passport photocopy in his duffel to take to the US embassy. Luckily, he'd also left his traveler's checks and most of his cash hidden in the room before taking his ill-advised evening stroll. Aside from the irreplaceable loss of his L.L. Bean desert boots, Lancelot was bloody but unbowed. He could make do with sandals, like the locals.

Getting a new passport proved tedious. Embassy functionaries grilled him about his reasons for being in Ethiopia. Did he know that the US State Department had declared the country unsafe for tourists? Craig shook his bandaged skull. Was he there to aid the Derg regime as a paid or unpaid advisor on political, economic, or military matters? Another shake. Why did he know a doctor in a remote region of Ethiopia? Craig improvised a touching story about Rolf having been a friend in LA, until the good doctor felt God's call to serve the poor in Africa. "He's a living saint. And I want to write his story for the *Methodist Quarterly*. That's why I'm here." *Now do your fucking job and give me a passport.*

Reluctantly, but dutifully, Craig's countrymen issued a new passport. It took seventy-two hours, during which time he was advised not to leave his hotel. Craig did as he was told, sending the concierge on forays to acquire a new wardrobe to mask his identity as an American begging to be robbed. He also stopped shaving.

Lonely, he sent another telegram to Rita, telling her he was in Ethiopia, about to venture into the dangerous unknown. He signed it, "Love Ya!" for spite, but there was a hollow-sick feeling in his gut that he might never see her again.

She responded less than six hours later. "Be safe, my love. Mario is jerk, by the way. Kiss, Kiss." He folded the telegram neatly and put it in his pocket.

Craig stood in the morning shade of a eucalyptus, across the dirt street from the clinic. The day was already hot. The air smelled of dust and dung. People streamed past carrying sacks of produce and pulling goats and sheep, bound for the market in the town square. He'd arrived in Sekota the night before, the two-day bus ride having taken three because of blown tires. He'd checked into the best of the bad hotels—the one with a safe to secure his valuables—and paced the room until dawn.

Except for his sunburned face, Craig might have passed for a local in his *shamma*—a loose tunic—cotton pants and sandals. The *shamma* covered a carving knife in a scabbard on his hip—courtesy of the concierge in Addis Ababa. He'd never wielded a sharp, serrated knife to do anything more brutal than cut into a New York steak—but he would now, in self-defense, of that he was certain. The "righteous wrath" that Rita had urged upon him was simmering below the surface. He'd been through hell to stand where he was now. Nobody was going to take him down without a fight.

Craig had staked out the clinic an hour before it opened in hopes of observing staff as they arrived. The Nikon was at the ready, wrapped in a greasy food sack to shield it from curious or covetous looks of passersby. No staff had come through the front door, but a line of peasants had formed outside, mostly women with infants or small children. When the door swung open, the people filed in. A little girl in rags began to cry hysterically and her mother pulled her inside.

Craig took a deep breath and crossed the street. He'd gain access to the clinic by asking for a clean bandage for his head wound. After three days on the bus, the bandage was dark with blood and caked with dust. He was just an American tourist passing through on his way to see the ancient churches of Aksum. Naturally, he had a camera, like any proper tourist. Perhaps the dedicated staff would pose for a picture? If not, he'd take some when they weren't looking.

There was a small waiting room, every seat taken. No receptionist. Just a metal door with a sign in Amharic. The room stank of sweat, disinfectant, and human misery. Craig stood against the wall, trying to ignore the stares of the other patients, many of whom looked half-dead from disease or starvation. The children with hollow cheeks and sad trusting eyes broke his heart. So he looked at the floor. This was no time for pity. The camera was waist high, his finger on the shutter release. Would Sabine Arnaud march through the door with her thick glasses and tangled mane of gray hair, dressed in a starched white uniform? He was ready if she did.

After ten uncomfortable minutes, an Ethiopian woman appeared with a clipboard. She was followed by a tall man, slightly stooped, with wire glasses and wispy white hair. It was Rolf, in a lab coat, stethoscope in one pocket. His eyes locked on Craig.

"Ah, I've been expecting you," Rolf said.

"Not me."

"You are *faranji*, are you not? I get about one a week. So, I've been expecting you. This way, please." His English was British, laced with a German accent.

"I can wait my turn."

"Nonsense, my boy. I give priority to foreigners. You have money to pay—not like these poor wretches. Let's look at that head of yours."

Craig hesitated, then followed Rolf through the door and down a corridor. "I'm Dr. Rolf. And you are?"

"Pete Harris," Craig said, improvising.

Rolf opened the door to an examination room. It was bare except for a heavy wood table covered by a sheet.

"Sit on the table, please. A blow, I presume."

"I fell and hit my head."

"Of course." Rolf put on surgical gloves and gently removed the bandage. His blue eyes were intense, but not unkind. Craig told himself that Rolf was a "good" Nazi, if there was such a thing, but his heart raced. He could smell Rolf's stale breath and the hint of sweet cologne.

"Nasty," Rolf concluded. "The wound is suppurating. It must be cleaned and disinfected. I keep our medicines locked up. Wait here. You can hang your clothes on that hook. I want to give you a proper examination."

"I'm not getting undressed."

"As you wish."

Rolf went out and closed the door. Five minutes passed. Craig was used to the games doctors played in the States. Cool your heels in the waiting room. Then cool your heels in the exam room while the doc sees other patients. But this was fucking Ethiopia. Craig tried the door. It was locked. He fought panic and cursed his stupidity for making himself vulnerable. But Rolf couldn't possibly know who he was or why he was there. Keep your cool, Lancelot. Wait a few more minutes, then pound on the door. Make a scene. And remember, you have a weapon. Craig put his hand on the knife. Would he really have the guts to use it?

The door swung open and Rolf came in, smiling, followed by a male orderly pushing a cart with bottles and bandages.

"Why did you lock the door?" Craig said. "I don't like being locked up."

"My apologies. Force of habit. Our patients are tribal folk—many have not seen a physician before. They get frightened and flee the clinic before receiving treatment. Or they steal from us—selling our medicines for food on the black market."

The orderly was lithe, darker-skinned than most Ethiopians, his face scarred. Craig offered a smile that wasn't returned. "This serious fellow is Mulat," Rolf said, selecting a bottle from the cart. "Speaks not a word of English. He's of the Danakil people."

Craig sat on the table and Rolf cleaned the wound. "This should have three stitches to heal properly. May I do that for you? I'll give you a local. The pain will be slight."

"Of course, Doctor. Whatever you think best. I'm sorry I got angry about the door. That was rude."

The pain was more than slight, but Craig smiled through the procedure. He wanted to be a good patient. After Rolf dressed the wound with a clean bandage, Craig extended his hand. "Thank you, Dr. Rolf. I'm so happy I stumbled on your clinic. You do wonderful work here. Perhaps I could make a donation to the clinic, as well as paying for my own treatment. Despite my appearance, I am not without means. I thought it best to dress like a local."

"Ah, an affluent American! Please, let me take you on a quick tour, meet the staff. The more you know about us the more generous you may wish to be."

Rolf led the way down the corridor. Craig had the camera ready. They entered a room with a table and four chairs, a copy machine, steel file cabinets, and coffeemaker. Mulat closed the door behind him.

"Sit down, Mr. Harris. There is much to talk about. When I saw you in the lobby, I thought you might be somebody else, a man who claims to be a friend of mine from Los Angeles. Do you know of such a man?"

"N—no," Craig stammered. "I don't know him."

"May I see some identification, Mr. Harris?"

"I don't have to show you anything." Craig stood.

Rolf said something in Amharic and Mulat blocked the door.

Craig produced the knife. "Tell him to get away from the door. Now!"

"Please drop the knife," Rolf said. "I think I know who you are. But I need proof. No harm will come to you. I promise."

"I'm getting out of here. I'll cut that fucker if he doesn't move. I swear I will."

Craig slashed the air in short, sweeping arcs and advanced toward Mulat, who stood his ground, grinning malevolently, mocking Craig with slicing jabs of his bare hands. Rolf shouted at Mulat and gestured for him to step aside. Which he did, reluctantly.

"You may leave now, if you wish," Rolf said. "But I would prefer you stay."

As Craig reached for the knob, knife at the ready, Mulat dropped to the floor and kicked his feet out from under him. Craig fell hard on his back and head and the knife was twisted out of his hand and placed at his throat.

CHAPTER TWENTY-FOUR

Mouth taped, tied to a chair with surgical tubing, Craig sat across the table from Rolf. They were alone. He tried to comfort himself with the thought that Rolf was the husband of Sabine Arnaud. He *must* be a good man. Craig meant him no harm, so there was no reason for Rolf to kill or torture him. But perhaps Rolf was a sadist, for sport, and Craig was his new toy.

Rolf stirred sugar thoughtfully into a cup of black coffee.

"Our Ethiopian coffee is superb, but very bitter. It requires sugar to be properly enjoyed. I'd offer you a cup, but if I remove the tape, you might shout for help. When Mulat disarmed you, your cries were horrendous, truly heartbreaking—which I quite understand. But I had to go out and assure my staff that no one had been harmed, and there was no need for the police. I told them the *faranji* had a psychotic break, but was now sedated.

"I'm not going to hurt you. But I must keep you restrained, for your safety—and mine. You are fortunate that Mulat obeyed my orders and did not kill you. He is a Danakil warrior and reacts to threats instinctively—with deadly force. So we cannot chat as equals, as I had hoped. I will ask questions and you will respond in writing. You held the knife in your right hand—do you also write with that hand?" Craig nodded.

Rolf got up, rummaged in a drawer, found a notepad and pen, and put them on the table. He worked Craig's right hand through the tubing until the wrist was clear, slid the notepad under Craig's flipper hand and placed the pen in his fingers.

"This is awkward," Rolf said. "Comical. But here we are. Please explain why you are not in possession of a passport or other identification." Craig wrote: *in hotel safe.*

"Smart boy. You must be at the Zagwe—our Hilton. Please write your full name and date and place of birth."

Rolf sipped coffee while the pen scratched.

"All right, Craig Louis Martin, write my name. The one I was born with—if you know it. I won't harm you if you lie, but I can't help unless you tell the truth."

Craig hesitated. But there was no point in playing dumb. He wrote: *Karl Heim.*

"Bravo! Nobody knows my real name. Not even my CIA friend, whom we shall soon discuss. You don't look like an amateur Nazi hunter. So I assume your interest in me is not predatory. You came here to find the woman you believe is my wife. Is that correct?"

Craig nodded.

"Greta is not here. She lives a solitary life in a place of her choosing. She is not well. Please write the name she was born with."

Rolf glanced at the pad. He did not look surprised.

"What is your interest in Sabine Arnaud?"

Must speak, long story.

"If I uncover your mouth, do you promise not to cry for help?"

Craig nodded.

250

"If I untie you, do you promise not to threaten me with violence, or leave the room until I say you can?"

Craig nodded again, but thought: *I promise nothing asshole.*

"I'm exhausted by this," Rolf said wearily. "I'm too old to be unpleasant."

He stripped the mouth tape off, unwound the rubber tubing, and patted Craig's shoulder affectionately. "I'll get you some water and coffee. In case you're wondering, the door is locked, and the key is in my pocket. You can take it by force, of course, and break your promise and leave. But that would gain you nothing—except your freedom. Which is not so free, is it, with the CIA tracking you?"

Craig gulped down a glass of water, asked for another, and drank that down. He sipped the coffee, without adding the sugar that Rolf suggested. He'd drink it black and bitter, as a small act of defiance.

"How do you know the CIA is watching me?"

"Carlos told me. He's my houseguest at the moment, a most unhappy man. Carlos is of Argentinian descent and works for the CIA station chief in Addis Ababa. Not the kind of thing he normally shares with a stranger, but tell me he did—after we got acquainted. He was instructed to find out what business you might have with me, and report back. Curiously, he wasn't told why you were important—just to follow you. Your bus kept breaking down, so he got here early to snoop around. I don't like snoops, so we chatted."

"You tortured him."

"Not in the sense you mean. But I needed the truth, so I had to break his spirit. It was not difficult. He's young, inexperienced, on his first overseas assignment. I was shocked to learn he was CIA. From his appearance, I guessed he was a Cuban advisor helping the secret police root out counterrevolutionaries. I sympathize with the

Front, the Tigrayan People's Liberation Front, to be precise. I treat their wounds, give them money to buy arms—for which I could be shot. If poor Carlos had been working for the Derg regime, Mulat would have eviscerated him and fed his entrails to the jackals for luck. As it stands, Carlos is a problem we need to solve."

"He's your problem, not mine."

"Ah, but he's here's because of you. His male pride has been crushed, and he may want to make me suffer for crushing it—which gives me pause in releasing him. Tell me your story, Craig, from the very beginning. All of it. Then we shall talk about Carlos."

Craig started with the clues that had led him to believe Sabine was his birth mother. Rolf was a good listener. He didn't interrupt and asked only the occasional question to clarify a point. By the time he finished his story, Craig was drained, but relieved. And he no longer feared Rolf.

"So it was Carol who led you to Ethiopia," Rolf said. "I was very fond of your cousin. She called me Uncle Karl, the poor dear. I urged her to marry Ashura—he's a kind and patient man and takes care of her, allows her to function and help others. She's much loved by the children at the mission. People like Carol were often sterilized in Nazi Germany—and the most severely impaired were euthanized. The first time I was instructed to euthanize one of my schizophrenic patients, I refused. My superiors said they respected my decision. And a month later I was conscripted by the Waffen SS and sent—"

"You said you'd help me."

"I fear I must."

"I don't have to see Arnaud, or know where she is. I just need photographs—proof she survived the war. They don't have to be recent. And I won't say where I got them or tell anyone she's still I alive."

"I can't do that."

"Why the hell not?"

"Because I must take you to her."

"Why? You must have pictures of your own wife."

"A few, yes."

"Then give me one—a copy if you can't part with the original."

"I'd need her permission."

"So ask her! Call her! Does anybody have a phone in this fucking country?"

Rolf smiled. "No phone. No electricity, indoor plumbing, or running water. She lives a monastic life. It is an arduous journey to reach her. If she hears your story, but prefers to remain dead and buried—will you honor that wish?"

"I'd convince her otherwise."

"What if you could not? I've never been able to change her mind about anything."

"She'd listen to me."

"Your goal, Craig, was laudable, at first—to find your birth mother. But now you seek vengeance. To punish those who made your life hell."

"I want justice done. I want the truth. She worships the truth."

"Indeed she does," Rolf said. "And I must take you to her. Greta would want me to—after what you have suffered because of her. And most of all, because I know she would want to see her son before she dies."

"I'm not her son."

Rolf got up and refilled their coffee cups. "Champagne might be more fitting, but, alas, I have none. You see, my boy, you were right all along. Greta—Sabine I should say—is your birth mother. She never met your uncle, who coincidentally adopted a boy some months after she left New York. You were correct, however, that we went to Kenya to find her son. And it was you, of course, that we sought. When Greta was in England, in the sanitarium, she got a letter from Alice saying that she'd allowed your uncle to adopt you, because he and his wife could not have children. And also because—no doubt another lie—your father refused to raise a child that was not his own.

"When we got to Kenya, Greta knew at once that Will was not hers. She was heartbroken and knew that Alice had lied about giving you up to ensure that she would never return to New York to be a part of your life. In any case, once we found ourselves at the mission, we decided to stay. There were orphans for her to mother and the mission needed a physician. Your uncle had no idea who we were, so our German identity was never in question. You should know that Greta never forgave herself for abandoning you."

Craig sat there in stunned silence. He wasn't sure what he felt, but it wasn't jubilation. He remembered Sabine's last words on the postcard she'd sent to Alice from England: *There is nothing to forgive.* She didn't much care if Craig was shipped off to Africa with a Jesus freak she'd never met. *Well, screw you, Saint Sabine.*

"I should care—but I don't. Not the way I thought I would. Maybe later it will mean something. I want to get what I need and go home."

"If you're wondering about your father—Sabine refused to tell me."

"I had a father...I don't need another..." His voice trailed off. Rolf sat quietly, waiting for him to speak. "I had a mother too, who looked after me...If she was here I'd get on my knees and beg her forgiveness for the way I treated her...." He sat there, heart pounding, not knowing what to do or say, an orphan. "How soon can we leave?"

"Go back to your hotel, pack your bag, clean up, and put on some decent clothes. Look like a tourist. We must pass through military checkpoints. You would be arrested on sight in that ridiculous disguise. We will be gone one night—perhaps two. If all goes well I'll drop you in Gondar, where you can get a flight out of the country. In any case, I must get back here on Thursday for scheduled surgery. I will fetch you this afternoon. I have supplies to gather and patients to treat."

"What about our CIA friend?"

"Carlos? I'll take care of it. You won't be involved."

"I don't want him harmed."

"On the contrary. I'll find a way for the poor lad to return to Addis a conquering hero."

Rolf stood and opened the door. He didn't need a key. "I lied about the door being locked. Never trust a former member of the Schutzstaffel."

Rolf drove slowly through the crowded streets, steering past women with bundles on their heads and men with goats on tethers. Some of the peasants waved and grinned when they saw the old truck, emblazoned with a red cross. The rear of the vehicle was packed with crates of food and medical supplies, including several tanks of oxygen. "Greta's slowly dying of emphysema—all those years of smoking. Once a month I make the trip to bring her oxygen—which she often wastes by helping some poor wretch in the village cling to life a bit longer. She's ready to die, I fear. Perhaps longs to die. Maybe seeing you will change that."

Once they cleared the outskirts of town, Rolf accelerated. They bounced over deep ruts in the red clay, passing small farms, scrawny cattle enclosed by pens of mud and sticks, round *tukuls* with thatched roofs. On the either side were towering *ambas*, flat-topped mountains, some with terraced fields of green and gold on their barren flanks.

Rolf told him about the famine that precipitated the fall of Selassie in 1974, and the further collapse of the agrarian economy brought on by the Marxist regime. "I've grown to love this noble and savage nation. When I first met Mulat, he wore a necklace of testicles around his neck. They looked like small dried gourds. Trophies from battle, like scalps. His people, the Danakil, have a saying: 'It is better to die than to live without killing.'"

"Himmler would have approved."

"Ha! A dainty, fastidious man—with a bad stomach."

"The banality of evil."

"Hannah Arendt! Greta's writing on evil, after the war, was far more to the point. I managed to send some of it to her friend Colson, without Greta's knowledge. She said that evil, when we are in its grip, is dull, monotonous, gloomy, boring. It's like the worst job you can imagine that you can't possibly quit. Because the moral imperative is one of duty, a terrible duty.

"I followed the Eichmann trial with great interest—though the outcome was never in doubt. He deserved to hang. Greta wrote a letter to the court, under a fake name, as a Jew who had survived the Holocaust. She begged the court to show mercy. If Eichmann was truly sorry for his crimes, he should be allowed to expiate his guilt by serving the new state of Israel for the rest of his life, perhaps by working on a kibbutz, or taking an administrative post where his organization skills could be put to good use. Can you imagine?" Rolf shook his head. "The mind of that glorious, impractical soul…" He looked on the verge of tears.

Rolf collected himself. "Greta believed that pure good, su-pernatural good, was only present here, in our world, in minute, almost imperceptible quantities. Like one drop of pure water in the deluge of a sewer. Not her words exactly, but words to that effect. I want to tell you, young man, that I saw it. I felt it. I swear to God I did and I do not believe in the God of my fathers, the God of the Bible, or the Koran, or the God of any book. I saw it, that one drop of pure good in my hell as a Nazi. It was a tear that Greta shed for me, her tormentor, to release me from evil."

Rolf began to weep and wiped his eyes with a bandana. He slapped Craig's knee, hard. "How happy I am to have lived to meet Greta's fine son. And to know that she will soon hold you in her arms."

Craig was moved, but speechless. He wanted to ask Rolf a thousand questions, but he could not. He didn't have the energy, or know where to begin. He had entered a new universe that he could not accept, that was not quite real, with a language he had not learned to speak. But still gnawing in his gut was the fear of being followed, captured, and perhaps punished.

"What did you do with Carlos?" Craig said, fearing the worst.

Rolf glanced at his watch. "At this moment, our friend is enjoying supper at my home, along with Mulat and my housekeeper. In about an hour, he will be on his way back to Addis to brief the station chief on his mission to Sekota."

"And say what?"

"As a writer, you will appreciate the story I concocted for the lad. Carlos will boast that through initiative and clever spy craft he discovered that the mysterious Dr. Rolf is aiding the TPLF, which in fact I am. So he recruited me as an intelligence asset. It makes perfect sense. And you, young man, are also an asset. Yes, you lied to the embassy that you knew me, but your cousin in Kenya told you I had contacts with the rebels, and you wanted to write of their war against Godless tyranny. And for that purpose I am taking you into the mountains to a rebel stronghold—which, in fact, I am—where you can meet these brave fighters and write of their struggle."

"Did he believe that bullshit?"

"It wasn't all bullshit—and he was grateful for the cover story. It allows him to return to Addis and perhaps salvage his career. If all goes well, the CIA will send me money to buy arms for the rebels, and I will supply your country with valuable intelligence to help bring down this ghastly regime. If things do not go well for Carlos—if his cover story does not salvage his career—then I suspect he may return to exact his revenge in some fashion, for what I did to him. As you well know, Craig, once a man has been humiliated by another man—he never forgets and rarely forgives."

CHAPTER TWENTY-FIVE

Near Lasta, Ethiopia. September 1977.

She awoke from sound and dreamless sleep, gasping, drowning, fighting for breath as dark currents dragged her under. Coughing, spitting blood, she sucked in hard for air until the panic eased, then flopped back on the mat, panting. Gathering the coarse blanket to her chin, she curled on her side, taking deep breaths and exhaling the spent air forcefully in white puffs. It was black and cold in the *tukul*, wind spooling through cracks in the walls of wattle and mud. Sabine was alone.

Three times this night she had been wrenched from sleep by suffocation. It was the same panic she had felt when the Gestapo shoved her head in a tub of black sewer water until she began to drown. Now she was condemned to relive that agony again and again until death by asphyxiation. Karl had explained the physiology of it to her. In sleep, respiration naturally slows, but her ruined lungs could no longer meet the body's minimal need for oxygen at rest. So she awoke gasping from the sound sleep she desperately craved.

Karl urged her to use oxygen at night, but the tank was empty now, the life-giving air had gone to save a feverish infant in the village. Sabine cracked the door of the hut and saw traces of pink to the east. The hellish night was almost over. She lit the fire that Leila had laid the afternoon before, poured water in the pot for tea, and placed it on the iron grate above the crackling flames. That much she could do for herself, but the effort left her winded. She returned to her blanket.

When the fire had cut the chill, she opened the door to watch the dawn from her mat. It was her favorite time of day. She loved to see the earth brighten before sunrise, imperceptibly at first, as if unseen footlights were slowly coming up, illuminating the grand stage of creation. Scrub and rock and trees took form, emerging out of the darkness in colorless bas-relief, the baked soil not yet ochre, the eucalyptus leaves not yet green.

As the last star paled into blue, and the horizon ripened from pink to red, Sabine shifted her body to face the peaks where the sun would soon emerge, flooding the land with light and shadow, color and warmth.

Waiting for the sun, she thought of how a toddler sees something bright and is so totally absorbed in her love for the shiny object that her whole body leans toward it and quite forgets it is beyond her reach. Then her mother picks it up and puts it near her. Or the way a hungry child cries with her voice and her whole body, tirelessly, to be given milk or bread. The grown-ups are touched, and smile, but she is deadly earnest. Her body and soul are concentrated on that single fact of desire. Nothing is less puerile than a little child. It is the adults who play with her who are puerile.

The sun's crown appeared, fanning rays above the mountains. The Egyptians were not wrong to worship *Ra*, giver of light and life, who showered his blessings equally on rich and poor, good and evil, pharaoh and slave.

Soon, Leila would walk up from the village with fresh goat's milk and water to last the day. She would chop wood for the fire and heat the cooking stone until the oil spit, then pour out batter in concentric circles to make an *injera* pancake to smear with honey.

Sabine felt like a sick child again, remembering how Mama brought breakfast to her bed on a tray: croissants and butter and fruit, and a *champignon* omelet lovingly prepared. But the sight and smell of food only turned her stomach. And she stubbornly refused to take one bite—despite her mother's pleas and tears. What a cruel and heartless child she was! *If only poor Mama could see me now*, Sabine thought, *gulping down warm goat's milk, licking honey off my fingers, and asking Leila for another pancake!* Now that she was dying, food was delicious and her appetite rapacious.

She lacked the will to write, and seldom read, but kept two books within reach: a Greek bible and Pascal's *Pensee*. Both were dog-eared, dusty, and disintegrating from use and exposure to the elements. Too weak to gather twigs for kindling, of late she had ripped out portions of the Old Testament, those she found repellent, to start the morning fire. Only the Psalms, Ecclesiastes, Isaiah, and Daniel remained. Pages from the New Testament, beginning with Revelation, might be her next burnt offering. But she was loath to desecrate her beloved *Pensées*.

When she first read Pascal as a girl, she became despondent, envious of Pascal's genius and humbled by it, knowing she could never ascend the intellectual heights to which he had soared, that transcendent realm where truth alone abides. When Karl told Sabine that notable literary critics had compared her writing to Pascal's, she thought it absurd—and blasphemous. Her posthumous oeuvre had been patched together from notebooks of stray and often contradictory thoughts, ideas recorded to be developed and refined, or discarded, later. Now her incoherent ramblings had been printed—without her editorial guidance or permission. "Were I not dead," she once raged at Karl, who split his sides laughing, "I should rain abuse on those foolish enough to praise my work!"

Increasingly, her thoughts turned to Paris, long before Hitler's rise to power, when she and Mama and Papa and André lived on boulevard Saint Michel near the Sorbonne. With her time short, too short for self-loathing, she recalled the happiness of her childhood and youth, before she made the irrevocable decisions that brought sorrow and pain to those she loved.

Her first memory, perhaps apocryphal, was of lying on the grass, mostly naked, in shorts, or even a diaper, at about age three—probably in the Luxembourg Gardens, where Mama took her and André to play. Mama was near, but Sabine was alone. Alone in the way that each of us is when we emerge from the Eden of infancy as a self-conscious, self-imprisoned Being, a Self, at the dead center of the universe, free and alone and mortal. She was on her back, the grass prickly on her bare arms and legs, looking up through leaves and branches at immense clouds drifting across the sky. And she felt something that she could not name…a shock, a shiver? Wonder? Perhaps the hint of Pascal's lament: *The eternal silence of these infinite spaces frightens me.*

After learning to read *Le Temps* at age six, it wasn't long before she tackled *Pensées* and discovered a kindred soul, along with the existential questions common to all humanity.

> *When I consider the short duration of my life, swallowed up in the eternity before and after, the little space which I fill, and even can see, engulfed in the immensity of spaces of which I am ignorant, and which know me not, I am frightened, and am astonished at being here rather than there; for there is no reason why here rather than there, why now rather than*

then. Who has put me here? By whose order and direction have this place and time been allotted to me?

Pascal never found a rational answer to these questions. And his famous wager—to live as a Christian because there was nothing to lose and possibly heaven to gain—seemed to her a mockery of true faith.

And what did she believe? After a lifetime of thinking relentlessly about the nature of God and man and truth, how would she answer those questions that arise in every human heart: Who put me here? For what purpose? If a loving, all-powerful God created the universe, why does evil prevail over good? Why must I suffer and die? *By whose order and direction have this place and time been allotted to me?*

She had come to the conclusion, of late, that we ask these questions only because of our imaginary position at the center, as a Self. We were all spoiled little gods, believing that we should be exempt from suffering and death. And we must somehow empty ourselves of this false divinity, to give up being the center of the world in our imagination, to discern that all points in the world are equally centers and that the true center is outside the world. This means we must consent to the rule of necessity in matter, and the free choice at the center of each soul. Such consent is love.

But perhaps these ideas would be found wanting too, if she had time to think them through. But time she did not have. How many breaths would she take before her last? Each breath was a whispered prayer for the next. In the end, she would die as ignorant and helpless as a child, as we all do, bewildered, incredulous: *Father, why hast thou forsaken me?* Perhaps that was the best we could hope for, to die on the cross of our spine and shoulders squared, expecting nothing—neither heaven nor hell. And by expecting nothing, perhaps gaining everything.

Sabine had often wondered, in her grief and shame over abandoning Craig, what it would have been like to raise her son to adulthood. If he had come to her as a troubled adolescent, with doubts about the existence of God and the meaning of life, what counsel would she have given him? Pled maternal ignorance of the divine? Recite Church platitudes? Or tell him what she did believe, though it might cause him distress?

She would have had to tell him the truth, of course, that she believed God's creation was an act of *de-creation*. In creating what was other than Himself, God necessarily abandoned it. Every human being was infinitely far from the good, and thus deserving of our compassion, no matter how unworthy. God abandoned our whole being—flesh, blood, sensibility, intelligence, love—to the pitiless necessity of matter and the cruelty of the devil. He keeps under his care only that part of creation that is Himself—the uncreated, supernatural part of every creature, the soul. That is the life, the Light, the Word...the presence here below of Christ.

She would also have told him that hers was a church of one, with a blasphemous creed, and he might do well to kneel at another, more consoling altar—or perhaps none at all. He should worship the truth, wherever he found it.

Sabine found herself craving a cigarette, absurd as the impulse was. Karl had confiscated her tobacco months ago. So she held the blanket close for comfort, and turned her attention to the path that came up from the village. When she saw Leila she would get up from her mat and go out to welcome her friend. She refused to be an invalid.

CHAPTER TWENTY-SIX

Not long after dozing off, Craig woke to the sound of a rooster crowing. He had been restless all night, listening to the Teutonic snorts and farts of Rolf on his nearby mat and anxious about what the day would bring. *I will meet my mother for the first time. And the last.*

Though Sabine's words had been part of his mind and heart since adolescence, the prospect of standing face-to-face, as her *son*, was beyond imagining. Would they shake hands? Tearfully embrace? What could he say to the woman he had worshipped like a saint? A woman who had also abandoned him to the care of crazy Alice? Would he struggle for words, act the fool in the presence of genius, betray his resentment? Fail to measure up? What if he saw disappointment, or even pity, in her eyes? *Yes, Mother—may I call you Mother?—I write jokes for a living. For television. That's my profession. I make a great deal of money. I wish I had done something more important with my life. Maybe, if you had raised me, I'd be different...better...but you weren't there....*

Craig got up and stumbled over sacks of feed to get outside. It was still pale dark, one stubborn star and Venus bright in the west.

Chickens clucked and scurried into violet shadows. The cool air smelled of dung. Craig could feel his hangover. They had stayed up late drinking *araki*, Ethiopian moonshine, with their host, Meles, before bedding down in the storage hut near the pen where Meles kept his goats and one scrawny cow. Before the fall of Selassie, Meles had been a *dejazmacth*, a local nobleman, with ties to the royal family. When the Derg seized his home and prosperous farm, his two sons resisted and were shot. Meles fled to the mountains with his wife, now dead from typhus, and carried on, living in a *tukul*, now a peasant.

Meles had done his best to prepare a feast for his guests, *kai wot*, lamb stew served with fiery *berbere* sauce. Craig had sampled the dish and now wished he hadn't. After relieving himself in the outdoor latrine, he pumped water into a bucket to wash his hands. Feeling his life had become unmoored from reason anyway—washing in water that smelled like a swamp while standing in chicken manure—Craig absurdly broke into song, from *Oklahoma*: "O what a beautiful morning...O what a beautiful day..." while drumming on the bucket with a stick. Rolf had slept long enough. They were getting an early start, whether the Nazi liked it or not.

Three hours later the sun was high and the day was hot. They had climbed steadily on the meandering dirt track, past scrub and juniper that gave way to prickly pear, aloes, and flowering cactus that Rolf called "candelabra trees." Near the crest of the ridge they saw baboons perched high among the rocks as a hawk wheeled in lazy circles against the hard blue sky.

Rolf stopped and got out with binoculars to scan the downward switchbacks that disappeared into the haze below. There was smoke rising out of the valley from several fires.

"When the army encounters rebels," Rolf said, "they burn every village in the area, kill the livestock, rape the women, steal anything worth stealing, all in the name of progressive socialism. So far, Lasta has been spared."

Rolf pointed beyond the smoke, to another expanse of barren mountains.

"Two hours more, if all goes well," Rolf said. "This is for you." He removed an envelope from the glove compartment and handed it to Craig. "To keep," he added, "if Greta will allow it."

Inside were three black-and-white photographs of Arnaud, each with a caption on the back. *Paris, August 1944*: Sabine smiling, among the throngs of Parisians waving at US troops entering the city. *Cairo, 1947*: Sabine on a terrace, in profile, a candid shot, gazing out at the city. *Kenya, 1959*: Looking older, hair streaked with gray, holding a black infant.

Craig stared at the photographs. *This is my mother. I came out of her womb.* It was real to him now. And he fought back tears.

"I chose these shots," Rolf said, "because she is not yet old, and the likeness is good. If you took a photo of her now, I think it would not serve your purpose. She looks…not well…" His voice trailed off.

As they came within sight of a burned-out village, they rounded a curve and Rolf hit the brakes. A military truck blocked the road, surrounded by soldiers with weapons raised. Craig froze. *Not again, please God, not now. Not this close.* He fumbled for his passport, expecting to be turned back, or arrested.

Rolf waved out the window and shouted something in Amharic. An officer approached with the casual swagger of a man who delights in issuing unpleasant orders. Rolf chatted him up like a friend, and produced a stack of documents emblazoned with red seals. The officer looked impressed, and morphed into a smiling public servant. He glanced at Craig's passport, came to attention, and waved them on with a sweeping gesture.

"Idiot," Rolf said, as he roared off. "He called me 'comrade' when he saw my forged papers with the signatures of terrifying bureaucrats. I can go where I want, and transport what I want—and my permits are never questioned. Why? Because most of this scum army is illiterate, and the ones who can read, like this thug, are too terrified of the regime to question any piece of paper with a pretty red seal on it."

An hour later, they reached Lasta, a tiny hamlet bordered by sandstone cliffs and eucalyptus. It appeared deserted until Rolf playfully tapped the horn, mimicking the opening beats of Beethoven's fifth symphony. Ragged citizens emerged, warily at first, then ran toward the truck, smiling and waving. Rolf shouted greetings and slowed, but did not stop, steering past barefoot children with emaciated limbs.

"They're hungry. I always bring grain for the elders to distribute as they see fit 'To each according to his needs' sayeth Comrade Marx. The peasants are better communists than the corrupt swine in Addis." Rolf kept waving and shouting. "I'm telling them I'll be back after we pay our respects to Grandmother—as they like to call my Greta."

Rolf started up a steep track. When they crested the hill, they saw the mud *tukul* and terraced fields behind it. Heart racing, Craig had the door open before they came to a stop. "Stay put," Rolf commanded. "I must prepare her, assess her condition. The shock of seeing you could kill her." He grabbed a tank of oxygen. An Ethiopian woman appeared in the doorway, robed in white cotton, her hair braided in plaits close to the skull until it billowed out at the nape of her neck. She followed Rolf into the hut.

Craig paced, edging closer. He could hear Rolf talking, but not make out the words. It sounded more like French than English. And he saw something white on the floor of the hut, like a ball or a pillow. A step closer and he knew what it was. It was hair. Arnaud's unruly mop of black hair had turned white. Rolf was on his knees, leaning in close, but her body was all in shadow.

Craig withdrew and continued to pace. He found himself praying before he was conscious of it, the prayers silent and un-ceasing...*Please dear God, my God, my father, please let her live, please let my mother live...please dear God...let her not die...let my mother live...*

In the midst of these repeated prayers, eyes closed to the blinding sun, he heard his name and felt a hand on his shoulder. It was Karl. He looked shaken. The Ethiopian was at his side. There was blue cross tattooed on her forehead.

"Go to her now," Rolf said. "I told her why you came. I have her on oxygen. Remove the mask to let her speak—but not for long. She is very agitated and fears for your safety. I promised I would get you out of the country tonight."

Sabine was sitting up, back against the stone hearth, a blanket covering her legs. The mask covered her nose and mouth, but her eyes were full of feeling, glazed with tears. She seized his hand and held it to her breast. Her hands were cold, dry, her chest bone. Craig tried to speak, but no words came. He felt giddy, as if he wanted to laugh. But he began to cry.

Sabine pulled the mask down, whispering hoarsely. "My son, my son, I am so sorry..." She struggled for words, chest heaving; Craig replaced the mask, kissing her forehead. "There, there," he said, sliding his arm around her shoulder. Her eyes never leaving his, she lifted her hand to stroke his cheek. A mother's touch. A mother's love.

An hour passed. Sabine was asleep. Rolf had gone to the village to distribute food and now returned. "I must wake her and tell her we're leaving. We can make Gondar by dusk. I know a man who can fly you across the border to Kenya."

"I can't leave now."

"She will not allow you to stay."

"Not allow it?"

"I promised I would get you to safety. Then I will carry out my duty in Soketo and return. I must be with her when the end comes."

"I'll wait for you."

"No, you won't."

"I want to take care of her."

"Leila knows what to do. I have instructed her in the proper use of the oxygen. It should last until I get back."

Rolf went into the hut to wake her. Craig stood outside and heard Rolf talking softly. He came out after a few minutes, teary eyed. "Go," he said. "Quickly."

Craig knelt beside her. He kissed her forehead and whispered, "I'll be here with you for a little while, to keep you safe. Karl will return soon." She looked alarmed, and then whispered, "Only a little while?"

"Yes, a little while and then I will go home to America."

He went outside. Rolf was in the cab with the engine turning.

"I told her I was staying. She wants me to," Craig said, getting his bag out of the truck.

"You're a liar." Rolf got out and embraced Craig. "Do as Leila instructs. She speaks a little English. The two tanks of oxygen should last four days if used sparingly—mainly at night to help Greta sleep. I will be back in two, perhaps three days. If she dies before I return, she will be cremated, as per her wishes. The site has been prepared...up there."

Rolf pointed to sandstone cliffs high on the ridge.

"A kiln, once used by Gnostic Christians, for the same purpose. To send the soul toward the heavens in fire and smoke. But I think she will not die if you are here. She will fight harder to live—to be with her son."

Rolf extended his hand. "If I am not back in four days... assume the worst. Make your way to Gondar. Ask for my friend Schmidt at the airport. He has a small plane and will get you out of the county. But don't worry. I'll be back. I must."

Leila and her sister, Zewdi, worked in shifts. They brought water, cooked, and tended to Sabine's bodily needs. Men came up from the village to visit, sinewy warriors with facial scars and broken teeth. They talked softly to Sabine, and sometimes wept without shame. Word had spread that the *faranji* was Grandmother's son, so all the citizens of Lasta who were not infirmed made the pilgrimage up the mountain to meet the young American. None spoke English, so Craig nodded and smiled as people talked to him warmly in Amharic, often with great emotion. A young woman presented him with the gift of a white embroidered *shamma*, which he took to wearing proudly,

Sabine had gained strength and now relied on oxygen mainly to sleep. Two days had passed. She could stand, and liked to sit in the sun with Craig in the morning, when it was still cool—and talk. Or rather, listen, because she wanted to know everything about Craig's life. So he talked and talked. And marveled that she found every mundane detail fascinating—as perhaps only a mother could. When he asked her a question, she often dismissed it, as if her life was of no importance. He kept waiting for her to say something about his father, but she did not. And he was afraid to ask.

After the evening meal, Leila and Zewdi went back to the village and mother and son were alone. Craig chopped kindling and made a fire outside. They sat on a flat rock with their backs to the hut, the oxygen tank close. The first tank was empty now—this was the second, nearly full. But Craig would have to make it last at least another day. And what if Karl didn't return—tomorrow, or the day after? Craig tried to put the thought out of his mind, but, of course, he could not.

They were quiet for a while. And then Sabine took his hand and began to talk. "You were patient with my questions, and now I will answer the question you are perhaps afraid to ask, about your father. Your real father is the one who cared for you, Earl, the man you loved and admired, who was so terribly wounded in the war. But I must also tell you of the man who impregnated me. He was not, I think, a bad man…"

"You don't have to tell me."

"I feel I must. Surely you will always wonder. His name was Alain…"

"Not Louis?"

"Oh no. But I did pick the name—for Louis Chartier. My first philosophy teacher—at the Lycées Henry IV."

"I recognize the name—from your biography."

"Ah, my biography—I've never read them." She seized his hand. "Please, I must go on about your father. I barely knew him. He was the friend of a friend, much younger than me. A member of the Resistance—brave, and very fair, with reddish hair. He never told me his last name—it was safer than way. Alain volunteered to get me across the border to Spain. From there I could make my way to Lisbon. We traveled by train, by foot, to the frontier—in the Pyrenees. We arrived at night and spent the night in a barn. A man, a guide, was supposed to meet us in the morning. It was wet and cold. Alain had a bottle of cognac—he offered me some to keep warm. I had a sip and burrowed in the hay and fell into a deep sleep. He woke me roughly in the night. He had become amorous, and was very drunk—"

"You don't have to say more. Please, don't."

"I must. I resisted, of course, I fought, but he was very strong. I don't think he was a bad man—drink can make some men violent and mean. When he had taken his pleasure I ran off and he was too drunk to follow. I made my way back to Marseille—to my mother and father. I was so ashamed—but of course I told them nothing. When I found out I was pregnant I was devastated. I hated the baby I was carrying…I even saw a doctor, but I couldn't do that…I came close, so close. But then I came to my senses."

Sabine began to weep, and then fought for air. Craig gave her oxygen until she calmed down. He wiped away her tears, kissing her on the forehead.

"I knew it was best to have the baby in America—so I could spare my family the shame. But when you were born, when I first held you in my arms, my shame turned to joy. I should have stayed to care for you, but Alice wanted a child so desperately. Her baby had been still born three months before. I thought I was being noble, giving her the gift of my beautiful son…" Sabine began to cry again and Craig held her in his arms.

"Alice was a good mother," Craig said. "A loving mother, and Earl was a good father."

They sat quietly for a long while, and then Sabine drifted off to asleep. Craig saw that she had oxygen, flowing at the correct rate, and lay down to sleep beside his mother.

The next morning, when the sun cleared the mountains, they sat outside on a stone bench, the sun warm on their faces. The light and shadows were beautiful and Craig placed his camera on a rock and set the timer. He put his arm around Sabine and they did their best to smile until the camera clicked.

"Please, would you make me a cup of tea?" Sabine asked. "You have told me of your life and I have selfishly told you so very little about mine."

Sabine talked throughout the day and into the night. Craig built a fire to keep them warm. She told him of her childhood, her youth, her time in New York and London and what she did in the war. And of her years with Karl.

All of Craig's questions had been answered. But Sabine had one more of her own, which she asked shyly, apologetically: "My son, my dear son, if it's possible, if you can, without danger or hardship or great expense, would you take my ashes to France and leave them somewhere in Paris? Spread them on the grass in the Luxembourg Gardens, where I was so happy as a child."

Craig promised, tearfully, that he would. He helped her to her mat and gave her oxygen to sleep. While Sabine slept, Craig wrote in his notebook, recording everything she had told him, and monitored her consumption of oxygen. The bottle was half-empty now and would have to last at least one more day.

Karl did not arrive on the third day. Nor the fourth, when Sabine Arnaud died in Craig's arms. After she took her last breath, her eyes did not look dead, but fixed eternally on something that perhaps she alone was destined to behold.

EPILOGUE

Paris, France. October 2018

The American standing on the Pont Royal, breeze feathering his white hair, looked good for seventy-six. Trim, clad in tailored jeans, black leather jacket, and scarf—very French—he gazed up the broad, sun-dazzled Seine toward Notre Dame. After a while, he turned west to face the bright October sun, more light than warmth, and feasted on the Grand Palais and Eiffel Tower.

To say that you loved Paris, that it was your favorite city, was an insufferable cliché. And the writer in him hated clichés. But he also loved the truth. And in the arms of your beloved, what words could be spoken, really, but the hopelessly banal: *I love you.* The words were tired, but the feeling was always fresh, standing on a bridge above the Seine, under blue skies, light scattered like sequins on the wide smooth water. He turned in a slow circle, marveling at the panorama of this ravishing, magical city.

For the past two decades, Craig had come to Paris in the fall to celebrate his birthday. This was his first trip as a widower. Rita had died in June, suddenly and painlessly, of a cerebral hemorrhage.

And his own health was in slow decline. Bladder cancer hadn't killed him this year, but it might the next. So he'd pretend this walk, with the weather glorious, on the final afternoon of his stay, was the last time he'd walk the streets of Paris—and savor it all the more. He knew, of course, on this *last* walk, where his steps must inevitably lead.

After crossing the Pont Royal to the Left Bank, he turned up Quai Voltaire toward the Latin Quarter. There was no hurry. The Panthéon didn't close for ninety minutes. He strolled along the quai, admiring the Louvre across the river, and browsing the small green bookstalls. There had to be more bookshops in Paris than any other city in the world. The French may have rolled over shamefully to the Nazis in six weeks, but its legions of cranky booksellers would battle the Amazon juggernaut to the last man.

Consciously, he wasn't looking for the book, *his* book, but the title caught his eye in a stack of old paperbacks: *Saint Sabine*. It was a dog-eared French edition of his "nonfiction novel" about Arnaud and his quest to find her. The spine was split, pages loose, the photo of the dashing author ringed by coffee stains. It had been a global best-seller in 1986. Craig had made a fortune from the book, the sale of the movie rights, and writing and rewriting a screenplay that was never produced. *Saint Sabine* was priced outrageously at four euros. But he bought it anyway. Amazon could go to hell.

Two other books about Arnaud had preceded his. Denis Colson had penned a short memoir of his friendship with Sabine, and Carlton Hays had written a six-hundred-page autobiography, after his forced retirement from parliament. *My Life as a Spy in War and Peace* was largely self-serving, but included three moving chapters about Arnaud. Near the end of the book, as Hays reflected on his daring life, he related an incident to show that even retirement was not entirely without risk. As he and his Scottish friend, Alister (formerly of MI-5), were leaving a London dog show, a crazy man came out of the shadows, punched Alister in the mouth and vanished. His dear friend had two teeth knocked out and required twenty stitches to repair the damage to his mouth. Craig came to regret this childish act of revenge on the man who had tormented him—but only a little.

Saint Sabine was published after Hay's mammoth tome, because Craig had spent more than five years researching it. He'd tracked down every living witness to Arnaud's exploits with the Resistance. Craig never did succeed in learning the fate of Karl—despite many letters sent to the authorities in Ethiopia. He was one of the nameless victims of the Derg regime, or perhaps a young CIA operative by the name of Carlos had exacted his revenge for having been humiliated by a master in the black art of interrogation. In either case, Karl Heim had paid for his war crimes.

When he reached the boulevard Saint-Michel, he went south, pausing at the brass 37 on the black door of the apartment house where Sabine had lived with her brother and parents as a schoolgirl. It was getting cold, so he stopped at a Tabac for a café crème. Then he continued his pilgrimage, past the sprawling Sorbonne, where he—the college dropout—had been invited one summer to lecture on the life and thought of Sabine Arnaud. Every classroom seat was filled, and students lined the wall to hear him. Glory days.

When he reached the steps of the towering Panthéon, its neoclassical architecture reminiscent of the Lincoln Memorial in Washington, time was running short. Twenty minutes until the doors closed. Perhaps forever for him—if this was indeed his last visit to Paris.

He showed his lifetime pass to the guard, issued by the French Ministry of Culture, of which he was justifiably proud. In the rotunda beneath the cupola, there was one gaggle of Japanese tourists looking at the marble statues. He went down the stone steps into the rosy light of the softly illuminated crypt. Voltaire, Marie Curie, Victor Hugo, and Rousseau were all buried here. He knew where to find Sabine Arnaud. Her ashes were interred, fittingly, near Jean Moulin—tortured to death by the Nazis in 1943.

There were few tourists in the crypt, so he stepped over the red-velvet guard rope and knelt before her tomb, crossing himself like the good Catholic she never was. Sabine would have appreciated the irony. It was only because of him that she was here, where she belonged, in the Panthéon. It was the singular achievement of his long life. If not for him, her grave would have remained overgrown with weeds in a chapel cemetery in England. Now she belonged to the ages, to France, enshrined with her greatest sons and daughters.

Craig removed a picture from his wallet, the photo he'd in taken in Ethiopia of mother and son, his Nikon perched on a rock. Today it would be called a selfie. It was the only photograph he had of Sabine and himself. Both were grinning at the camera—happy and a little silly. Sabine was swarthy, looking more Ethiopian than French, with a mane of white hair. And bone thin. But there was no mistaking the joy in her smile. He slid the photo into a tiny crack between the stones in the crypt. If this was his last trip to Paris, he would leave the precious photo with her.

Craig stood and kissed the stone where her name was carved. Below it, were the simple words of tribute that he himself had suggested to the French authorities:

Philosophe   Patriote   Héroïne de la Résistance

APPENDIX

About Simone Weil

Simone Adolphine Weil (1909-43) was perhaps the greatest moral and spiritual philosopher of the twentieth century. She was born in Paris, of parents who were non-observant Jews. Simone and her older brother, André, displayed evidence of genius from childhood. The two gifted children were inseparable, but prone to violent arguments; both were short-tempered and stubborn.

At the Sorbonne, Simone acquired the pejorative nickname "red virgin" because of her radical politics, mannish clothes, and asexual nature. She was often described as a kind of alien being, *not one of us*. After university, she taught philosophy at a girls' lycée and was active in the labor union movement. For a time, she worked in unskilled factory jobs to understand the plight of the underclass. When France fell to the Nazis in June 1940, she fled to Marseille with her parents, who obtained visas for them to sail to New York in May 1942. From there, Simone went to London in December 1942 with the hope of returning to France to fight with the Resistance. Always in poor health, Simone was given an administrative job with General de Gaulle's Free French Forces, drafting papers on the political and social ideals that should govern postwar France. Diagnosed with tuberculosis, she was hospitalized in London and later transferred to a sanitarium in Ashford, Kent. She died of tuberculosis and self-starvation on August 24, 1943. Her premature death was brought on, at least in part, by her refusal to eat more than the starvation rations of her countrymen in France.

Simone's father and mother died in 1955 and 1965, respectively. André was a preeminent mathematician of the twentieth century, spending the last part of his career at the Institute for Advanced Study in Princeton. He died in 1998. André's daughter, Sylvie Weil, born in September 1942, is a professor of French literature and the author of several works of fiction. Simone had the joy of holding her infant niece in her arms before sailing from New York for England.

Abbreviations for Weil sources in English

FLN   *First and Last Notebooks* (Oxford University Press, 1970)

GG   *Gravity and Grace* (Rutledge Classics, 2002)

SL   *Seventy Letters* (Oxford University Press, 1965)

SW   *Simone Weil: an anthology* (Weidenfeld & Nicolson, 1986)

WG   *Waiting for God* (Harper Perennial Classics, 2009)

Chapter Notes

PRELUDE

The poem is adapted from "Thunder, Perfect Mind," one of the Gnostic texts discovered in a cave in upper Egypt in 1945. Interested readers will find *The Gnostic Gospels*, by Elaine Pagels (Vintage Books,1981) a good introduction to these fascinating, often heretical texts from early Christianity.

CHAPTER ONE

3.   *Nothing can have as its destination anything other than its origin.* (FLN, 79)

7.   *To wish that the world did not exist is to wish that I, just as I am, may be everything.* (GG, 143)

Those who are unhappy have no need for anything in this world but people capable of giving them their attention. (WG, 64)

CHAPTER THREE

30. Weil's plan for a corps of frontline nurses is detailed in a letter she wrote from New York in July 1942 to Maurice Schumann in London (SL, 144). General De Gaulle, when told of Weil's proposal, is reported to have declared her a lunatic. There is no record that the two ever met to discuss it.

33. *There is a reality outside the world…* (SW, 202)

34. *Risk is an essential need of the soul…* (SW, 114)

CHAPTER SEVEN

74. Arnaud's remark that a tree is rooted in the sky. (SW, 66)

    Arnaud's remarks on the concept of "de-creation." (GG, 32)

77. Arnaud's description of her mystical experience is drawn from Weil's account of her encounter with God in a letter to Father Perrin. (WG, 21)

    *The pure taste of the apple…*is from a letter Weil wrote from London to her parents in New York in June 1943. (SL, 189)

CHAPTER TEN

107. *We are the crucifixion of God.* (GG, 89)

109. *Absolutely unmixed attention is prayer.* (GG, 117)

CHAPTER ELEVEN

118. Arnaud's comments about the paradox of God and faith are drawn from the following passages:

A case of contradictories which are true. God exists: God does not exist. Where is the problem? I am quite sure that there is a God in the sense that I am quite sure my love is not illusory. I am quite sure that there is not a God in the sense that I am quite sure nothing real can be anything like what I am able to conceive when I pronounce this word. But that which I cannot conceive is not an illusion. (**GG**, 114)

Religion in so far as it is a source of consolation is a hindrance to true faith: in this sense atheism is a purification. (**GG**, 115)

CHAPTER FIFTEEN

163. *Humility is attentive patience.* (**FLN**, 111).

   Suffering is to move either toward the Nothingness above or towards the Nothingness below. (**FLN**,117)

   Father, in the name of Christ, grant me this… (**FLN**, 243).

165. Craig's remarks about Christ wanting us to prefer the truth to himself. (**WG**, 27)

CHAPTER SEVENTEEN

185. *When I think of Christ on the cross I commit the sin of envy.* (**WG**, 29)

CHAPTER TWENTY

211. *Imaginary evil is romantic and varied…*(**GG**, 70)

   Two ways of killing ourselves: suicide or detachement. (**GG**, 15)

   It is the innocent victim who can feel hell. (**GG**, 72)

CHAPTER TWENTY-ONE

222. Arnaud's reflection on last judgment. (**FLN**, 152)

CHAPTER TWENTY-FIVE

260. Arnaud's thoughts on the purity of little children. (**FLN**, 325)

263. Arnaud's thoughts on the false divinity of self. (**WG**, 100)

264. Arnaud's thoughts on our infinite separation from God. (**FLN**, 103)

EPILOGUE

Simone Weil is not buried in the Panthéon, but on my last visit to Paris in 2018, Simone Veil (1927-2017), a holocaust survivor and prominent figure in French politics, had recently been interred in the Panthéon, in the same crypt as Jean Moulin. I thought this a fitting honor as well for Sabine Arnaud.

Acknowledgments

My heartfelt thanks to my brilliant editor, Meg Storey, whose advice was invariably correct, if not always friendly to the author's ego. My thanks also to friends and family who read early drafts of the novel during the seven years I struggled to write it, offering encouragement and critical insights, without which I might have abandoned the project in despair. Those generous souls are (in alphabetical order): Al Austin, Ed Kromer, John Matthews, Becky McCann, Beth McCann, Scott McCann, Robert Rosell, and Linda Slater.

53204017R00175

Made in the USA
Middletown, DE
11 July 2019